A STORY THAT COUL

The NAPPERS

A NOVEL BY

NICK RONDI

Contributing Writers

SEAN RICHARDSON - CARY ALEX - PAT MULCAHY - FRANK PELLEGRINO

First Edition

PAGE PUBLISHING, INC.
New York, NY

First originally published by Page Publishing, Inc. 2015

ISBN 978-1-62838-995-1 (pbk)
ISBN 978-1-62838-996-8 (digital)
ISBN 978-1-62838-997-5 (hardcover)

Printed in the United States of America

PROLOGUE

The good news is you won't need a dictionary to read my book. I wrote it in every day language because I wanted to make it easy for you to enjoy reading it.

As we all know writing is cathartic, especially when you're writing about events which actually happened. Writing "The Nappers" helped me bring back so many memories of growing up in East Harlem. It was the East Harlem of 40's, 50's and even up to the mid 60's that still run through my veins, much different than the East Harlem of today. A community is made up of its people, not the bricks and mortar of which it's constructed.

These days, when I go back to East Harlem which is often, I sit outside of the famous Rao's restaurant with the owner Frank Pellegrino discussing the by gone era of East Harlem. Between Frankie greeting his guests and saying hello to the passersby's, we mostly reminisce about the good old days, but we both agree that some of those days were not that great.

Sitting on 114th Street and Pleasant Avenue talking with Frankie and some other East Harlem natives is not only therapeutic but it also makes me day dream of the good days. It's the vestiges of those memories that are my body and sole.

Being a New Yorker is like growing up in the whole world. If you continuously look around, you'll see everything. If it's not in New York, it doesn't exist, it wasn't made yet. That's how we New York lifer's feel. You got a problem with that?

As a young boy growing up in the streets of a neighborhood like East Harlem you're seduced by "the Life". That was then. These days I turn on the TV and low and behold, there's a so called ex mobster either being interviewed or making believe to be and analyst on documentaries about the mob. These so called ex-mob personalities, betrayed not only their friends but also their family to save their own asses. How can anyone give credence to anything they tell us? Law enforcement makes deals with these low life's, but at what cost. What about the pain, suffering and carnage they caused and left behind. These rats wind up getting rewarded by the same government they pissed off most of their lives. And what about all the people they screwed. What kind of life were they left with? Nothing but sorrow and misery! We all make choices about what we want to do with our life. No matter what one does just be true to it. Whether a Doctor, a Porter or being in "the life". If you heart is in it, it'll show in your eyes. That's the genesis of "The Nappers" story.

As the story plays out, you too may be seduced by some of the characters. I wish what you're about to read never happened, but it did. It cast a dark light on my East Harlem. By the time "The Nappers" was done, so was the neighborhood. It looked like 1945 Berlin.

Many of the men I knew then and some who I still know are men of their times. Some of them are sages; they know life, and they know how to live it. Hey kid, don't just look down the street; make sure you always look around the corner.

In the end it comes down to one thing. It's not who we were, it's what we became.

I believe circumstances influence the course of our lives. Often we are victims, but most of the time we can control our destiny, because we know right from wrong.

When good people act out of anger, vengeance or hate, only bad things can come from it, usually heinous, unforgivable actions. The characters in this saga are real, though their names are fictitious-—then again, what's in a name? Because they're all gone, this story can be told now. Some of the years and events as they appear in this story may not be exactly when things actually occurred, but nevertheless, the story is based on actual events. And until this day, many of the facts still remain a mystery.

It's a story of many loves, or tragedies: I'll let readers decide which side of that fine line they want to walk. You can see it as a doomed passionate love story between two people, Joey Rendino and Carol Reedy, or of love between two brothers, Joey and Vinnie Rendino. It's also a tale of unexplainable actions which took place in the Life during that time, which left confusion and many unanswered questions. Last but not least, this is a love letter to a neighborhood, a real community that was dismantled piece by piece in the name of urban renewal.

The Nappers takes place during the post-World War II era and chronicles the life and times of people I grew up with in East Harlem, once the largest concentration of Italians in this country. Today few Italian Americans are left in what we still call East Harlem. Those of us who climbed the ladder of success in the American tradition, including many I still know from the old neighborhood, might echo the words of our narrator, Vinnie Rendino: "Now I live in a nice house on the north shore of Long Island, and own a condo in Florida; I did good, but I would give it all away for just one day of how it used to be."

Nick Rondi, 2015

CHAPTER ONE

One thing they always get wrong…

Say a guy places a big bet with money he doesn't have, then he loses. Now he owes a lot of money to some guys that nobody wants to owe money to. If you watch a lot of movies, you gotta figure this guy's pretty much dead, right?

Wrong. That's the last guy they're gonna kill. They may even step up if somebody else has a beef with the guy and tell them to hold off. He's on the hook, and as long as he's afraid, you know he's gonna make the vig every week for as long as they tell him to. That five grand he bet, it's much better for them that he doesn't have it. They'll clear twenty off him before they're done, easy.

The thing you don't want to do is to get too lucky. Maybe your pals get busted for a job, and somehow you walk away clean. If you stay too lucky for too long, somebody's gonna notice. And if the wrong people notice, you may have a problem. They might say, how come this prick was never pinched? Keep an eye on him. Who does he meet? Where does he go? And they usually don't wait too long to figure it out. The fact that the question came up is enough of an answer.

The street is treacherous. You gotta watch every step and move you take. The street is a line you better know how to walk. And sometimes, caution's mistaken for weakness. My brother Joey instilled in me that survival is the key. That's why I'm alive to tell this story. Even though he taught me everything, I wound up using those lessons better than he did himself. It's funny how things turn out.

I'm in my seventies now; I've got three grandchildren. Some nights if I get into the vodka too early, I get sentimental about my brother. I know the thrill of his life was Carole Reedy, but that's a story all its own. My brother Joey Rendino was, and still is, a legend in our life, one that's fading into memory, like the neighborhood that was our world.

I'm the second son. You could say I was a knock-off of my brother. I'm 5'9", and Joey was almost 5'11". Some people in East Harlem said Joey Rendino was as vain as any woman with his perfectly tailored suits in sharkskin, silk, and mohair. His Egyptian cotton shirts were always monogrammed and custom made by Sulka on Fifth Avenue. Sometimes, he wore a Stetson with the brim turned up.

I dress off the rack, then and now. Part of being the second son is being less conspicuous and blending in, like a tiger whose stripes make it harder to see in the jungle foliage.

I've had to piece this story together from many sources, and for my own reasons. I needed to know why Joey crossed lines he shouldn't have—ones he taught me, his most eager pupil in the Life, not to. I know it wasn't just about the money, because he didn't act out of selfishness. He was as giving a person as I've ever known. He was cool, calm, and always courteous. He never showed much emotion. Even though I knew him better than anybody, I rarely knew what Joey was really thinking or feeling. But, I do know for sure that if Joey could have foreseen all the pain and heartache he'd wind up causing, I doubt very much that he would have taken the course he did.

My brother owned the streets in East Harlem. He never walked fast; in fact, you could say he strolled, with the confidence of a guy whose looks turned heads with his piercing blue eyes and jet black hair. He flowed with perfect timing. Same thing with his charm: he knew how to turn it on and then be a wise guy a minute later.

He was a gentleman, but also scary. He could look right through you. I didn't have to own the streets because I was Joey's brother. Everyone knew the way he had my back.

I first saw my brother kill someone in the summer of 1951. What I eventually figured out was that killing someone had absolutely nothing to do with earning money, yet it had everything to do with money. Even before Joey got into the Life, he'd been telling me for years how it worked: the code of honor and the traditions of respect and tribute.

As close as we were, Joey never told me what he was up to when he stayed out all night. Sooner or later, I could see that this level of secrecy, even from family, was just another part of the Life. Living this way made me an observant kid, eager to figure out where I'd fit in someday in the world Joey managed to keep completely hidden, which, of course, made it all that much more exciting. Even if I spent hours searching our apartment, I never found anything that would give me a hint of what Joey was really up to. I wanted to be part of it, no matter how much Joey didn't want me involved. If he was in it, I had to be, too.

It was just my brother and me in our tiny apartment on the second floor of a tenement on 105th Street (or as they used to say in East Harlem, *a Hun'Fifth)* between First and Second Avenue. We lived in what was called a railroad flat, with the bathtub in the kitchen. Even if he came home late, Joey would take off the top of the tub to take a bath and then put it back when he was finished. The next day, I could use the top as a chopping board for onions for my pasta sauce.

During the long summer days and way into the night, Sinatra blared from jukeboxes all over the neighborhood. Everybody was out on the street or hanging out on the stoops. We used to say that when you were sittin' on an East Harlem stoop, you never knew who you were sittin' on.

Even in the grip of hot and humid weather, all I could think about was girls. I figured it was time for me to get a real girlfriend. Yeah, I'd been laid—anybody who had two bucks in his pocket could get laid. But with the girls in this neighborhood, forget it! It seemed like every girl had a brother, father, or uncle who was connected, so they were all off-limits. I spent the summer hanging out with my neighborhood friends at night and earning money during the day working in Joey's club, the Pioneer, where I washed the espresso cups and pots and kept it looking respectable, no matter what was going on inside.

The Pioneer was on the ground floor of what was known as a doubled storefront. Joey and I lived upstairs, like any other small business owners. There was a front entrance to the club on the left, and a few feet to the right was another door for the rest of the building. The fire escapes were in back. Inside was a private back room with booths lining one wall where card games were held, a small kitchen, and a door that led to a back yard. All the street-level windows were blacked out, making the Pioneer look like a private club. In those days the club even had its own stickball team, also called the Pioneers.

Most nights, I lost my days' pay playing cards. Late one Sunday evening, my friend Jamesy Russo and I wanted to start a card game on our own. We were always told to stay off the block where the club was located if we were going to do anything that could attract attention. So, we set up our game on a well-lit stoop further down 105th Street between Second and Third, one of the quieter blocks of East Harlem. We decided to play "bankers and brokers," a game where the cards are divided into bundles and the banker determines the limit of the bet. The "brokers" bet against the bank. High card wins. As luck would have it, I was the banker that night. Maybe I wasn't so lucky after all.

After we all bet, I turned my bundle over and moaned, "oh shit," when I saw the deuce of spades. This made my friends crack up because I'd blown my money on the first deal. Since I was out of the game, I volunteered to stick around and keep chickie, that is, watch out for the cops.

I walked down the steps from the top of the stoop where the game was going on to get a better view of the action on the block. As I looked across the street, I could see Gino the Zip pacing back and forth in front of his window. He was called the Zip because that's how we used to describe Italians who were born on the other side. The whole neighborhood knew Gino, and most people shared the opinion that he was as tough as the street gets. In his forties then, he was a dark-skinned, balding, barrel-chested guy who made his money pushing junk. On the record, this was completely forbidden, but everybody knew what the Zip was up to. Though Gino was immensely disliked, he was also feared, which allowed him to get away with it.

Gino was one of the first in the neighborhood to see that you could make more money as a middleman and at the same time be less exposed. He had a major connection for pure heroin in Italy that always came through, no matter how dry the streets were. Gino didn't have to worry, since he only dealt with people who had juice. The Zip was in the good graces of some old-timers still holding power in New York in the 1950s and 60s. He did the right thing and gave them a regular taste. If you were gonna push junk, you had to know the right people—and pay quite handsomely for the privilege.

From the bottom of the stoop, I watched Gino alternate between looking out his window and pacing back and forth in front of it. The rhythm had a hypnotic effect. Because I was still staring up at the Zip in a bit of a trance, I barely noticed Teddy O'Neill, the beat cop, as he approached.

"What are ya, peeping in people's windows, son?"

I snapped out of it and said, "Nah, just got bored with the game."

Alfredo Balducci, whose father owned the local butcher shop, laughed and yelled down from the top of the stoop, "Yeah, he lost all the money he made this week on the first hand and then got bored... bullshit."

"Not too much of a lookout, are you, Vin?" the cop said.

Teddy wasn't the worst of the cops in East Harlem. A burly six footer with a thick brogue, he observed the laws of the local street—the ones that weren't always on the books—and kept his head down with the brass.

When I started to answer, Jamesy Russo cut me off, "Yeah, he's not too good at cards, either."

O'Neill said, "Look, boys, you know I don't give a shit what you're doing, but let me tell you, McCleary'll be on the beat in about a half hour."

As O'Neill walked away, Jamesy mimed jerking off, one of his favorite gestures. We played a few more hands just to feel like we could, like the bone-headed teenagers that we were. But we all knew the game would end if McCleary caught us. He was the one cop we all called "sir" and didn't mouth off to; that's how much respect had been bullied into us. And we knew that if McCleary caught us playing cards, he'd chase our asses off and pocket all the money. So, we had to find another spot anyway if we wanted to keep playing.

It was real hot out, almost 100 degrees. When I looked up again at the Zip, I could see he was wearing an athletic undershirt and mopping sweat off his brow with a handkerchief. It turned out that Gino was waiting for a call about the pay-off he was due that night. Little did he know, people he trusted who owed him big money were plotting against him. On the street, it was said that Gino'd been seen with FBI agents and NYPD narcotics detectives; supposedly, he gave up two out-of-town drug dealers. Even though it turned out to be bullshit, the story made its way up the ladder. When it got to the top, it was bye-bye, Gino.

A little after 11 p.m., Armondo Manna finally made the call Gino'd been waiting for. Armondo was a big man in the neighborhood. He drove a baby blue Caddy and owned a successful restaurant at the corner of First Avenue and 104st Street that gave him a bird's-eye view of the action in East Harlem: who came, who went, and with whom. It was directly across the street from the first public housing project in the neighborhood. An immaculately kept place with black and white tiled floors, Armondo's had a coal-fired brick pizza oven and seating for about fifty people. By neighborhood standards, Armondo's was classy, with its marble-topped bar and back courtyard where bocce ball was played in the warmer weather. Even though East Harlem was changing, everyone still looked out for each other for the most part. Italians, Irish, and some blacks were all in the mix. Jewish and German merchants still owned delis and bakeries here and there.

Apparently, Armondo had gotten the word to go ahead with the move on the Zip that very afternoon. It had taken time to get the blessings of some people close to Gino, but money prevailed, as it always does. It makes you see the light, even if the light is black. Later, I found out from Joey that five or six weeks earlier Armondo had instructed my brother to get close to Gino, even act like he wanted to score some H in order to win his trust.

It wasn't hard for Joey to win people over with his seemingly effortless charm, especially guys like Gino, whose paunch and dark complexion didn't exactly make him a local lady-killer. As a matter of fact, no one ever remembered seeing him with a lady. Maybe he figured getting close to Joey would improve his luck. This was Joey at his best. Even though he was aware of the Zip's toughness, Joey did what he was told to do without asking why; that was part of being in the Life.

Joey had to believe that Armondo was part of the conspiracy and was using him and Al "Hicks" Aurelio, who was fifteen years older than my brother, to take care of the situation. People always wondered how Al got his nickname. He used to say that he became a hick in Attica because of "all the cow fuckers up there." We laughed when he told us how one of his fellow inmates robbed a bank and then tried to get away using a horse and wagon: "What a bunch of dumb hayseed cocksuckers!"

Sitting at the bar in Armondo's place, my brother and Al Hicks overheard the call Armondo made to the Zip. I pieced this together after the fact from my own sources and what I got from Joey in dribs and drabs. When Armondo informed the two of them that Gino would be at his luncheonette on 105th in about fifteen minutes, they were both surprised; it seemed a little too public for what they were going to do, right in front of the place Gino owned. Joey never liked to do this sort of thing in the neighborhood. But, Armondo was clear: it had to be done this way. The Zip felt safe on his block, and there was no more time for romancing him.

Joey and Al left Armondo's through a side exit and got into the black sedan waiting at the curb. To make sure there were no surprises, they wanted to make one pass of the area where Gino was going to meet his fate. Though I couldn't see who was in the back seat as they drove by, I was able to make out Ralph "Smitty" LaPore, Armondo's driver, at the wheel. That's when I knew something was up. Since he was looking at the Zip's building, Smitty didn't see me standing by the lamp post.

From the street, I couldn't hear everything that was going on in the Zip's apartment, even though all his windows were wide open in the summer heat. But I'd heard the phone ring and had seen the Zip disappear from the window to answer it. After a minute, he reappeared briefly, looking down the street both ways. To cover myself, I went back to being a look-out for the card game. As the stakes got higher and my friends one-upped each other, they'd gotten louder.

"I got a ten," Fredo yelled.

Richie yelled even louder, "Well, here's the king. Whaddaya got, Jamesy?"

"I can't believe I got the fuck'n deuce of spades, you cocksucker!"

Everybody laughed except Jamesy. I looked at him and mimicked jerking off, the way he always did. When the Zip hit the street and saw us, he started yelling, "Hey, get outta here!. People gotta work tomorrow! Go on, get the fuck outta here!"

He squinted at me, a skinny kid in khaki pants and decent leather shoes. My pants were always pressed. That was my disguise: as casual as I looked, I plotted all my moves with care, from where I hung out to exactly what I wore once I left the apartment. Maybe it came from spending most of my early years after our parents died in an orphanage before Joey and I got to live together. I was always aware I had to make my own way in the world;. there was little or no margin for error.

I was still leaning against the lamp post when Gino shouted at me from across the street, "Vinnie, what're you doin' hangin' with these shit-heels? Don't let your brother hear about it."

As the Zip walked off, we could hear him muttering to himself, "Little cocksuckers, gotta come here, breakin' balls."

The game seemed destined to break up. When Fredo and Jamesy and the rest of the guys made their way to the pool hall, I went my own way. For one thing, I had no money left; what I did have was a hunch.

"I'm gonna go to the club," I lied. "I'll see youse all tomorrow."

At this point, all I knew was that Gino had been hanging out with Joey a lot lately. Even as the Zip walked away, I wondered if he was going to meet a cop or a Fed. That's how the street version of the game "telephone" got your imagination fired up. Was Gino working with another family? Whatever it was, I had a strong suspicion that Gino was going to meet a contact, and maybe he was even plotting against my brother. For now, I figured that if I followed the Zip to check out the situation, maybe I'd see something valuable to bring to Joey.

Gino stopped outside of his luncheonette and looked at his watch as he lit a cigarette. Meanwhile, I was crossing Second Avenue walking east. The door to Barney's Bar and Pizzeria was open, making the warm summer night even hotter. The music from the jukebox seemed to serenade the entire neighborhood with a mix of classic Duke Ellington, from the Other Harlem, and Count Basie and Tommy Dorsey. It was the tail end of the big band era before rock and roll ruled the airwaves. We played Italian music, opera and songs full of old country wisdom and humor, only in the home.

I could smell the aroma of fresh-cooked coal oven pizza and tap beer as I cruised along, taking note of the many open windows in the apartment houses along the avenue. Except for the music and the laughter from the pizzeria, all was quiet. When I hit the curb, I had to jump over a puddle of water, the remnants of a fire hydrant kids had opened earlier to keep cool.

Then, I saw the sedan pull up with Smitty at the wheel. I stopped in my tracks at a closed newsstand on the southeast corner of 105th Street. Inside the car, I found out later from Al Hicks, he and Joey had discussed the night's mission. My brother reminded Al that the Zip was always punctual.

Al said something along the lines of, "The sooner this rat's gone, the better."

Later Al told me that Joey wasn't having it; my brother didn't care what people said. As far as Joey was concerned, Gino was no rat, and Al knew it.

As much as my brother trusted Al, whose family had helped us out after our parents died, Joey was always his own man, whereas Al was in Armondo's back pocket.

Al reminded my brother that they had a job that needed to be done.

"Al, c'mon, we all know the Zip's a major junk pusher," Joey told him. "Tell me, who the fuck did he ever put in jail? Somebody owes him a lotta money, so they put out a wire he's a rat? Bullshit, the fuckin' color of blood is green."

"Hey, Joey, we shouldn't even be talkin' about this. You know better than–"

"Yeah, yeah, I know, just do the fuck'n work. Meantime, we end up with the leftover bones after some cocksucker, who wouldn't even step on a roach, eats the meat."

Al shook his head. "*Madonna*, Joey, c'mon, you can't go around talkin' like that. You're gonna get both of us whacked."

As the car with Joey and Al inside pulled up, I could see from my position at the newsstand that Gino was standing outside his luncheonette, waiting. When I saw my brother and Al Hicks get out of the back, I tensed up inside but stayed hidden as best I could.

Gino smiled. "Joey, what, Armondo's got you makin' drops now?" I heard him say with a laugh. "What did you do to piss him off? What's doin,' Al?"

Joey looked at Al; neither of them smiled. Later, Al admitted to me that he knew Gino wasn't a rat, even if only Joey acknowledged it. They both knew the score. This was the fuckin' street, and they had to do what they had to do without asking questions.

As the truth suddenly dawned on Gino, he went white in his normally swarthy face. Joey and Al Hicks drew their pistols and shot Gino several times: POW, POW, POW.

After a pause, the Zip got one final shot in the head for good measure.

Joey and Al looked around for a few seconds to make sure Gino had no back-up. As Joey turned to get back in the car, he noticed me with a "What the fuck just happened" look on my face standing by the newsstand. Al never noticed me, nor did Smitty, who was focused on the getaway.

I knew what Joey was thinking as he drove off: what the hell was his kid brother, the one he wanted to protect above all else, doing on that street? I knew he'd have to confront me soon, though not that night since he didn't plan on coming home right away, but it would be soon. Joey and Al had to make sure they covered their asses concerning the law, though they weren't too worried. People in the neighborhood still didn't see or hear anything they weren't supposed to see or hear. It seemed that everybody in East Harlem acted like Helen Keller: deaf, dumb and blind.

Once the job was over, the name Gino Pinetta was never mentioned again around the neighborhood. Everybody accepted that he'd had it coming. As soon as people heard the gunshots stop, they'd started trickling out. When they saw that it was Gino who'd taken the hit, a few people started to laugh.

One old guy who'd lived in East Harlem all his life said, "Looks like the Zip needs a zipper!"

Gino lay there dying, and nobody in the neighborhood gave a fuck. They didn't even call the ambulance until they were absolutely sure he was dead.

CHAPTER TWO

Joey was initiated into the family in early 1951. To this day, my brother is talked about, though not in my presence. Most people won't mention him if I'm around; they don't want to offend me. Joey was a handsome, well spoken rising star in our world, and most people can't help but remember the best of him.

He was class all the way. For a while, custom-made clothes and soft leather shoes were the only things he spent money on. While his friends were gambling or drinking, he was building his wardrobe; when Joey focused on something, he got pretty obsessive. He'd shut out everything else, think through every possible angle, and then do it exactly right.

The only place I ever really topped him was in the kitchen. My brother knew how to cook, but he could never get that last spark, the difference between a good meal and a great one. It's an instinct, I guess. My brother never quite had it, but I did. Thinking about it, Joey and me in the kitchen, him tasting my sauce—always made with the freshest of tomatoes—might have been my proudest moment in his eyes. You couldn't always tell with Joey; he hid that stuff behind a poker face. But I knew what he was feeling and thinking about me every time he raised the spoon to his mouth.

I think he'd be even prouder of what I did with my place, Big V Deli, on Second Avenue between 105th and 106th. It was a real Italian deli, a throwback to the days before all the Puerto Ricans started moving in. Even they came in for my sausage and peppers, my homemade mozzarella, and my eggplant parmesan. So did some of the Italians who moved to the Bronx and the suburbs after the GI Bill helped them move out and up, Americana Italian style. Who could blame them? The tenements were home, but a lot of them didn't have central heating or even a tub in the kitchen like ours. Some had a common bathroom, one to a floor. The only light came from the window facing the street or the air shaft. People who grew up here come back to the old neighborhood to shop and eat 'cause there's no place like East Harlem, once the biggest Italian American community in the country. At one point, there were 5,000 people living on a single block.

Back at the turn of the century, Mulberry Street, in what's now considered Little Italy, couldn't hold a candle to East Harlem. Many Italians came to Harlem from downtown for more light, air, and a bigger sky. Even if the apartments were tight as a tick, Harlem has that uptown feeling, a sense of possibility. That's something money can't buy.

Big V Deli grew over the years. I couldn't say the same for Joey's club, the Pioneer, which, I have to admit, got a little worn around the edges. After my brother died, I left the Pioneer just the way it was, even if it's mostly old-timers hanging out there now, still playing cards and drinking espresso. You can't deny that there are ghosts in the walls. If those walls could talk, the stories they would tell might make your hair stand straight up.

Maybe Joey wouldn't have liked me clinging to the past, but it was the only way I could keep him alive in the neighborhood. I guess that's why I left the Pioneer just the same, raggedy edges and all. Frankie Chiaro and his even dimmer brother Swifty are still there, the last holdouts from the old days, still hanging on to traditions we honor, like the Giglio Feast and the Feast of Our Lady of Mount Carmel. Frankie Chiaro was Joey's friend: strong, tough, and could always be counted on to back us up at the club if things got out of hand. His loyalty was unquestioned even if he wasn't the sharpest knife in the drawer. Sometimes, he drove Joey and did errands my brother cooked up for him. His sister Nadine, who Joey liked to say had the biggest mouth in East Harlem, cleaned our place for us every couple of weeks.

Sometimes, what I heard on the street amounted to half-truths. In terms of who was pregnant, who hadn't paid their rent on time, and who missed Mass the previous Sunday, Nadine was the only reli-

able source. But, there were others who spread false rumors on purpose to pit people against each other. Nadine always told it like it was.

Some years ago, Big V moved to the Italian section of the Bronx off Arthur Avenue, but it's still in operation, with my son Joseph at the helm. I never called him Joey. You can't step in the same river twice, as that famous Roman general used to say. Even though I'm supposed to be retired, I still go in at least three times a week to putter around in the kitchen and bother my wife Rosemarie, who's younger than me and helps Joseph run the show.

Nadine's here too, still calling Joey Rendino the handsomest fuck she ever met. Who would have guessed that Nadine, all 5'1" of her, with hair dyed the color of Tang, would be one of my last links to the Harlem days? I remember most vividly one morning when Joey walked into my deli when it was still located in East Harlem. There was a good-sized line on this bitter cold day at about 9 a.m. I heard Nadine tell Joey that I was in the kitchen. I asked Nadine to help out at Big V when the Dew Drop In, a cheerful, over-lit luncheonette where she worked on Second Avenue between 106th and 107th, was demolished to make room for low-income city projects.

I could also hear Joey teasing her, as he did on so many occasions, "Hey, Nadine, make sure you butter the rolls. And the coffee better be hot, not like your usual."

"Nadine, you want me to go and wake up Swifty? He'll bring his dog in for breakfast, and it'll shit all over the floor so you can clean it up."

Nadine had it with Joey's horsing around, "Hey, go fuck yourself, you fag! And take my two retarded brothers with you!"

Everyone on line for their breakfast started laughing out loud. Nadine's shtick was part of the show at Big V Deli, one you didn't want to miss. When I moved the deli to the Bronx, she was part of the traveling show.

I wouldn't have this story without Nadine and Al Hicks, who revealed so much to me on his deathbed.

It's my history, and I'm lucky to have a piece of it still with me.

Our mother died two weeks after giving birth to me. She'd

been bleeding a lot during and after the delivery, and by the time the doctors were able to stop it, she'd already caught the infection that killed her. In those days, there wasn't a lot they could do. She tried but couldn't breastfeed me, so the midwife obliged. Joey was always at her bedside. By the second week, she'd lapsed into a coma and never woke up.

She got to see me just once before we lost her. All this, of course, I was told years later; Joey was forthcoming about information like this. He was there when our father brought me into the room and asked my mother, "What should we name him?" Still spent from the delivery, she was too weak to even hold me. Finally, she told my father, "Name him Vincent," after his dead brother.

In those days, life was often short and brutal. Our father, Antonio, died just before Joey's thirteenth birthday. I don't have many memories of my father, but from pictures, I could see that he was solid, like a bull ready to charge at the slightest provocation. He was a mechanic who got hit in an accident at Mel and Marty Lester's father's car lot, where he worked. "Pop" Lester and his kids grew up on the Lower East Side and moved to East Harlem during Prohibition.

Marty's father felt responsible for our father's accident, even if it was just a freak thing and nobody's fault. After Antonio had seen a truck back up too quickly, he rushed over to push a new co-worker, a young guy who wasn't yet alert, out of the truck's path. The young man survived unscathed, but Antonio was killed instantly.

The Lesters were devastated. They spent weeks fighting in the courts, trying to find a way to keep custody of Joey and me before they finally realized that they couldn't fight the city. Marty's father kept up the rent on my parent's apartment on 105th Street and maintained it the entire time Joey and I were in the orphanage. When Joey managed to get out, he went to Marty, who handed him the keys to our parents' apartment and gave him a job. A few months later, Joey was earning his own money working in construction, but he made it a point to be available if the Lesters needed him.

I spent most of my childhood in the Catholic orphanage on First Avenue run by the Sisters of Charity. After a year or so, I could hardly remember life being any other way. The orphanage let Joey see me only once a week.

When my brother turned eighteen, he spent a year trying every legal way he could to get custody of me. He knew they'd make it very difficult for him to adopt someone at his age, not to mention that he'd been upstate in juvie for a stretch. But, it was in Joey's nature never to stop trying. And at least he could show he had a job. On paper, he was a member of the laborer's union.

Finally, Joey's friend Al Hicks helped get me sprung from the nuns. It was Al's father, Santino, a prominent guy in the local fruit and vegetable business, who eventually came up with the plan to get me out of there. Santino set it up through some people Armondo Manna knew. Armondo's connections extended to the church and every other institution in East Harlem that needed contributions. There was a story told around the neighborhood that one day one of his men needed money for an operation for his kid. He wanted it to be legit, given the circumstances. So on the inside of a matchbook cover, Armondo wrote: "Backed by Armondo Manna, a loan of $1500." Armondo told his man to bring it to the bank manager on 116th Street and First Avenue. This way the bank knew they'd be covered if anything went bad. The neighborhood then was one big web of connections, and they trailed you all your life.

Al Hick always admired Joey, how he handled himself in the streets and respected his elders in the neighborhood. Al took my brother under his wing when he was just a teenager. Al was a good judge of who belonged in the Life, and it turned out that Joey was a natural.

By the late 1940s, the fruit and produce markets were well established in the Bronx. The markets moving out of East Harlem enabled many new players to get involved in the market. Though there was room for everyone to make a living in this flourishing business, some of the new breed broke the long-established rules between the vendors and truckers:

DON'T TRY TO STEAL CUSTOMERS
DON'T UNDERCUT PRICES
DON'T INFRINGE ON TRUCK ROUTES

The Papa family was a tough Bronx clan who didn't give a fuck for anyone or anything. Mario, the patriarch of the family, was a vendor who also had a truck route in the Bronx. After he died and his three sons took over, the shit really hit the fan. Other drivers were beat up, their trucks damaged, and their inventory trashed.

The Papa boys approached Santino, who ran the market, and demanded more space so that they could expand by hook or by crook. They started intimidating his customers and their competitors. Santino's large supermarket stops were growing, but the Papas' antics were causing problems with the entire market.

Al Hicks' people at the market were being affected, too. So, Al went to Armondo and filled him in on the problems being caused by the Papas. He also told Armondo that the Papas weren't with anyone; they were just a bunch of fuck'n cowboys. They did what they wanted to do whenever they wanted to do it. After listening, Armondo told Al, "Do whatever you want to do—whatever you think is necessary."

Al knew he couldn't talk or reason with the Papas; when he discussed it with Joey, my brother agreed.

For weeks, Al and Joey watched the Papas' every move; the brothers were predictable to a fault. Angelo was the oldest of the Papa clan. Al Hicks couldn't remember the names of the other two. These crazy bastards seemed to think they were invincible, that no one would ever fuck with them.

The Papa brothers would get to the market at 11 p.m. to get ready for the next day's business. Their workers would unload the trucks and reload them with whatever new produce they received that day. Angelo stayed in the office with one of his brothers all night. By 4 a.m., the trucks were ready to roll. The youngest brother, one of the drivers, took care of all the call-in orders.

Every morning when he left the market, he would stop at an all-night luncheonette on Southern Boulevard in the Bronx, about a five minute drive away. He always left the truck running when he went into the luncheonette to get a container of coffee and a bite to eat.

To make this move, Al Hicks recruited one of his relatives who worked at the market; Al never let me know which one because he was still alive when Al told me the story.

Since Al's relative and Joey knew every move the Papas made, they decided to wait on a side street by the diner where they wouldn't be noticed but would be able to see as the young Papa approached the diner for his morning ritual. At about 3:30 a.m., they found a parking spot on a nearby side street. As sure as shit, at about 4:05 a.m., they saw the truck approaching and pulled out. They caught up to the back of the truck and followed it as it pulled in.

When the Papa's truck stopped, Joey got out of the car—now right behind the truck—and quietly snuck up behind the driver's door. As the young Papa opened the door and stepped out, Joey hit him with an axe. WHACK!!!!!! The poor bastard never knew what hit him. Given that it was about 4:15 a.m., the luncheonette and surrounding neighborhood were quiet. With the truck running, no one could hear a peep. It was all over in seconds.

As Al's relative watched Joey smashing the Papa with the axe, he got out of the car, walked over to Joey, and handed him a pump action, sawed-off shotgun. Joey got in the truck and drove back to the market as Al's relative took off in another direction. As planned, Al was waiting at the market in another car. Joey pulled up and parked in one of the Papa Brothers' spaces. He jumped out of the truck, walked briskly to the Papas's office, pointed the shotgun point blank at the other two members of the clan, and blew them away: BOOM… BOOM…BOOM…

Joey jumped into the waiting car. He and Al were gone before anyone knew what had happened.

Al told me it was Joey who mapped out every aspect of the move.

When Al met with Armondo, he went over every detail of what had happened and let Armondo know that it was Joey's plan. Armondo was so impressed that he told Al he'd found himself a real gem and insisted that he meet my brother.

I don't know for sure, but I think this was the first piece of work my brother did on the record. I can't help but think about the fact that back then people died over grapes and watermelons. Today, many more people die because of oil.

I guess my brother was right: *the color of blood is green.*

Joey always had my back. When I first got out of the orphanage with Santino's help, I was set up with a foster family, the Gallos, who were paid a fee by the government to take care of a troubled kid (Joey said this proved the government was just another sucker, paying somebody to do what he wanted to do for nothing.). They met me once, so they knew what I looked like in case anyone ever checked. Then, the Gallos cashed the check each month and signed whatever paperwork came their way.

If anybody came by, their story was going to be that I was out of the house with my brother because it was important for me to see my family—Joey, period. But, they didn't have to bother keeping up the show, nor did they need the spare room filled with children's clothes and the other stuff that they kept around for the first few years.

The only time an inspector from the city came by, the Gallos got nervous. But, as it turned out, the inspector was checking out the building because his daughter was moving in. After seeing the address on my paperwork, he just wanted to make sure it was a safe place to live. In the six years the Gallos cashed those checks, only once did someone come to their door. As far as the authorities were concerned, I could have been dropped to the floor of the ocean like a stone.

Joey never let anybody have reason to investigate the situation. He kept me well-dressed, partly because he wanted me to stand out from the Irish kids, whose tailoring was far less sharp than the Italians, even at that age. My brother wanted me to look good enough so that no social worker looked twice but not so good that someone would take notice from the other direction, either. This was the beginning of my education in how to make myself fit in. Even later when Big V Deli was doing great, I never went for custom tailoring or the pinkie rings, gold chains and medals, and crosses that the wise guys wore.

Joey and I ate decently, and he made sure I always went to school, even if school was never my brother's favorite place. He was bored with the whole thing and left after the eighth grade. Later in life he regretted it. A teacher in his reform school got him interested in William Shakespeare, whose work he came to love. Though he'd never seen the plays performed, he heard the words over and over in his head. As an adult, Joey often resorted to quotes from the Bard even in everyday conversations. The same teacher had tried to get him interested in acting, but Joey didn't enjoy pretending. What made Shakespeare so great to Joey was his grasp of everyday tragedies and triumphs. Even with all the "thees" and "thous," there was nothing fake about the action in Shakespeare's plays, as far as my brother was concerned.

Joey encouraged me to be interested in school. He didn't think I knew what he was up to; but, years later, I found out that after I fell asleep at night, he'd force himself to read every book I brought home from class. In terms of math, my brother thought numbers only made sense as a way to keep score. I was better at it, though Joey and I could both do quick math in our head up to a point. We got it from our mother, who once had her own business making artificial flower arrangements for schools and funeral homes in the neighborhood. She even kept her own books.

Once I hit junior high, Joey came to enjoy history vicariously through me. Whenever he quizzed me on the class work, his questions would come from a different angle. He'd read between the lines, imagining the characters that the history books felt were too unimportant to document. He'd ask me stuff like, "Do you think those farmers really cared who they were paying a tax to? Do you think the slaves gave a fuck who owned the country they were slaves in?"

One of the reasons Joey left school was that when he tried to bring in ideas like this, none of his teachers ever appreciated it.

Joey made me feel obligated to go to school every day. What the hell happened as a result? My truant friends got much better than me at shooting pool.

The day after Gino got clipped, I lost my gaming money—yeah, again. I was outside Joey's club smoking with a few of the kids from the neighborhood when Carole Reedy bummed a cigarette from me. That was the year that Carole and some of us graduated high school.

I was surprised because I didn't even know she smoked. Joey was friends with her brother, Danny, who worked at their father's bar in Hell's Kitchen. I didn't know any of the Reedys very well. What I did know was that Carole and Danny's father, Mike, a former dock worker, did well enough with the bar to support the family; this much Joey'd told me.

Carole was a stunner, a classic Irish beauty with red hair and bright green eyes. She was the girl every boy wanted and grew into the woman every man craved. Even in a Catholic school uniform, she had a look that said "class." Maybe it was the fact that she carried herself with poise beyond her years. When Carole got older, one of the local wise guys told her she was a cross between Maureen O'Hara and Rita Hayworth—not that she would have given any of those guys the time of day.

She may have been a high school girl, but as the daughter of a saloon keeper who grew up in East Harlem, Carole was plenty street smart and knew better than to encourage attention from the local players. Besides, she had eyes for one man only.

The day she bummed a cigarette from me, I extended it with an ease I hoped looked real. "Thanks, Vin," she said, with a friendly smile that telegraphed her confidence. She knew I would never make a move on her.

I was spared the need for small talk when Carole headed off in the direction of the pool hall. A moment later, I spotted my brother striding down the street in his usual confident way; Joey always walked like that. He knew everybody in East Harlem, and people were friendly to him wherever he went. I watched him stop at a newsstand, where he shook his head at an item screaming from the front page: "Gangster Slain on East Harlem Street."

Then, I saw two of the nuns from the Sisters of Charity walking down 105th. The Sisters hadn't always been easy on me in the orphanage; they weren't easy on anyone. Most of the nuns were Irish and retained a suspicion of the Italian kids, especially the boys. Still, my brother had a lot of respect for the work they did. He crossed the street to give them a few of the big bills in his pocket.

"Thank you, Mister Joey," they chirped in unison.

I had to laugh when I saw this turnaround in attitude. When Joey heard me laughing, he called me over.

"Those two must pray for you every night, Joey. You never miss. 'Thank you, Mister Joey,'" I said, imitating them.

"Hey, don't joke about the sisters. They do the right thing. They help people."

Joey looked up and saw Carole standing in the crowd of teens by the pool hall.

"By the way, keep Carole away from the pool room."

"Why?"

"Because I said so, that's why."

"All right, Joey, jeez…"

I had to run to keep up with my brother, who continued with the stream of patter as we walked,. "There's gonna be a game tonight at the club. Vin, pick up some bread and some cold cuts. Make sure the joint's clean."

This wasn't good. Now I knew that Joey had seen me when the Zip got whacked. Starting off like this—with something unimportant, something he'd already told me—meant that my brother was way pissed. He wasn't gonna talk about the stuff that really mattered.

I just nodded, trying to look as nonchalant as possible, the same pose I'd perfected when handing Carole Reedy, Miss Bombshell, a smoke. "Me and Frankie, we took care of it already," I assured Joey.

"Good. So who you hangin' out with in there?"

"Aw, Jamesy, Richie, 'Fredo, everybody, you know?" I looked off into the distance. Knowing the rhythm of Joey's conversations, I counted silently, "*One... two... thr—*"

My brother grabbed me. "Why were you out on the block last night, ya dumb prick? What the fuck was that about?"

I braced myself, but Joey didn't hit me, just held onto my shoulders. I told him calmly, "I didn't see nothing, Joey. You don't have to worry about it."

Joey smiled, just a little, but caught himself. "That's not the point. I told you I don't want you getting involved in this shit, and I meant it."

"I know you want to take care of me, Joey, but I know the score."

This made Joey tense up. He almost did slap me then. "Don't think that, kid. This is something you gotta be born to, and you ain't. Forget what took place last night. It never should've happened."

But, when my brother looked me in the eye, he knew this was one battle he might lose. He was dealing with a teenager; if he gave me a rule to follow, I was gonna do the opposite.

Joey switched tactics. "If you're so bored and you want to start moving, use your brains—you're good at math. Listen, I gotta meet up with Armondo, but you're comin' home for dinner tonight. I'm cooking."

Looking back, I'd remember this as an important conversation with Joey because it was the first time my brother discussed these things with me on anything approaching an adult level. I knew better than to argue, especially when Joey was at least broaching the subject of the Life. The clues were there; I could read my brother better than anybody. Maybe someday soon I'd drive the car for him or something. I knew I could do a better job than Frankie.

Almost everyday I fantasized about things I could do with Joey to get close to him. I made mental lists before I went to sleep, like some people count sheep. In my mind, I decided I was a natural with firearms and imagined going with Joey to a shooting range and amazing him by hitting all the targets on the first try. But, there was plenty of time for that. Now, I needed to make a nice little stash of my own money instead of blowing my brother's playing cards and other bullshit.

I decided to do what Joey had recommended, something I was good at, numbers. A few weeks later, when Joey walked into Barney's pizza joint, he saw me with a notepad keeping a record of the bets on a numbers game. From the look on my brother's face, I knew he didn't approve, but he put $10 on 1-4-6. I have to admit, I thought I'd bought myself some cover working at a place like Barney's, now being run by an associate of Al Hicks. I was amazed that Joey could walk so casually into the pizzeria after having killed Gino just across the street, but nobody said anything about it.

And, of course, the next day, his numbers hit. Joey decided to take the money and a stash he'd built up and buy a new car. The next day, he pulled up at Armondo's, where the local crowd was lounging outside on the hot and humid day because the inside of the place was even hotter. Everybody got a good look at Joey's new Oldsmobile 98.

Even Armondo was impressed. "Look at the size of that fuck'n car," he muttered.

"Whoa, Joey, that's a big fuckin' car," Al Hicks repeated.

"Yeah, the price was big, too. I dealt with that friend of ours you sent me to. He fucked me. I could've paid $900 less at Marty the Jew's brother's dealership." He smiled bitterly. "Leave it to our friends to fuck us."

Joey knew Armondo was skeptical about dealing with Jewish people, so my brother made it a point of praising the Lesters whenever he had the opportunity.

Armondo shook his head and turned to Al and said,. "Okay, Al, next time Milo sees that piece of shit from Gothic Motors, raise the vig a half-point."

Al nodded.

It wasn't the overpricing of the car that vexed Joey. It was about a friend taking advantage of another friend. The seeds of his rebellion had been planted, and they would only grow with time.

CHAPTER THREE

I'm not sure exactly when my brother and Carole started to see each other. Joey kept it secret for a long time. He wasn't embarrassed, really; he just didn't want people thinking he was messing around with some teenage girl. Robbing the cradle didn't exactly fit the tough guy mold.

I figure she was maybe sixteen, and he was about twenty-two, when they started seriously hanging out. A lot of people would judge him for that, but, I know that nobody judged him as harshly as he judged himself. Of all the things he did in his life, all the sins he committed, this was the one thing that really bothered him. He was worried he was going to corrupt her. He loved her so much that he didn't want her falling in love with someone like him.

But, it was too late. She'd been in love with him from the first time she saw him. I don't know what age that was.

Given that I've got two granddaughters, I know how old a sixteen-year-old girl can look to an adult. But I'll tell you one thing, something that makes all the difference: Joey loved Carole until the day he died. And, to this day, I believe she still loves him. Sure, when they met that six years gap in age was a big deal. But, if he were alive today, would it matter at all? Hell, no.

When Joey was sixteen, Carole was ten. He thought of her as Danny's kid sister, always hanging around when he was in the house. Though his sister's behavior annoyed Danny, Joey thought it was cute. Even when my brother was a teenager, women flirted aggressively with him. Joey would often have to excuse himself before he got embarrassed (which always led to a show of anger on his part). Carole just liked to be around my brother, who knew even then that she'd grow up to be something special. She had the looks, the quick wit, and native intelligence to leave the neighborhood behind at some point; Joey was right about that. In some ways, Carole never did leave the way my brother might have imagined.

Her brother, on the other hand, was always reaching for something he could never quite grasp, which was why he idolized my brother. A hothead, Danny admired Joey's self-possessed cool. Even though my brother knew Danny Reedy wasn't always as level-headed as he was, Joey considered him a loyal friend who would have his back no matter what. Joey had tons of acquaintances, but, aside from maybe Al Hicks and Frankie Chiaro, my brother didn't have many friends he could rely on in that unquestioning way.

When it came to Danny's parents, Mike and Katie Reedy, they didn't think Joey was a bad influence on their son. They knew Danny: if anything, they thought Joey might protect him from getting into serious trouble, which Danny might have courted on his own. Then again, they were worried about Joey's influence on Carole. At first, Mike and Katie considered Carole's feeling toward my brother to be nothing more than a cute little crush. But, they started to become concerned when Danny and Joey were sent away upstate together. Carole didn't come out of her room for two weeks and ate almost nothing. Her parents willed themselves to believe her depression was for her brother, not the beautiful Italian boy.

It was Carole's dumb ass brother's idea that got Danny and Joey into trouble to begin with—even though Danny told his parents it had been Joey's. They got caught for lifting Mr. Minkoff's DeSoto. When the cops picked them up, Danny was in the back seat reading a porno magazine and smoking a Camel because of the he-man image he thought it gave him. He may have been loyal to Joey, but he was a real jerk-off.

The night of Mike and Katie Reedy's twenty-fifth anniversary party, Joey didn't say a word to Carole when she first walked into Reedy's pub, where just about everyone in their life had gathered to celebrate. All of Danny and Carole's friends had come for the occasion, too. Located on the south side of 55th Street near Eleventh Avenue on the lower level of a three story walk-up, the pub was jam-packed.

For the occasion, I wore my best leather jacket. I needed to keep up my image as Joey's younger brother. Most of Carole's girlfriends weren't half as good-looking as she was. Gorgeous women don't necessarily hang out with other women just like them because it can breed jealousy and resentment.

Though he kept his distance at first, Joey couldn't take his eyes off Carole; I noticed this even from across the room. Carole Reedy was wearing a bit too much make-up, including bright red lipstick, and was dressed in a slim skirt and tight sweater whose V-neck dipped a little too low. She was away from the nuns and took the liberty of dressing and looking like a modern-day woman.

When Joey looked at her, he didn't see a teenage girl desperate to be noticed. He saw the woman emerging from within; the way the light hit her red hair, the way her smile opened up her heart-shaped face.

Even if he'd been in juvie, Joey might as well have been a golden god to Carole, she'd confided in Nadine Chiaro, who combined an encyclopedic knowledge of neighborhood news with a motherly touch that few young girls looking for advice could resist. They'd all drop in at the Dew Drop even though the coffee tasted like dishwater, and the hamburgers always arrived half raw. None of this mattered; the girls came for Nadine's patient ear and insight into life.

Nadine's earthy language gave an Irish girl like Carole an opening to disclose love life particulars she'd never be able to share with her own strictly religious Irish mother. Carole didn't think she'd make it with a guy like Joey, she told Nadine one day on the way home from school. Her breasts hadn't grown as fast as the other girls'. Her mother refused to let her wear make-up to school. The nuns forbade it, anyway.

On another occasion in the Dew Drop, as Carole sipped a cherry cola she wailed to Nadine, "I'm not even Italian!" She honestly thought that Joey would never want to be with a little Irish girl like her.

"He's a good-looking son of a bitch," Nadine acknowledged. Even if she could see as clearly as a fortune teller with a crystal ball that Joey Rendino would break Carole Reedy's heart, Nadine swore on our pastor Father Fanelli's cassock that she'd keep her mouth shut at this stage of the game.

How did I know this? Nadine Chiaro, source of all info on Carole Reedy as the years went by.

Carole had invited a number of friends from school to her parents' party, including Nicky Tortino, one of the many boys who aspired to have Carole as a girlfriend. The way he was acting that night, he seemed to think he might have a chance with her, but Carole wasn't the least bit interested in Nicky. He started sneaking drinks the minute they got in, not even noticing that he was mooching off of Carole's parents.

Across the crowded bar, Joey signaled to me. So, I brought over two glasses of vodka. We clicked our glasses and downed the shots. It was the only time I ever saw Joey drink. "Vin, who's that guy Carole brought?"

"Nicky Tortino, he's in my homeroom. Fuckin' jerk."

"They serious, or what?"

"What do I know, Joey? He may think Carole likes him, but I never seen 'em together that way. He's just one of the group she hangs out with sometimes."

Joey watched as sickness overcame Tortino, who rushed to the bathroom with both his hands over his mouth—amateur hour. Half the bar erupted with laughter because if someone got sick this early, everybody knew it was going to be a good party. When I went over to tell Carole that she shouldn't be embarrassed by some chump, she'd already rushed to the bathroom to check on Nicky. Embarrassed, she didn't want her parents to think badly of her friends. After I went back to the bar, I realized that Joey was well aware of what was going on. He had a look in his eyes that would have scared the shit out of anyone.

What happened next was so fast that people barely noticed.

Mike and Katie Reedy didn't see it; Danny was too drunk to take it in. But Joey did. He saw Carole running out of the bathroom red-faced, a torn strap on her dress floating behind her. As she ran past him, he even swore he saw a handprint on her face. Later in their relationship, the only time they ever discussed Nicky Tortino, Carole told Joey that he had been wrong about the handprint. By then, Joey could have believed that if Nicky Tortino had hit her, Carole would've killed him all by herself.

Joey sat there, seemingly as calm as ever, watching Nicky Tortino exit the bathroom and slowly walk up to the bar. By chance, the only empty stool was directly next to Joey. Nicky plopped right down and was scanning the bar for leftover drinks when his eyes met my brother's.

"You still got a little bit right here, kid," Joey said, gesturing at the side of his mouth.

"Oh, thanks." Nicky rubbed his sleeve against his cheek, trying to wipe the puke away.

"Nah, it's right there," Joey said, pointing emphatically.

Nicky wiped harder, getting frustrated. "Did I get it now?"

"Christ, kid... here, let me."

Joey picked up a napkin and leaned in close. He grabbed Nicky by his elbow and pulled him off the stool. "Come on, we're leavin', Nicky. You've had too much to drink. Some fresh air'll do you good." He walked out of the place calmly with his arm around Nicky's shoulder.

Though I tried not to let Joey see me, I followed them outside in case my brother needed backup.

Given that a few guests were lingering outside the pub, Joey kept walking towards Tenth Avenue so he wouldn't make a commotion where people were standing. He almost pushed Nicky as they walked, but made it look as though he was only nudging him along. Before they reached Tenth Avenue, Joey pushed Nicky closer to an old tenement building. His tone was stern, but his demeanor remained calm: "Nicky, I'm gonna put you in a cab. Go home and sober up, and never, I mean never, come back here anymore, UNDERSTAND?"

By this time, Joey had the kid up against the brick wall. Nicky looked at Joey in a drunken stupor and said, "Why? What the fuck did I do?"

Now, Joey spoke with more force, "It doesn't matter, just do what the fuck I tell you to, you little prick."

"Hey fuck you, Joey, I'm going back inside."

As Nicky started back toward the pub, Joey grabbed him by the collar and banged him hard against the brick wall.

"Listen to me, you little cocksucker. I'm trying very hard not to give you the buck-wheats you deserve. You're a nasty, disrespectful little prick. Take this money, get in a cab, and get the fuck home."

I could see my brother starting to lose it. I hoped Nicky would listen, but he didn't. He started cursing Joey again. Before he could get one more "fuck" out of his mouth, Joey started to slap the shit out of Nicky.

Without thinking, I stepped in to stop Joey, something you never do, as I learned later in the Life. To my surprise, Joey looked at me, gave me a twenty, and told me to "put this little shit-head in a cab."

I'll never forget the way my brother looked; he even scared the shit out of *me*. Nicky finally got the message. Joey put the fear of God in him. Nicky Tortino never went near Carole Reedy again.

When Joey went back to the pub to retrieve his hat and coat, I followed once I'd sent Nicky on his way. No one at the party knew what had gone on outside, but the anger on Joey's face seemed to fill the room and tell a story about something the other party guests could only imagine.

When Joey walked back into Reedy's, Mike looked at him and shrugged. He figured Joey had to have his reasons to manhandle Nicky. He was glad my brother had dragged the kid outside instead of making a scene at the bar and ruining the whole night. Thank God Katie was in the backroom at the time and hadn't seen a thing.

The following week, Nicky walked up to me in the school

yard on a Friday. I was in a hurry to get to the Pioneer, so I shot him a cold look and walked away.

But Nicky came running after me, even though I tried not to acknowledge him. "Hey, Vinnie, wait!"

"Nicky, get the fuck out of here before I give you the beat'n my brother should have."

"Vinnie, you don't understand. I want you to take me to your brother. I want to apologize. Please, Vinnie, do this for me. Here's the twenty you gave me for the cab. Take it, take it."

I told him, "Keep the money." I could see how shaken this kid was. I told him I couldn't bring him to Joey's club, but I would make sure my brother got the message.

I started to feel bad for him. Hey, we all make fools of ourselves somewhere along the way. Last I heard, Nicky Tortino was doing very well on Wall Street.

Although Mike was happy that Joey had handled the situation with Nicky, he was very disappointed that his son, Danny, hadn't taken charge. He felt that since it was his family's place, Danny should have straightened out Nicky Tortino himself. What the whole incident did do was clarify Mike Reedy's view of how Joey felt about his daughter.

A few nights after the incident in Reedy's, Joey waited for Danny outside the pub on 55th Street. Joey had asked me to drive him; of course, I was thrilled to have a chance to get behind the wheel. The only reason my brother and I ever hung out in Hell's Kitchen, Irish turf, aside from going to special parties, was to visit Danny, who'd gone inside to check on an errand for his father. Joey was in the backseat of the car reading his newspaper when Carole Reedy appeared at the window, as if out of nowhere.

"How are you, Carole? Everything all right?" Even though he wasn't on his own turf, Joey acted like he owned these streets, too.

"Hi, Joey."

They stared at each other for a long moment: neither could think of a single thing to say out loud that wasn't better left unsaid. Finally, Danny appeared behind his sister. He ignored me behind the wheel and punched Carole in the shoulder, dodging her response as he got into the car. "Let's go, Joey. Leave the kid here."

Carole just watched as we pulled out.

The next night, Frankie told me there was a message at the Pioneer for Joey, telling him to be at Reedy's at 9 p.m. I overheard my brother ask, "Did Danny call this in?"

"Nah, I think it was his sister. Maybe there's a problem over there," said Frankie. By this time, I knew something was up because Joey was even more tight-lipped than ever. If Nadine hadn't given me the lowdown, I'd never have known how much Carole really meant to my brother.

Joey was cautious. He drove by the pub twenty minutes early and parked down the block. After killing his lights, he scanned the streets and windows. Not a minute passed before the passenger door opened and Carole got in and said, "Are you always so early when you have a date?"

Joey looked at her and said, "I didn't know I had a date. I thought Danny might have had a problem."

"Well, Rendino, Danny doesn't have a problem. You have a date with me. Does that answer your question?"

"Yeah, okay, now that I've been told I have a date, where would you like to go, Carole?"

"Let's park by the East River and watch the boats and talk."

But when they got there, Joey hardly had time to get out two words before she'd leaned over and cut through them. Because what Carole really wanted was Joey—right there, right then, all the way.

My brother and Carole Reedy first made love in the back of a 1949 Ford that Joey borrowed: this was before he bought his Olds. It wasn't exactly how he would've planned it. He would've planned to take her to a hotel. He would've planned on roses and champagne. He would've planned and over-planned and laid it on far too thick. He would've done all that because he genuinely loved her.

He wanted something better, he'd explained to Carole, something more romantic, for her sake.

Carole had thought about this moment for a long time. She hadn't discussed it with her girlfriends, the way other women might have. She confided only in Nadine, who had her ups and downs with men yet retained a hopeful attitude towards love. Carole knew she'd never get practical advice from her mother Katie. Not only was Carole too young in her mother's eyes; she'd been raised in a strictly religious home. Irish families discussed the birds and the bees even less than Italians did.

Nadine had warned Carole that Joey was a street guy, as much as she liked him; but Carole knew her own mind. Once she'd decided she wanted Joey Rendino, Carole went after him like a woman on a mission.

Later, Carole told Nadine that her experience with Joey had been exactly what she'd expected intellectually, but emotionally it was something else entirely. Seeing how Joey looked the moment he lost control was something Carole would never forget.

At this, Nadine had let out a long sigh as she put down a cup of coffee in front of Carole. "Honey, you're just a kid," she warned her.

Carole told her what she'd also told my brother, "I'm going to get my just due in this life. But, it won't be worth much if I don't have Joey with me."

That's how Carole was: once she made up her mind, she acted without fear. Though she'd grown up on the tough streets of East Harlem, she was ahead of her time in her sense of independence. This is what I realized only looking back at the way she loved my brother. When she'd first seen Joey Rendino, Carole Reedy wasn't even a teenager. To her, he always was, and always would be, Just Joey. As for Joey, he knew Carole could be stoic, tender, and even arrogant at times; but she never overwhelmed anyone with any of it. She was sexy, smart, beautiful, and charming. Yet, I'd seen her reduce grown men who hit on her to awkward little kids.

Joey loved her for all of those qualities. There was another thing that made Carole Reedy different: although she'd gone to Catholic school, she never took to the religion the way most of the women in our community did. I think she found the Church hidebound, especially the way the hierarchy regarded and treated women. Carole never saw herself as less than a man's equal. Nevertheless, she related to and loved God in her own way.

When Carole was considering going to school in Boston, Joey encouraged her. He loved her enough to know he wasn't good enough for her. He wanted her to be free, to get away from a neighborhood where most people don't even go south of 96th street. At Boston University, Carole's assigned roommate was a grad student from Switzerland. When discussing the courses they were planning to take, her roommate asked Carole to take a chemistry class with her. Since chemistry had been Carole's favorite subject in high school, they both enrolled.

Eventually, Carole Reedy became one of the first female success stories in the fragrance industry, but all of that was yet to come. Years later, her boss Stephen Aronson would say that she was the perfect blend.

She was then, and she still is.

CHAPTER FOUR

Joey never told me about the money he was making. Years later, other people filled me in. Though he was tight-lipped on his finances, he always schooled me on street life. Rule Number One: "Observe, and don't ask a lot of questions. Never speak unless spoken to first."

And always watch your back.

After I graduated high school, I started making my own moves with the help of Al Hicks, not my brother. Al would lend me money at 1%, and I'd turn around and lend it to other people at 3% or 4%. Nine times out of ten, the guys who borrowed were working off gambling debts. Getting paid back from these mooks could get complicated. Sometimes, it was easier to move "extra" stuff that came in on the docks: televisions, just getting popular; radios, still a force; and all kinds of liquor. Al made sure none of my action overlapped with Joey's.

As for Carole, she was working on her own life. Until the day she left for Boston University, she thought Joey was gonna beg her to stay. She lost that bet she'd made with herself. Joey fought every impulse he had because he always believed that she was destined for something better. He couldn't stay away, but he never once suggested that she shouldn't go to Boston. Joey put in the lion's share of the money that paid for her education, though Carole never had an inkling; nobody knew but me. I'm not even sure what Joey said to Mike Reedy to get him to agree to take the money without hurting his pride. But, that was the kind of thing Joey would always do. He could almost convince you that you were doing him a favor by taking the money; that's how much he enjoyed it.

When Carole left town, Joey stayed in East Harlem building up a reputation on the street but never quite saving as much money as he should. He even got arrested a few times. They were just fucking with him, but Joey found out that he was now expected to grease some of his own palms. That was the problem with a reputation; people expected you to take care of yourself. Navigating on his own also gave Joey a chance to do some things independent of Armondo and the other old-timers in the neighborhood. Only once did my brother take me on a real job with him, only because he had to keep the crew especially tight—just Joey, Frankie, and me, people Joey felt he could absolutely trust.

As I look back, I can see how my brother began to mark his own turf, one that wasn't always strictly aligned with the local powers that be.

I remember the day Katie Reedy died of ovarian cancer. She was only fifty-two, way too young for someone to go. At the time, Carole was away at school in her sophomore year. My brother stayed with the Reedys throughout the entire ordeal. When it came to Carole and her family, Joey was always sensitive to their needs. He took care of all the expenses and arrangements for the funeral. He even bought Carole an airline ticket so that she could get back to East Harlem in time for her mother's wake and services.

To make sure Katie would be remembered in the neighborhood, Joey made a large donation in her name to our Lady of Mount Carmel on 115th between First and Pleasant Avenue for repairs to the beautiful interior, the work of thousands of immigrant Italian artisans in the early part of the twentieth century. The way Joey jumped in allowed Mike, Danny, and Carole to deal with their grief without having to handle practical things no one wants to think about at times like that.

Though the Reedys weren't Italian, they were honored in East Harlem for their decades-long devotion to Our Lady of Mount Carmel. Nadine Chiaro always said that Katie Reedy knitted more crafts for the annual Christmas bazaar and fundraiser than almost everyone else combined. Although Nadine had a mouth like a truck driver, she counted herself, like Katie, as one of Father

Fanelli's best friends in the parish.

If Nadine liked you, the odds were everyone liked you. She liked the Reedys, especially Carol, and since Katie did her part to help Mount Carmel, so did Nadine. Who else would clean the rectory twice a week for nothing and make sure the good father had his favorite Chianti at Christmas and on all important feast days?

When it came to the type of dress in which Katie would be laid out and buried, Nadine helped make the decision. Carole trusted and valued her opinion. Katie was as straight up and down conservative as you could find. Together Carole and Nadine picked out something for Katie that fit her image. When Katie Reedy was laid out for viewing at DePaolo's Funeral Home on Second Avenue, Carole was overwhelmed by the number of people who came to pay their respects and press prayer cards into her hand as they passed by. As emotional as the experience was, it also helped Carole focus on the fact that she needed to think about the future.

After the wake, hundreds of people from the neighborhood came to Our Lady of Mount Carmel for a mass conducted by Father Fanelli in Latin—that's how they did it then. When Carole broke down sobbing against my brother's shoulder, Joey cried a few stoic tears, too. Though Mike Reedy saw this, as far as I know, he never told Joey how much the small display of emotion moved him. But, from where I was sitting in the church, I could see it on Mike's face. Danny showed no emotion whatsoever during the Mass. Later, I found out that after the funeral, he got so drunk that he passed out in the back room at Reedy's Pub. This was rare for a practiced drinker like Danny, but then again, this was a special occasion. When a parent dies, you begin to face eternity yourself.

Yeah, Mike Reedy appreciated all Joey had done for the family in a time of need; but he still didn't like the way my brother sneaked around with his daughter. He knew about their relationship, though Carole thought he didn't. As much as he liked and respected Joey, Mike knew that my brother was a street guy: that was his lot in life. But, Carole's father was also aware that coming between them would only drive Carole and Joey away. Whether Mike Reedy liked it or not, his daughter and my brother were in love, and he knew it.

Whatever his concerns, Mike had to acknowledge that Joey showed him and his family respect. Mike had run his pub honestly every day for twenty years, holding his head high. He'd even paid taxes on the full cash register till, saying it was his duty not to short change the country that gave him the chance to earn an honest living.

Then one day, Jerry Shay, who controlled the action in Hell's Kitchen, had two of his Irish thugs, the Boylan brothers, pay a visit to Reedy's Pub. The action in Hell's Kitchen then was still dominated by the Irish mob. Jerry Shay was a quintessential Irish hood, over six feet tall with dirty blonde hair and a casual way of dressing. Because he was quiet, when he got serious, his demeanor was that much scarier. The Irish come in two sizes: the ones who never shut up and the ones that are the classic "silent and cunning" type—that was Jerry. The Boylan brothers were as tall and fair as Jerry Shay, and just as mean.

At Reedy's, Billy Boylan just stood by the bar while his low-life brother Hughie, a pot-bellied thug disliked by everyone, even Jerry Shay, and said loudly, "I'm gonna help Mike out, get him some new customers."

All they wanted was a cut of the action. When Mike said he'd give him a piece of whatever new business they brought in, Hughie laughed. For a few weeks, Hughie ran a dice game every night in the back room of Reedy's. The only people who came brought their own booze and complained about Mike's prices. The Boylans brought in six to twelve low-lives, like themselves, who were so loud that they scared away many of the regulars, who numbered from forty to fifty customers on any given night. They were ruining Mike's regular business.

Since the Kitchen had only become more Irish in the twenty years he'd been open, Mike Reedy wasn't sure where to turn. He couldn't go against Jerry Shay's people, no matter how legitimate his complaint. He'd need to partner with another bunch of local thugs who were just as strong, which might cause trouble in a turf war. And, Mike certainly couldn't go to the police. The pub would be burned down the same night, possibly with the Reedys locked inside, a fate even worse than what the Shay crew might do.

He did the only thing he could think of: call Joey. When my brother met him at the pub and heard the story, Joey fumed in his own controlled way. He wasn't going to rush into anything, but he wanted to find a way to keep an eye on the situation. He managed to get himself into the dice game, but when he kept winning, Hughie Boylan began to notice him.

One night, Joey asked me to drive him because Frankie was busy at the Pioneer. My brother let me in on a few details about what was going on in Mike's place. He knew I cared about the Reedys, too. Two weeks to the day after they started, Joey told me, the dice game run by the Boylans stopped.

Mike chased off the remaining guys who were just looking for some action. One night as Mike was locking the heavy wooden door at closing time, Hughie showed up flanked by the younger, more physically fit Billy, who looked around the pub as he had the first time, without saying a word.

"Hey, Mike, glad we caught you. I figured this would be a good time to pick up my cut," Hughie said grinning.

Mike didn't respond. He stayed behind the bar where he had a shotgun within reach, he told Joey later, filling him in on everything that had gone down with the Irish hoods. Mike Reedy was at wit's end.

"I'm figuring twenty percent of the register, ten for me and ten for my brother," Hughie had told him—as if Mike Reedy were the sole support of the Boylan boys.

"Hughie, maybe we had an arrangement, but you're supposed to be helping this place," Mike said firmly.

"Are you kidding me? We tried, but this place is what it is. There are plenty of bars just like this one. What you got here's nothing special, Mike, hate to tell you. Like it or not, we're your partners for as long as you're in Hell's Kitchen."

"Bullshit! I've been here since you were in grade school," Mike Reedy said angrily. "I've never been bulldozed in my life," Mike sputtered to Hughie Boylan. Given all the years he worked on the West Side docks, he may have been a little hunched over when he walked, but Mike Reedy was nobody's patsy.

"You better do what's right here, Mike. You got a very pretty girl going to that school, where is it? Somewhere up in Boston? We know a lot of people up in Boston, friends who can make sure she's safe. You know what I mean, Mike? They can watch her all day and all night. Or, it can go the other way, if you know what I mean."

Staring daggers at Hughie, Mike had fought the impulse to draw his gun, which would only have made matters worse. Hughie smiled, poured himself a drink, and toasted Mike. Billy licked his lips with an odd look on his face.

After a long pause, Mike finally said, parsing his words carefully, "You picked the wrong day, Hughie. I put all the money in the bank on Friday. It's Saturday. I can't get it out till Monday. I can give you something from the register tonight, but business has been a little slow these past few weeks…"

"Hey, it's okay, Mike, I trust you. Anyway, if it turns out that twenty percent ain't enough, we can always take a flat fee. You go to the bank on Monday, you get the envelope, and I'll see you here, *partner.* Remember, I've been easy on ya, but I'm gonna want an envelope every week. Your guinea friends don't hold no weight in the Kitchen."

After Hughie downed the last of his Jameson's on the rocks, he and his brother finally left Mike Reedy in peace to take a shot from the bar himself as he pondered his predicament.

When Mike repeated the story to Joey, my brother knew that Mike's broad face would have been turning bright red listening to these low-lives, the way it did when he really got pissed.

When Mike got to the part of the story when the Boylan's started talking about possibly doing harm to Carole, Joey almost went ballistic. Once he calmed down, my brother started to plan how he was going to fix these Irish cocksuckers.

First, he'd meet Hughie a few times with Jerry Shay, but he still needed to get close. In a few weeks, Joey made Hughie feel like they were long-lost brothers. My brother had access to a loft in the South Bronx not far from the Willis Avenue Bridge that was sometimes used for crap games. The day before he planned to take out Hughie, Joey asked me and Frankie to wait at the loft the following night. He told us almost word for word about the conversation he had with Hughie.

"Hey, Hughie, how's it goin'?"

"Not so bad, Joey. How's Harlem?"

"Nothin's goin' on here. What's happening with you Irish mutts?"

"We crazy Irishmen always got somethin' goin' on."

Joey said, "Hey, pal, see ya later."

"Good, Joey, meet me at that joint on Eleventh Avenue."

Joey had smiled as he hung up the phone. After putting on his best camel hair overcoat, he went to meet Hughie, who got into my brother's impressive Olds and directed him to an Irish-owned dive a few blocks away. When they arrived, the craps game in the backroom had already ended.

Joey said, "Hey, pal, fuck the game. Maybe both of us will save some money. Let's go bouncing. Later, I'll take you to an after-hours joint like you wouldn't believe. The broads from the Copa and some of the locals go up there after work. We're gonna score tonight."

When Hughie got all worked up at the mention of the girls from the Copa, Joey knew he had him. He told me and Frankie that this would be easy as taking a piss off Pier Six, Joey's favorite place at the end of 106th.

After five hours of taking Hughie to places he'd never been, Joey knew it was time. They pulled up in front of the loft in the South Bronx in an old warehouse whose lower floors housed a tool and dye factory. In those days, the South Bronx still had a lot of small manufacturing, perfect cover for illegal activities on the upper floors. Huge padded freight elevators that opened directly into each space could be locked on individual floors to keep out city inspectors.

"Joey, you wop bastard, only you could know about a place like this."

"Fuck you, you Irish prick. Follow me." They both laughed.

Joey got Frankie to buzz them into the loft, which was furnished with a fake crystal chandelier and long red velvet couches. When Frankie and I went to the loft earlier, we'd placed little candles in holders all over to complete the bordello look—a total contrast to the factory's exterior.

As the freight elevator went up to the eighth floor, Hughie slurred, "When we get up there, you're takin' a drink with me, Joey, you fuckin' guinea. No more'a your bullshit! You're havin' at least one real drink. I'm the only one who's been drinkin' all night."

"Sure, Hughie, soon as we get upstairs."

As the door to the loft opened, Joey could see that Hughie was impressed by the gaudy interior: yeah, this was definitely the type place where you might find some ladies from the Copa after hours. Frankie stood at the door dressed in a tux his father had handed down to his older brother, who passed it down to Frankie. Even though Frankie had outgrown it in turn, he had no one to pass it down to yet and still wore it when he needed to.

"Frankie, how's things? This is a friend of mine, Hughie Boylan."

"Well, bring him in. It's a bit slow now, but it's gonna pick up in a while. I was starting to think you weren't gonna show up tonight, Joey."

Joey shot him a look as Frankie held the door open for Hughie. As Hughie stepped over the threshold into what he assumed would be a night of forbidden pleasure, Joey swept forward and knocked his legs out from under him. Then my brother stepped into the dimly lit loft and slammed the door I was hiding behind. It had seemed like an eternity since I'd first heard the sound of the freight elevator's clank as Joey and Hughie came up. At this point in my life, I'd done little to practice what I had learned from Joey on the ways of the street. All I'd done was drive him around. This was my first real taste of the Life. Joey may not have wanted me this close to it, but when it came to a move like this that was supposed to be off the record, Joey needed only people he could truly trust.

Alcohol dulled Hughie's reaction; he didn't have much time to be surprised. I'd drawn a pistol after coming out from behind the door, but Joey quickly stepped in front of me and pushed my gun aside.

Hughie Boylan fell like a rock slab collapsing in a pile at a quarry. When his head struck the floor, it seemed to bring him out of his stupor. As the Irish hood raised his head and tried to roll over and get up, Joey fired and hit Hughie right through the eyebrow, exploding the back of his head all over the plastic tarp Frankie and I had laid out in advance. The scene was like something out of a horror movie. Hughie's remaining lifeless eye seemed to stare back at me, until finally I had to look away.

Frankie loosened his bow tie, reasoning that the disguise no longer mattered. He always had trouble breathing with the top button buttoned. "Hey, Joey, what about the body?" he asked.

"Ah, we're just gonna prop him up and leave him sitting at the bar," Joey said.

Frankie accepted this and started for the body.

I started laughing to calm my nerves as Joey said, "Wrap him the fuck up and let's get outta here!"

A few nights later at the Pioneer, Joey chastised Danny for letting his family get involved with people like the Boylans and Jerry Shay.

"How the fuck did you hook up with that scumbag to begin with?" Joey asked him. "I'm sorry he's dead, 'cause I'd like the satisfaction of killing the cocksucker all over again."

"It was my dad who got taken in by him," Danny told Joey as he sipped an espresso.

Danny Reddy was the only Irish guy I ever met who liked that kind of coffee, cementing his status as an honorary Italian.

"Dad thought he'd be good for the pub, and he didn't want

any trouble from the neighborhood thugs," I overheard Danny say as I straightened up the kitchen in back with Frankie. "A neighborhood guy and all… I thought he was real too Joey, until he started making moves on us."

"They'll only take as much as you let them, Danny. Don't let them push the Reedys around, or they'll never stop."

"I know, Joey, I know," Danny slurred. Knowing the problems his father was having, Danny had been drinking heavily, though never where Mike could see him. On the way to the Pioneer, Danny had stopped and had more than a few: the espresso was a way to disguise all the booze on his breath. "You played it great. You walked him right into the garden."

"Yeah, but he never got to smell the roses. Remember, it's off the record, okay? You can never tell a soul."

"So it's done? I mean, done?"

"Yeah, he's with Peter and Paul."

"Oh, thank God! Thanks, Joey, I didn't know what we were gonna do. We both fucked up, but this pub is all Dad has."

Danny leaned back in his chair, relieved.

"Danny, you're not listening to me! You never mention this because it never happened," Joey insisted, raising his eyebrows to show Danny how serious he was. "My people don't know about this, and the reason I didn't tell them is because it didn't happen, period."

"I owe you, Joey."

"You don't owe me for this or anything else, Danny. And neither does your father."

Danny leaned forward, spilling coffee on the table. "Shit!"

"Fucking concentrate! Are you listening, Danny? Don't ever, *ever* talk about this again."

Without anyone else knowing, Joey had kept Armondo in the loop the entire time, a fact I learned only later from Al Hicks. If my brother hadn't kept Armondo up to date, he would have been inviting deadly retribution. Once Hughie threatened Carole, Armondo didn't just give Joey permission to kill him, he ordered him to. Joey knew he'd need Armondo's backing when sooner or later Jerry Shay showed up asking about what had happened.

"I'll make sure it stays off you, Vin and Frankie," Armondo had told Joey when my brother filled him in on the plan. "Christ, I can't believe one of Jerry's boys would do that. A lotta these young guys got no class, Joey, you realize that? Not like your brother—you raised him right. I've been hearing some good things about that kid, Joey, really good things."

Al Hicks told me later that Joey was not that happy that Armondo had taken notice of me.

That same week, Jerry Shay and Billy Boylan arrived at Armondo's club for a meeting Armondo had called earlier in the day. Al Hicks and a few of his boys were there, keeping an eye on Billy from their positions at the bar, but nobody expected serious trouble. Men like Jerry and Armondo never tolerated violence when they were doing business.

"Jerry, you and me, we got a lot goin' on, so I thought we should have this sit down. This beef should be put to bed before it goes any further."

"We do have a lot goin' on. That's what don't add up about all this. Hughie was with us, you knew that. He made the move on Reedy's pub with our blessing. We get a piece of everything in the Kitchen, always have. You know that. But, we don't talk about it. Hughie just gets whacked."

"And he was my fuckin' brother!" Billy interjected.

This was a major violation. Billy Boylan may have wanted vengeance, but he had no right to talk to Armondo Manna that way. In fact, just talking to Armondo without prompting would've been frowned upon. Jerry Shay was quick to shut him up just with a head movement.

"It wasn't without cause, Jerry. You know Mike and Danny… Do you know Carole? Mike's youngest?"

Jerry shook his head no.

Armondo went on, warming to his task, "Well, this guy's piece-of-shit brother threatened her if Mike didn't come up with money,. and this piece-of-shit Billy was there that day sittin' at the bar."

Billy exploded, "That's bullshit!"

Jerry looked at him, then back at Armondo.

"Billy, go out and wait in the car."

"You're standing for this shit? Fuck it!" Billy stormed out of the restaurant.

Al Hicks and the other men at the bar watched slightly dumbstruck. With a wave of his hand, Armondo indicated "ignore it," and turned back to Jerry as if nothing worth noticing had happened.

"Let's get down to it. The Reedys are East Harlem people, and Joey loves them. You get me? Now, there's a bar on 96th Street and First Avenue where your people take action. For years, we've been lookin' the other way. And there's the carpenters' union you want to get going—it's in the works. All I'm saying is that there are bigger grapes out there for us to pick. Let's put this Hughie bullshit to rest…

"And by the way, hot-heads with emotions that can't be controlled are bad for business. Understood?" Armondo smiled at Shay in mutual understanding.

Jerry thought for a few moments and then extended his hand. "Understood, over and done. Come on, Armondo, take me to the bar, I wanna have a drink with some of the boys."

Billy Boylan never made it home that night, and nobody investigated the matter all that closely when his body was discovered lying in the road with two bullet holes in his chest. After all, he was just some Irish punk. He didn't even have any family left to complain about the total lack of interest in the investigation from local law enforcement.

CHAPTER FIVE

Joey never told Danny that Armondo had approved the move on Hughie Boylan. Joey was never a hundred percent sure what Danny might say once he got a few drinks under his belt, so he kept him in the dark as much as possible. After that, Joey stayed out of Hell's Kitchen for a while. He didn't see Danny as much. The first time he went back was for Carole's graduation. Even then, out of respect for Mike Reedy, Joey didn't stay long.

He told me that his relationship with Mike was not as cordial as it used to be after the Boylan incident. Now, Mike knew for sure that his daughter was dating a killer, and he had to live with the fact that he'd taken advantage of the situation when he'd been pressed. Whenever he saw Joey and Carole together, Mike Reedy felt as if he'd traded his daughter away in the bargain. Joey didn't like to see the way it ate away at Carole's dad. Mike's white hair was getting whiter all the time, his stooped posture even more pronounced.

At Carole's graduation party, I saw Mike Reedy talking to one of his oldest friends, Jeff Riordan, who'd worked on the docks, too. On the way to the men's room, I lingered just long enough to overhear the gist of their conversation.

Jeff asked Mike, "Who's that kid with Danny?"

"Oh, that's Joey. He grew up with Danny—you know, Joey Rendino? But now Carole's the one who's always going on about him."

"After four years in Boston, she's still interested in some New York knock-around street guy?"

Mike nodded. "I can't say I like it much. I know what he does with his life. But he's never treated our family with anything less than respect, especially when my Katie died. He did a lot for us during that difficult time."

This time, Danny used his sister's graduation party to cover his drinking. He and Joey had a booth (his side of the table was filled with empty glasses, while Joey just sipped his club soda). Danny was having a ball making Joey laugh shyly with his dirty jokes. He could always get to Joey that way; he was one of the few people that my brother allowed to act like that around him.

I was in the next booth with Helen Connor, an open-faced, buxom girl who'd gone to grade school with Carole at St. Anne's on 110th. So far, our less than sparkling conversation had been limited to my supposed career helping my brother run the Pioneer and Helen's plans to attend school to become a beautician. She, too, was a regular at the Dew Drop, where Nadine Chiaro held court for lonely old men and young girls in need of advice in equal measure.

I saw my brother look up as Carole chatted at the bar with a big Irish guy dressed in a lumber jacket and construction boots, even at a graduation party. When he took off his jacket, you could see a tattoo on his forearm of a heart with a dagger going through it. I heard Joey ask, Danny, "Who's the face at the bar Carole just said hello to?"

Danny turned to look. "Oh, that's Timmy Green. He's a good guy, Joey. He did time with Spike up in Greenhaven. He just got out." Later, I found out that though he was a wire lather by trade, Timmy also dabbled in drug dealing—a fact Danny decided to omit.

Spike had been the bartender at Reedy's for a bit more than a year. Dedicated to all the Reedys, he'd become one of the family quickly. Tall, rake thin, and pale around the gills, he always wore a bow tie behind the bar. One night, Mike had found him digging through the garbage cans outside the bar. Spike had looked up at him, his eyes full of fear that Mike was going to be another in a series of people who abused him, hitting him or chasing him away: that was the way the world had worked for Spike since he'd fled the orphanage.

Mike Reedy had made a snap decision: "Hey, kid, you know how to pour a beer without fucking up the head?"

At first, Spike (whose real name was Thomas Dineen) was

a trainee. He slept on a cot in the store room, and Mike kept him fed. After a few months, Spike was working more shifts than Danny and doing a better job. Carole was the one who named him Spike. He'd copied her father so perfectly; it was like they were twins, "Mike and Spike."

Years later after her father died, Carole found it hard to watch Spike behind the bar because the resemblance to Mike was so strong. Other times, she'd stare at him and take comfort in it. She and Spike had grown close over the years. Spike loved Carole in a way that combined a sister, a lover, and a best friend.

Trying to sound like a streetwise funny man to impress Helen, I went up to the bar and said loud enough to be heard back in the booth, "This is the only joint I know that serves corn beef and cabbage with marinara sauce. I love it! Gimme some more of that Russian water!" I held up my glass to have it filled with vodka.

Helen looked over at me warily, as if rowdiness was not her style. She'd been nursing one Guinness for over an hour and a half.

"Another one, Helen?" I suggested a little too loudly as I sat down again. Danny heard me and turned around and smiled, well aware that I was getting nowhere fast.

"I'm good, thanks," she said with a forced smile.

It was beginning to dawn on me that Carole and Helen were very different women, despite their shared Catholic school education.

From the booth where he and Danny sat, Joey watched Carole bend over the jukebox, flipping through it and finally making a selection.

"Hey, Joey, whaddaya say to a broad's got no arms an' no legs?" Danny said in a boisterous voice. He'd had at least four Irish whiskies with soda on the side—not that I was counting.

Joey looked up and saw Carole approaching. They locked eyes just as Danny hit the punch line: "Nice tits!"

When Danny laughed loudly at his own joke, I saw Helen blush the color of a ripe tomato. By now, I knew this night was a total wash as far as getting laid was concerned.

Joey had to chuckle when he saw the look on Carole's face.

By then, she might have been a college graduate, but this was still her family; she had to take Mike and Danny as they were.

"Sorry, is this a bad time? Did I interrupt man talk?" Having grown up with an older brother, she'd never let Danny embarrass her over something like this.

Unfazed, Danny looked up at her and said, "Hey, Dumbo, we was just talking about you!"

Joey laughed. When Carole scowled, Joey laughed even harder.

"Yeah, ha-ha—listen, jerk, Dad needs you!" she told Danny. "I think he wants you to help surprise me with a cake."

She turned to Joey. "Can you believe my brother? He calls me Dumbo because my ears stick out a little."

Danny stumbled to his feet. When Joey started to stand, Carole held up her hand. "Uh-uh, not you, Rendino, you stay right there. No more avoiding me." She leaned back, listening to "All My Life" from the jukebox. "This is my favorite song in that old jukebox, C-16. I used to come in here after school and listen to it over and over."

Joey was torn inside. He wanted to embrace her but felt it would be disrespectful towards Mike, who'd made his feelings plain. On one level, Joey agreed with Mike; but, on the other hand, he still couldn't look at Carole at this close range without wanting to kiss her.

Carole cocked her eyebrow and began imitating Joey's accent. "Oh Carole, you look so ravishing tonight. Did you wear that dress just for me? Because nobody, but nobody, could fit in it the way you do. I just can't take my eyes off of you."

She tilted her head and returned to her own voice, "Oh, Joey, you're making me melt. Joey, Joey… Aren't you even gonna give me a kiss to wish me luck?"

Joey finally smiled at her. "How can I if your goddamn lips don't stop moving? You know I wouldn't do that in front of your father."

"I'm not hiding this anymore and neither can you. We have to bring this out in the open, Joey."

"You sure about that, kid? Your father isn't going to be too happy…"

"Don't give me that bull, Joey. You don't think he doesn't know you've been coming up to Boston to see me all this time?"

By the time, Helen got up to go to the ladies' room; I could see Danny and Mike Reedy coming out of the kitchen with a "Congratulations" cake in the shape of a mortarboard. Scanning the room for Carole, Mike spotted her next to Joey, and was temporarily taken aback. Across the crowded pub, Danny flipped off the jukebox and turned down the lights as Mike lit the candles on the cake.

Carole turned her attention from my brother to the celebration, though I discovered that they'd made a plan for her to call Joey that evening at Armondo's. She made him promise he'd answer, but now she had to act surprised for her father.

I saw Joey kiss her hand as she slid out of the booth. "Carole?" When she turned back, he leaned in close and told her that her ears were just perfect the way they were.

Even though Nadine hadn't filled me in on the details of this relationship, I knew by then that my brother was a goner. Love conquered all.

Carole smiled at Joey's words before turning away and walking across the room towards Mike. The crowd burst into a spontaneous applause as they sang "Congratulations to You" to the tune of "Happy Birthday." Then, Carole blew out the four candles on the top of the cake that each represented a year she'd been in college. By the time she looked back, Joey was already gone.

Shortly afterwards, I too was stumbling back to the apartment above the Pioneer after dropping Helen off at her place on 107th, where she lived with parents who'd be watching what time she came home. I got a peck on the cheek goodnight, and that was that.

After the party, Joey and Carole started going out on the town in public. They shopped at Bergdorf Goodman's and B. Altman's and dined at the Stork Club and the El Morocco. He took her to places like Santo's, the hottest Italian restaurant in the city; Joey couldn't hide it from me as I watched him get dressed in his sharpest clothes. But, out of respect to Mike, he'd never pick up Carole at the pub.

The next day, Joey told me Santo had greeted them like local royalty: "Joey, *bella senorina*, welcome!"

When Joey noticed that Armondo was eating there, too, they'd acknowledged each other with a nod. Armondo had eight or nine other men sitting with him, along with assorted wives or girlfriends, at a very crowded table.

Joey asked Santo if he'd saved my brother's favorite table on the other side of the room. Joey didn't want to be too close to Armondo and his entourage.

Santo laughed, "Of course Joey, follow me."

Though Carole had applied for jobs everywhere in the fragrance industry, she'd been having trouble getting in the door. When she looked over and saw Stephen Aronson, the head of Creative Flavors and Fragrances, sitting at a nearby table with his boyfriend, she grabbed Joey's hand: this was the man she's been trying to get in to see for months.

Joey asked her, "Who is he?"

"He's the one who could help me jumpstart my career, Joey," Carole explained excitedly.

After Aronson's mother emigrated from Eastern Europe she'd started what eventually became a multimillion dollar fragrance company—an American success story known all over the world.

As Joey and Carole talked about how to approach the head of Creative Fragrances, a waiter interrupted: Armondo wanted to send over a cocktail and a bottle of wine.

My brother started to say thanks, but no, when Carole jumped in. Though Joey wasn't a drinker, Carole enjoyed her own form of moderation, which involved getting extremely drunk once in a blue moon, or otherwise sticking to a reasonable amount of wine. "I'll have a double Bombay martini on the rocks with olives. As for the wine, whatever Santo suggests would be just fine with us."

As the waiter poured, they lifted their wine glasses to toast Armondo's generosity. It was clear from Joey's description of the night at Santo's that Carole had enjoyed herself enormously.

She'd told my brother, "This place is fantastic. Now I know why it's impossible to get a table. You've got Wall Street people, politicians, movie stars, neighborhood people, and who's who in the mob. It's like Shakespeare and Damon Runyon dining together."

Joey laughed. "Sure, King Lear and Little Caesar."

"Who would believe my Joey's so well-read?"

Conferring with Santo later, Joey found out that Aronson dined at the restaurant at least once a week, usually with his boyfriend, a lawyer named Charles Bryer. The next time Aronson made a reservation, Santo let Joey know, so he could provide an introduction.

Given that he was approaching Aronson on Carole's behalf, my brother made a point of dropping his East Harlem accent as much as possible. When the perfume executive invited him to sit down, Joey told him, "I won't take up a lot of your time. I waited because I didn't want to disturb you while you were eating. I know who you are, and I want to tell you about a friend of mine named Carole Reedy, someone you may want to consider hiring. She's not only a wonderful person, but also very knowledgeable in the fragrance field."

Though Aronson took stock of Joey at a glance, he also observed that my brother wasn't coming with threats or insults; he'd approached respectfully. Stephen was impressed with what Joey related about Carole as he laid out his case but didn't push. Joey simply told Stephen Aronson that he'd do well to pay attention, and maybe take an interview—just to give Carole a shot. Then, Joey shook hands with both Aronson and his companion and ordered them a bottle of wine.

On his way out, Joey took Santo aside and said, "Give 'em anything they want, but don't give 'em the check."

Carole Reedy got her interview: as they finished the wine, Stephen and Charles agreed that at the very least Stephen should see what all the fuss was about. And, if she could control a guy like the man they'd just met at Santo's, maybe she'd be able to whip a team of assistants into shape.

I often think about Joey and Carole's relationship. Although Joey was always trying to push her away, he probably would have wound up living to a ripe old age with her no matter how awkward their relationship might have become as Carole climbed the company ladder. But, as fate would have it, Joey got pinched by the Feds, and sent to Leavenworth.

CHAPTER SIX

I was driving Joey one night; I don't even remember why. Maybe Frankie was tied up. But, I remember pulling up near the Pioneer and seeing cars double-parked in front, with assholes in suits sitting in the front seats. Joey told me to back up, but by the time I got the car in reverse, we were already blocked in. Joey looked at the car and said, "If this ain't a fuckin' pinch, I'll go jerk off an elephant."

He was right: that night the elephant was on his own.

Armondo set up the lawyer, but it was a foregone conclusion. The best Jack Friedman could do was plea bargain it down to two to six. After that, Joey never really forgave Armondo. He always said that prison was just one of the realities of the Life; but, in this case, the whole thing was about putting money in the forefront. It was all about greed, and fucking everybody else. So, Joey got fucked.

As far as anybody knew, the guy was just another deadbeat with a bad habit at the track. He'd borrowed from Armondo a few months back. Every once in a while he was late with the money, but always came through eventually. What nobody realized was that his money was coming from the Feds, who wanted to keep their new informant safe. They always managed to find a way to get it through their budget. Once he knew they'd cover him, the informant's bets grew bigger and his wins even less frequent.

This guy was giving up information on everybody—a whole bunch of the big players in the heroin trade in New York City. All tolled, when the feds swept in, it was one of the biggest drug busts of all time, implicating over forty guys. But, this was partially due to the fact that the feds cast a wide net in order to justify the large sum they'd paid to just one informant.

Joey had gone to the guy's place two or three times for Armondo. As far as the court was concerned, they had my brother on tape picking up money, making him part of a conspiracy to distribute drugs, along with twelve other guys who were left hanging after the rest of the forty had their beefs thrown out. What could Joey say in his defense—that he was actually working for a completely separate and unrelated loan shark operation?

Seeing the mess they were in, Joey figured that the sooner the twelve of them all pled out, the sooner they'd manage to serve their time and be released. He couldn't plead out on his own because that would be like saying they were all guilty. And, if they didn't all agree, Joey would be considered a rat. Luckily, they all understood his logic and went along. My brother got transferred through three different facilities in five days; It got to the point where Carole lost track of where he was. For his part, Joey was depressed, and he didn't want to get in touch with anybody yet.

Since my brother was arrested on a drug conspiracy, the question arose as to whether he'd violated the code of the Life; but Armondo stood up for him and explained that it was a bad beef. Armondo sent word through the lawyer, Jack Friedman, who had plenty of government connections, that Joey was off the hook as far as the administration was concerned. Joey didn't seem as happy with the news as Armondo and Jack had expected. For all his contacts, Friedman hadn't been able to make the charge go away altogether.

"Even the Feds know I'm not pushing junk!" My brother was furious with his lawyer. "This never should have been brought to the table."

"Calm down, Joey," Jack Friedman told him. "You know, it's all part of the Life."

"It's all part of my cock," Joey ranted to me on the phone. "Fuck them old greaseballs! What the fuck do they know about how we have to earn in the street? They're all sitting on their fat bellies. Let's see if any of them fat rich cocksuckers can do time."

At the Dew Drop, Carole told Nadine that when she got the call a few weeks after Joey's arrest to come in and meet with

Stephen Aronson, she almost didn't take it; she was so distraught and broken-hearted. What was the point of getting her dream job if she didn't have Joey in her life?

"You gotta look out for yourself," Nadine cautioned. "Joey can't help you from where he's parked right now."

In the end, Carole went, but she cared so little about the interview that she wasn't even nervous. To Stephen, Carole Reedy appeared unflappable as she explained her ideas for less costly substitutes for certain ingredients that would have the same effect in the final product. Essential oils, she suggested, could be diluted with neutral-smelling oils like coconut.

Aronson couldn't follow all the science; his highly-paid, well-recruited staff handled that. But, he could see that Carole had a lot of ideas and figured she'd be less expensive than a man. If it didn't work out, he could get rid of her and nobody would complain; but he had a feeling the fiery Irish girl would work out just fine. Though Stephen Aronson never mentioned Joey, he'd followed the trial and was pleased to have a chance to help Carole without my brother in the picture. He saw her as one of the few people who had the potential to help him follow through on one of his long-term goals: to break into the European markets. Not to mention that he had a strong suspicion that his marketing and development man in France would find Carole irresistible.

Carole had both street smarts and a polish she'd obviously worked hard to acquire. That combination was just what Aronson was looking for.

CHAPTER SEVEN

Joey didn't like having visitors in prison. Besides, he was all the way in fucking Kansas, a place about which I knew nothing about except for what I saw in The Wizard of Oz.

My brother and I kept in touch by writing to each other and talking on the phone from time to time. Of course, Armondo knew a few people inside, so Joey never had trouble with the guards or any of that. But, without my brother around, there was no money coming in. Joey had loaned out some money to people in the neighborhood. A few kept their word and paid me back while Joey was in prison, but it didn't add up to enough. And, without Joey, there was an opening for others to horn in on his action.

Al Hicks sent me out on a few jobs, nothing major yet, just testing the waters: picking up money from this guy, setting up a meeting with that guy. It was always me and somebody else; I never went out on my own. Joey wouldn't have let it happen if he'd been out; but he knew there was nothing he could do from where he was. So, he kept quiet.

The first time I was sent out solo, the driver handed me a gun. "Just in case," he said.

I checked it, and then stuck it in my waist. From the minute I walked inside the bar where the pickup was to take place until the minute I walked out, I thought I was gonna have to use the piece. The guy who owed the money was acting weird, and the light was playing tricks. There were two or three guys, kind of Slavic looking, standing in the shadows; turned out that the guy was just a little drunk. He gave me the full payment.

That was the night the Life started to seem real to me. You'd think I might have started thinking about how crazy this whole way of life was as I watched Joey get sent away, but it hit me once when Smitty handed me a gun I didn't even have to use.

And it was different now that I was alone. For the first time, I didn't need my brother to look after me.

This Life, it's a lot like smoking cigarettes. When you're a kid, it looks cool, even sophisticated. The fact that the older guys won't let you in, just makes it that much cooler. So you start up. By the time you figure out that maybe your brother was right about the Life, it's too late; you don't know how to stop. When I realized that I wasn't sure I wanted to be a part of it, I already was, and there was no one around me who had any idea how to get out. In this Life you can never quit—and you better hope you never get laid off.

Joey didn't need to adjust to prison life because he'd had a taste of it as a teenager. In one of his letters, he explained to me that the guards were pretty much like cops; if you find the friendly ones and treat them okay, you'll be fine. As for the other prisoners, they knew about Joey. My brother didn't have to walk in alone and prove himself. The Italians made it clear that not only was he with them, but a guy like Joey wouldn't even need their help. They spread his rep, which was enough.

The Italians and the blacks had bad blood between them. Whenever a new Italian inmate arrived, the black prisoners would try to get him alone to beat him up. It was the same the other way around. Sure enough, his first day in the yard, Joey might as well have been wearing a sign on his back that said, "New white guy" as a sea of black faces eye-fucked him. Barboni, a thuggish guy from the North End in Boston who was doing time for extortion, told Joey to forget it; but Joey kept scanning the yard silently.. Joey's gaze stopped at the basketball court, deep on the "colored" side of the yard. Spotting the biggest guy on the court, who was dominating the plays and scoring at will, my brother started walking towards him.

Barboni was dumbfounded, but he gestured to the others, who began to follow Joey until he brushed them off. "Stay here, guys. It's okay."

Though segregation wasn't officially practiced, unofficially the white guys stayed on one side and the black guys on the other.

As my brother continued to cross the yard slowly, all faces turned to watch the only white guy in the crowd other than the guards. Still, Joey walked calmly towards the basketball court.

The game stopped. The big man holding the ball turned around slowly; he didn't like having his game disturbed, since inmates only had so much recreational time. But, when he saw Joey coming, he grinned.

They stared at each other for what seemed an eternity, but lasted all of maybe ten seconds. Joey never looked around, never acknowledged anyone other than the huge black man—well-muscled, over 200 pounds—in front of him. Finally, Joey blinked and smiled. "Let me ask you something… you still buyin' your pizza by the slice out in Brooklyn, ya dumb fuck?"

The black inmate smiled broadly and embraced him cheerfully, "Joey Rendino, what the fuck?"

"I can't believe you're here, Higg. I figured you guys had your own prisons down South, you know? I didn't know they let you mingle."

Over the years, my brother had told me all about Clarence Higgins. They'd met in the Orange County Correctional Facility as teenagers and had trusted each other ever since. After the showdown in the yard, Higgins warned his crew to stay away from Joey. Higgins let it be known that if anybody got out of line, he'd take care of them before Joey could even ask.

Even with friends to protect him, Joey stayed to himself and spent a lot of time reading. The guards let him keep a small shelf for books, where he lined up most of Shakespeare's plays. But, he read anything he could get his hands on—anything to forget about what was going on outside. Sometimes, he asked me to send more of the plays so he could catch up on the ones he hadn't read.

In my letters, I tried to keep him up to date on what was going down in East Harlem. I made it pretty clear that things were changing. Some people were making big bucks selling property to the city. But, they were selling out their own people, who were being forced out of the neighborhood in droves as the tenements were razed in the name of "urban renewal." No one could say that the tenements were ideal, but to tens of thousands of people, they were home. Small businesses—my friend Jamesy's Dad's fruit and vegetable market, the Jewish deli Joey'd hit up as a teenager, bakeries, Fredo's dad's butcher shop, hair salons and barber shops—were being torn down to put up high-rise projects. The problem was that most of the people moving into them were black and Puerto Rican: 'cause they made so little, they were able to move into the projects, according to the city regulations. A lot of the Italians didn't qualify.

For Joey, the neighborhood was sacred ground—an extension of family. To him, the selling out of East Harlem was a major crime—one that demanded some kind of response.

In her letters, Carole begged Joey to let her visit; but he pleaded just as strongly for her to stay away. He didn't want her to see him as a prisoner. And, he was still trying to convince her to unshackle herself, knowing that it was the right thing, even if neither of them really wanted it. After more than a year, Carole insisted on seeing Joey. I helped her set it up because I wanted to go, too. Carole was my ticket to Leavenworth, Kansas.

We drove for days, passing flat fields full of wheat and other grains. The middle of the country was a flat as a pancake, like I'd always heard. There wasn't a high-rise in sight outside of Chicago.

"Hey, Carole," I said, trying to lighten up the mood in the car. "Maybe we can convince some of the hayseeds out here to buy some tall buildings from us. They'd be tourist attractions."

My attempts at humor were falling on deaf ears. Since we'd left New York, Carole hadn't said much other than that she loved her new job. Her main worry was her father's health and her brother's drinking: so what else was new? Now that Carole was the *de facto* mother in the Reedy family, she had to worry about Mike and Danny, who needed all the help they could get.

Her mood got even more apprehensive as we approached the prison itself, its high fences topped with vicious-looking barbed wire. This was where her Joey spent his days and nights.

I'd never seen my brother look as humble as he did when he walked into the visiting room. He'd made a point of shaving. (He tried to keep himself neat, even while in prison, as if this somehow removed him from the worst aspects of his surroundings.) But, his uniform was a drab reminder of the situation, and as glad as he was that Carole and I had made it out to Kansas, Joey's face betrayed a hint of sorrow that we were seeing him like this. For her part, Carole managed to hold back her reaction, to convey nothing in her face about how much it hurt her to see my brother confined. She only broke down later. I did my best not to show my emotions; I knew this is what Joey wanted, and expected, of me.

I waited as Carole approached my brother with a restrained kiss; she was dressed more conservatively than she might have been in the city. There was no point in standing out from the crowd in a prison waiting room. Carole Reedy did that anyway, just by showing up. On a nearby metal bench, hard as a rock, I sat waiting, trying not to eavesdrop on a personal conversation; but I got the gist of it.

"Joey, I wanted to wait until I could tell you face to face... I got the job with Aronson! You remember, I pointed him out to you–"

"At Santo's, of course I remember. That's great, kid, I'm happy for you. And remember, you owe nobody, nothing. You deserve it. This is that Creative Fragrance thing, right?"

She smiled. Joey never really understood what was involved in her business, but at least he was interested. Some men might have felt threatened, but not Joey, as Carole had often said to Nadine when they discussed her career goals.

Carole pointed out to Joey that she was the first women Aronson had hired as something other than a secretary. "We're creating fragrances, flavors, all'a that good stuff that intrigues me, Joey—the stuff that makes people feel and smell good."

For a moment, my brother pretended to be jealous; later, he admitted to me that he was relieved Aronson hadn't mentioned Joey's name to Carole. He didn't want her to know about his role in getting her the interview.

"This Aronson guy, did he try anything with you, Carole? I know I'm not there, but I can still—"

She laughed, "Oh my jealous Joey."

"What's so funny? Carole, these business guys, you don't

know–"

She had trouble holding back the laughter long enough to explain, "No, that's just it, Joey—Stephen's queer."

"No shit, he's a fag? I guess that makes sense."

"Yeah, I'd be more worried leaving him alone with you! But that's not the important news. I'm making a special cologne, just for you."

The success of Old Spice had shown fragrance companies the mass market potential for men's colognes, Carole told Nadine the last time she'd made it to the Dew Drop. But, Carole kept Joey's special blend a secret. Nadine understood why an ambitious woman like Carole Reedy would be eager to make headway in a new market; things were different now for smart women—they had options.

"I haven't figured it all out yet, Joey," Carole told my brother with great excitement to distract him from his grim circumstances. "All I know is that I was inspired by the way you smell after we've made love—musky and earthy. I'm going to call it *Just Joey.* And we'll never sell it."

Joey didn't take her seriously. "Anything named after me will just smell bad," he growled.

"Just you wait, Joey. I'm gonna hit it out of the park, even if it takes me a while to get it just right."

Momentarily overcome, my brother had to look away. I pretended not to hear any of this from my bench.

"Yeah, well, I guess I have some time to wait anyway…"

"Oh, Joey, I'm so sorry, I didn't mean to bring anything up…"

"Carole, don't worry, I'll do my time as easy as pissin' off Pier Six. You just keep doin' what you're doin', okay? Take any opportunity that comes along. Don't allow me to hold you back, ever."

Given that Carole was beginning to tear up, Joey stopped himself. After she and Joey hugged, the guard on duty let her give my brother another chaste kiss. Then, she excused herself to go to ladies room in order to compose herself.

"I'm sure you two have lots to talk about, too," she told me on her way out.

Joey turned to me for the word on the street.

"You hear Al Hicks is being moved up?"

"Of course I did. Word travels faster in here than it does in East Harlem. In fact, I've been hearing something you may not know. In a few months, they're gonna open up the books. When they do, Al Hicks is gonna propose you."

I'd suspected as much, but nobody had mentioned it for sure. I was torn: on the one hand, I wasn't sure I wanted formal initiation into the Life. On the other hand, what the hell else did I have going? Nothing—not to mention that some part of me thought I might pull off something that would make Joey proud of his kid brother.

"Are you gonna take it, Vin?"

"Are we goin' through this again?"

"All right, you know what's best. Let me give you one piece of advice, besides 'don't do it…' Don't make the Life your life. Find something else if you see half a chance. Open your own place, anything legit. You don't want to depend on Armondo or anyone in our world for your living, okay? Use the Life to your advantage. Don't let the Life use you."

Finally, my brother was talking to me as an equal. I knew Joey was sincere in trying to discourage me from getting made, but I also knew he'd accept it. In fact, he expected it. Why else would he have been so careful in schooling me about how it worked: what to do, what not to do? And, I knew Joey wanted me to be my own man, which was the key to making him proud of me. Of course, we loved each other; but we weren't cut from exactly the same cloth. We didn't even look that much alike. I was much darker, to the point where the guys at the Pioneer called me a Puerto Rican and started making jokes about what our mother was up to while Antonio had been at work.

The guards were signaling that visiting time was almost up. Joey kept looking at me for a response to his cautionary words. I just nodded.

"So, this is how it's gonna go down. Somebody's gonna take you to a house, or maybe the back room at a restaurant. Al and Armondo will be there waiting with a whole lot of people. Some'a them you know, some'a them you don't. This is important: they're gonna ask you if you know why you're there. You say 'no,' you have no idea. Let them tell you. Then, you gotta act surprised and grateful, of course. Act like this is the only thing you've ever wanted your whole life. Al and Armondo, they'll make sure it's done right. Then you'll be part of a tradition… you poor fuck."

That night when the lights went out, when nobody could see or hear him, for the only time in his adult life Joey felt truly sorry for himself. He told me this when he got out. For a year, it had been building up inside him. Joey said he felt trapped, as if every inch of the prison was coming down on top of him. And, he told me he was sorry he couldn't necessarily protect me from all the terrible things life might have in store.

He longed for Carole, realizing that she'd grown up and was becoming successful in her own right. Now, she might be able to spread her wings and finally get away from him. Even though he wanted her to leave, believing it was best—that he was poisonous to her—Joey suddenly admitted to himself that if she really did leave, it might kill him. What was even worse was realizing that it might be too late, that she might be too in love with him to leave, ever. This was the worst of all, he confided to me one night in the apartment when I'd come home late.

Joey always waited up for me like a vigilant parent. He agonized not only for his kid brother, but also for himself.

In prison, Joey had come to realize that he was going to be in his early thirties when he got out, with no better prospects than the ones he'd had at twenty. He'd still be working the same job, one that didn't have a whole lot of room for advancement. My brother didn't have the ambition or knowledge to make it any way other than the one he knew. He couldn't go to medical school; he didn't know anything about the stock market. He couldn't fix an engine, or sew an inseam.

The Life was one big dead end, but it was all he had. And once he got out, Joey knew he'd have to start over completely from scratch. My brother also knew that the neighborhood diminished his earning potential greatly. You take the people out of the neighborhood, you remove the money: who was gonna play the numbers or meet for cards in Joey's club? The new people in East Harlem didn't know Joey, didn't have to respect him. He'd have to come up with his own way to become a big earner. If

Joey was going to start over, it wasn't gonna be at some two-hundred-dollar a week, no-show job for a friend of Armondo's.

In prison, he'd still been operating in a way: the relationship that Higgins and Joey had greatly eased the tensions between the blacks and the Italians. Joey told his people, "Hey, you gonna do business with these guys on the outside. I know you done business with some of them already. It don't make sense not to be civil on the inside."

People opened up and trusted Joey, people like Babe Marsano, one of the toughest people in East Harlem, a workout freak who kept himself in excellent shape while locked up. There were others, too, not only from New York, but also from Philadelphia and South Jersey, who became friends with Joey while he was inside. They knew that Joey was Armondo's main man—his workhorse.

In our clan, dealing drugs was officially a no-no; it simply wasn't allowed. The punishment was death. But, what Joey discovered in Leavenworth was that this was complete bullshit. Armondo had been behind the whole move on Gino the Zip. Armondo knew Gino wanted to be a part of the Life because the Zip had been chomping at the bit. He'd told the Zip he was gonna take him in, but only if Gino gave up a hands-on role with his heroin connection. Armondo would make sure his outside people handled all the moves. Gino Pinnetta had fallen for the whole thing, lock, stock, and barrel.

As usual, if it hadn't been for Al Hicks, I never would have known these details.

My brother may have been raging inside, but he never revealed his true feelings to me. Still the seeds of revenge had been planted. Al Hicks explained that Joey'd held back because he didn't want to plant the same seeds in me. He wanted me to follow a different path: deep down, my brother always wanted to protect me. What pained Joey most was that this was not the life of honor he thought he'd been brought into. And now I was a part of it, whether he liked it or not.

As his release date approached, Joey didn't fall asleep at night with a specific plan in mind. He just knew that he needed a way to earn real money, but he didn't want to take it from the people of the neighborhood. Anybody who was sticking around deserved to keep what they had. My brother wanted to take it from the people who'd ruined East Harlem; he just didn't know how.

As it turned out, he didn't have to wait long. When a busload of fresh inmates arrived the next day and Joey heard who was onboard and what they'd done, the wheels in his head started turning right away.

CHAPTER EIGHT

What can I say about those two redneck bastards, the Miller brothers? It's funny to think about the fact that for all the ways they were central to my brother's fate, I never actually met them in person. Rusty called the club once, so I heard his voice, beyond that, I only know what I heard from people who did meet them. Wherever they went, they were the craziest people in the place. They weren't afraid of anything. They grew up in one of those mountain families running moonshine down South, where they learned to fight and kill. They always laughed when they heard Joey talk about guys in New York paying off the cops. The way they told it, down there, you didn't pay them; you scared them off.

Ronnie, the younger brother, was the better looking, but that was only because Rusty had the face of an old catcher's mitt with barely-faded acne scars. Ronnie had longer blond hair, less greasy than his brother's black hair, but in the same way that Burger King is less greasy than McDonald's.

At first, the brothers meant everything for Joey. Once they came into his life, they led directly to all that followed. But, as good as it all seemed, it was hollow at the core. It would all fall apart eventually; that was their doing, too. I don't blame them, though. Without Joey they never even would've come north.

The Miller Brothers were notorious troublemakers who were transferred into Leavenworth after they more or less pissed off the entire prison population in Atlanta. Bored with serving their sentences, they started selling fake drugs to other inmates and even some guards. They burned a whole bunch of guys that way pretty fast, selling pencil shavings and flour from the kitchen.

They didn't do it for the money so much as to show everybody that they didn't give a fuck. Nobody knew quite what to make of them. After a guy came after Rusty with a shiv, Ronnie broke the guy's arm in three places and then stabbed him in the neck with the shiv anyway after he was helpless.

Ronnie got a month in the hole; they couldn't prove it wasn't self-defense. But, another convict said something about it to the warden. Rusty spent the whole time trying to figure out who'd talked. Word got back to him that it was Firpo, a huge, bald, offensive, smelly fuck to whom the Millers had sold a full quarter ounce of oregano.

When Ronnie got out of the hole, he and Rusty watched Firpo for four days before he actually took a shower. Once he got in, everybody cleared out. In walked Ronnie, fully dressed.

"Hey, motherfucker, I heard you wanted to get me alone, away from my brother. So here I am. You got something on your mind?"

"You redneck cocksucker, you're coming for me? I'm gonna fuck you up and rip your redneck face off."

As Ronnie got closer, Firpo punched him in the mouth as hard as he could. Ronnie backed up, wiping the blood off. "A punch like that makes me homesick for my mother."

When Firpo charged him, Ronnie dodged. He jumped on his back and began strangling the giant, who was 6'8".. Firpo was putting up a good fight. As soon as Ronnie felt like he was losing momentum, he shrieked like a banshee and bit Firpo's ear, ripping half of it off and holding it between his teeth.

With Firpo screaming at the top of his lungs, Ronnie rabbit-punched him twice in the ear wound. Two quick punches and an uppercut knocked Firpo to the ground. When Firpo looked up at him, as if to say, "Ok, so maybe I'll give you this round," Rusty pulled the ear out of his mouth and smiled before swallowing it in one quick gulp. Then he looked at this brother on the other side of the shower. "I think I'm gonna bite off his nose next, big brother." Rusty walked over slowly as Firpo struggled to his feet. "You oughta learn how to keep your mouth shut, you dumb motherfucker."

"Fuck you! Your bastard brother just ate my fuckin' ear!"

Rusty grinned. "Your ear? Shit, he bit off a guy's dick in the last joint."

Ronnie was getting impatient after tasting a little blood. "Let's finish off this motherfucker."

The Miller brothers looked at each other, sharing an unspoken thought. Then, Rusty stepped forward and said,. "I'm gonna jerk off and come all over your bald head, you ugly motherfucker…"

He open-palmed Firpo in the neck, then slammed an elbow into his nose and punched his chest. Firpo stumbled, falling again, bleeding from the nose. Overwhelmed by the pain, he leaned over and vomited.

Rusty laughed as he kicked Firpo in the chest. Ronnie turned on the shower to wash the blood and vomit away and then, like a child who becomes eager to steal a toy only when he realizes his brother is playing with it, Ronnie jumped onto Firpo's back with his knee, and began slamming his face into the tile floor.

A few days later, Ronnie found out that Firpo hadn't said anything after all. A different guy blabbed to the warden, a black guy that hadn't even been in the room. He'd made the story up, based on what everybody knew had happened, because he knew it would score points with the warden.

Before the Millers could get their revenge, the warden had them transferred to Leavenworth. Word about the two crazy rednecks spread fast. Joey was intrigued. Outside, he wouldn't be caught dead with trash like them; inside prison they were good company.

They always had good stories: shootouts at 80 miles per hour on back roads in Georgia with other moon shiners, or the time Rusty walked up to a guard and just started punching him in the face repeatedly, even while two other guards broke their batons on his skull. They told Joey how they injected pure heroin into the black junkie, just to see his reaction. The crazy son of a bitches laughed, saying the black motherfucker must have still been sleeping. That's how sick these two lowlifes were.

Joey interrupted one of the Millers' many story sessions, "Let me ask you two maniac fucks: What's the most you guys ever got on a job? Did you ever rob a bank, anything like that?" Where was the money in being a crazy bastard, my brother wanted to know.

"Banks! Nah, banks, that's not the way to do it, Joe. Best score we had going, we'd set up a deal with a nigger drug dealer then steal whatever he'd got on him. Some of them, if they had enough money that you could tell they mattered, we'd kidnap 'em and get paid off."

Since this was just another story with nothing funny in it, the Millers moved on to another tale of outlaw derring-do. But a few nights later, as he was drifting to sleep, Joey had his epiphany. He knew exactly what he was going to do when he got out—how it was all going to work for him, to get back in the game on his own terms.

CHAPTER NINE

Joey got transferred to Danbury in Connecticut for the last two months of his stretch. By then, he'd been inside for almost four years, plenty of time to get the details of his reentry plan set in his mind. But, he hadn't said a word to anybody. Walls in prisons have ears. As he left Leavenworth, he got word to the Miller brothers that they should come east when they finished their time. He owed them that; they'd given Joey an idea of what to do when he was released from the joint. And, he needed people nobody in his world knew at all.

Big-time drug dealers couldn't run to the law if they got snatched. They couldn't even go to wise guys because drugs were forbidden in that world (at least officially). And, given the embarrassment, they'd pay and shut up. It was this mentality that allowed Joey to execute his plan and gave him a way to compete. It was money and, at the same time, satisfaction. He could take revenge on all junk pushers while keeping up his image with Carole. He wanted to hurt the people Armondo protected. In the end, he might even get a shot at Armondo himself, at the top of the vicious food chain.

Joey got out of prison in the spring of 1960. Frankie was there waiting for him at 7 a.m. sharp, driving Armondo's brand-new Cadillac. I would've been there, but I'd had a little trouble of my own and was hiding out at Lake Carmel, near Mount Kisko in upstate New York. Joey knew that, and it was the first place he had Frankie drive him.

Just my luck—the whole time Joey's in prison, everything's fine. But, right before he gets out, Al Hicks sends me to some Greek fuck that'd lost a bundle on a dice game. The guy gets busted a week later and says he'll help the law get to Armondo. But, all he really had to offer was me, the only guy he'd seen. Next time we meet, he's wearing a wire. Now, I was the guy the Feds were looking for.

Al Hicks advised me to lay low while Jack Friedman worked it out. Since I had a lot of time to kill in that house on the lake, I worked on a few new recipes. Food is my heritage and the thing that grounds me, especially since I grew up without a mother. Sometimes, I got recipes not only from Mrs. Lester, who kept an eye on me and my brother after our dad died on her husband's car lot, but also from Nadine Chiaro, who makes the best pasta e fagioli I've ever eaten. Often, Nadine left some in the apartment for me and Joey after she'd finished cleaning. When I make one of her dishes, like lemon chicken or special ricotta cheesecake, I remember all the things about East Harlem that were laden with flavor and life and love— not just the hard facts of the Life.

"I'm going crazy cooped up in this fuckin' rat town, Joey," I told my brother with disgust after he and Frankie showed up at my hideaway. Still, I was happy that the humble little rental was my brother's first stop on the homecoming tour. He looked thinner but well muscled.

"What do you mean? How many barmaids and waitresses you fuck these days? You been on the lam, what, not even a year, living like a prince, getting your johnson serviced on a regular basis, and you fuckin' complain. You know where I just was?"

"All right, Joey, you made your point," I admitted, grinning at the memories of the local social scene, where my competition consisted of overweight, mostly married guys with no idea how to sweet-talk the ladies.

"I'm glad you understand. Listen, Vin, this greedy cocksucker Armondo, who's now our boss, set you up the same way he did me. In my case it was a junk pusher who was a rat, for you, a craps shooter who owed him money."

"Hold on, Joey, it was Al Hicks who sent me to see that Greek fuck, not Armondo."

"Why do you think Al was made a skipper, you fuckin' jerkoff? He won't make a decision without Armondo. I got transferred to Danbury two months ago. You were on the lam less than a week before word was sent to me. Listen to me, Vin, I loved Armondo like the father we barely had. He put me in the Life. I thought he was about honor and respect and loyalty. Shit, all he's about is money. This prick bleeds green. For as long as I can remember, I wanted to be in this life. I always believed that if I lived by its code, some day I would get my just deserts. The way things are goin' now, who the fuck knows how it's all gonna wind up?"

Until then, I hadn't fully realized the effect prison had had on my brother. "You never talked to me like this before, Joey—you never opened up. Now, let me do the same. They put Smitty out to pasture on a fuckin' construction job, after all the work that poor fuck did, as if you don't know. They passed on Smitty because he's a brokester. I'll stay true to the Life, you know that, Joey, but most of the moves being made these days are about who's the best earner."

"Thank God you're seeing the light. Look, from what they told me, Jack Friedman is trying to work out a deal, right?"

"Friedman refused a three year offer. The Greek changed his mind. He won't testify. I could cop to eighteen months. The Feds are really pissed, but what can they do?"

"Now that I'm back, I'll make sure Al stays on top of it." Joey started to laugh. "Can you do eighteen months?"

Knowing he was breaking my balls, I gave him some of his own medicine: "Easier then a piss off of Pier Six, brother."

Still laughing, Joey messed my hair. "Okay, Vin, don't get so touchy. I'm just breakin' your shoes."

Joey and Frankie had stopped at a diner to pick up some food before they got to my place. With Frankie in another room, my brother and I shot the shit for about another hour, catching up on things in East Harlem that had changed in Joey's absence.

Finally, they had to go. On his way out, Joey stopped and said to me, "One other thing, Vinnie—I'm gonna stay with Armondo. I'll report right to the top. The fox will be sittin' pretty in the henhouse. 'Let me embrace thee, sour adversity, for wise men say it is the wisest course.'"

"I remember, Joey—*Henry the Fifth*."

"*The Sixth*, ya dumb mutt," he said with a smile, giving me a big hug. "Stay here and be safe. You got it easy, kid. From all I've heard, I wish I didn't have to go back to East Harlem. I feel like I don't have a place to go back to."

"Don't worry about that, Joey. Nadine's been taking care of the apartment. It's all dusted and everything."

"The way Nadine cleans, I'll be lucky if I don't start sneezing as soon as I walk in the door," my brother said, grinning. "Well, at least I've got a little corner I can still call home."

On the ride back to Manhattan, Joey didn't say a word. He loved Frankie and trusted him completely, but he didn't want to show any emotion, knowing that Frankie wouldn't know what to make of it. Inside, Joey was raging. He couldn't believe Armondo and company had never checked out the Greek, especially after my brother's own brush with the law.

Joey always had one rule above all others: keep it out of the neighborhood. But, he couldn't help but fantasize about the Miller brothers kidnapping Armondo, cramming his fat gut into a van, and leaving him tied up in a basement until his people came through with some money. He knew it was a risk too stupid to consider. At the same time, it was exactly the sort of thing Joey was planning. Yeah, it would be treacherous to execute his scheme in the neighborhood; but weren't the players in East Harlem exactly the ones who deserved to be my brother's targets?

Joey was also starting to wonder about the new blood and how their arrival had changed the order of things. While he'd been gone, a lot of people had come into our Life who didn't belong, in Joey's eyes. He had to acknowledge guys he did not respect; all they were good for was earning money. To him, the Life was more than that.

The truth was, if Armondo and Al Hicks hadn't paid Jack Friedman's legal bill, Joey might have done more time. In addition to all the bitterness he'd built up inside in jail, my brother was even more pissed off that he was obligated to them—just another thing eating him alive. After Armondo had brought Joey into the Life, he'd also kept my brother from getting too big to deal with, but he'd always kept him around. Joey was starting to feel like Armondo's puppy, a pit bull that got sent out to deal with trouble but was never allowed to eat at the family dinner table. After being tossed aside for the last few years, Joey was now being fed scraps. And worse, it looked as if I were going to be tossed aside, too.

Though Joey wasn't sure what Armondo was up to, he knew the old spider did nothing by accident. He moved slowly. Armondo didn't sound too bright when he talked—unless you listened to the intelligence behind his words. Everything he did was by design, and was meant to benefit him in some way, even if nobody else could see how until it was too late.

CHAPTER TEN

Joey was returning to an East Harlem vastly different from the one he'd left. Though he'd seen the writing on the wall for years, he had a difficult time accepting it. He tried to convince himself it was never going to happen.

When Joey was just a kid, Mayor LaGuardia had started to get a hard-on for the mobs. They didn't even use the word "organized crime" back then. No matter what you called it, LaGuardia wanted to break it up. In some ways, he was ahead of his time: how long was it before J. Edgar Hoover even acknowledged what was going on? That was part of LaGuardia's problem: If he wasn't getting any federal money, how could the city fight the organizations? As it happened, they figured out how to kill another bird with the same stone.

The city had a long-term plan to revitalize neighborhoods, but they could cherry pick which ones. So, they started in East Harlem. They figured the whole organization was living or working in a twenty block radius, right? Everybody was making their money off the community. Combine that with the arrival of a bunch of poor immigrants, mostly Spanish-speaking and hard to employ; the city took uptown land, seizing it by what they called "eminent domain," and opened some housing projects, high-rises that completely altered the local streets. East Harlem was starting to look more like downtown but with cheaper building materials. I'd seen kids' Lego sets with more class and character. These projects looked like something out of our 1950s schoolbooks about conditions in Communist countries.

At first, it was just the one, and everybody got used to it. The people who lived there, mostly black and Puerto Rican, stuck to themselves; nobody bothered them. But, we all suspected that the city wasn't gonna stop at one or even two. The plan was to keep tak-

ing land and build more and more projects until the neighborhood itself was a goner. That's not to say there weren't buildings in East Harlem that didn't deserve to be demolished: but not the whole damn neighborhood.

Joey had heard about this years back. He'd mentioned that Armondo let it slip one night that he was putting a lot of his money into property in the neighborhood. Given that this wasn't the way Armondo did business—he usually took money out—Joey asked him why. Armondo told him about the city's plan and explained that he (along with a few other men he knew, men with enough money to burn on a project like this) was buying the land in order to protect it. If the city wanted to take it from him, let them come after him. He wasn't going to roll over like Paulie Varano, who'd sold off his apartment building without a fight.

Joey took Armondo at his word and never thought about it again. Then, in prison, my brother heard on the grapevine that the city had made a deal with several "private landowners who wished to remain anonymous." They were selling out the whole neighborhood. Armondo made a mint off a the city. He and a few other guys could have fought it. It's not to say they would've stopped it, but they might have limited the damage. Instead, the whole neighborhood was gutted. A lot of people had to leave, moving to Astoria, Queens, or the Bronx, or even into the projects if they didn't have enough money to go anywhere else.

It not only angered Joey, it saddened him. He used to tell me about the Chinese. He'd read a lot of history, about all the wars they fought and how they built that Great Wall. He told me that the Chinese think in dynasties that last for centuries. Armondo thought he was thinking long-term, five years ahead of everybody else, but Joey saw the next step, the step Armondo didn't see, or didn't care about—that the new neighborhood wasn't going to have earning power in the future.

Families were moving out, and the ones that were moving in couldn't afford to blow money on numbers games. Without the extra money from the numbers, a lot of places couldn't stay open. By the time Joey got out of prison, Louie and Ernie's beloved pizza place had moved to the Bronx; Half Moon, a local favorite for its veal dishes, was out on Long Island; Little Guisseppe's Italian deli, where they made the best hero sandwiches on the planet, had to close. And how long did DeMarco's Clam Bar last? It was gone after forty years in business.

In the end, the only major change the city made to East Harlem was forcing people to use bigger locks on their doors. The neighborhood used to be able to police itself: now you had bartenders in social clubs with shotguns instead of baseball bats. The crime was still there, just less "organized." The "organized" guys just moved to other neighborhoods. Guys like Armondo had real political clout they could've used: How was it that Mulberry Street never got touched? Before this all started, East Harlem was the real Little Italy. There were more Italians living there than in the rest of the country put together. The block Joey and I lived on, 105th, had more people crammed into one block than anywhere else in the world, even in China.

When Frankie picked up Joey at Danbury, he gave him an envelope with $2,000 in it. He said it was money he'd put aside after all the expenses of the club were paid. Where was the envelope from Armondo? What was he going to do, wait until Joey got to his restaurant and make a big splash in front of everyone? It never happened. Instead, Armondo offered Joey a small piece of a monte game on the West Side. Just as Joey thought, nothing was going on in East Harlem.

Joey took the destruction of East Harlem personally. He blamed a lot of people besides Armondo; but I never really knew how much of it was true and how much of it was just Joey being bitter.

The first place Joey wanted to go once he settled back into the old neighborhood was Fox Brothers, a clothier and haberdasher. Joey knew the tailor, Ralph, and for twenty bucks his clothes would be altered to a T within an hour.

The next time Frankie and Joey came to see me upstate, they ranted on about the decline in the quality of food in East Harlem now that so many of the Italian places had disappeared.

"We knew that fuck Armondo wouldn't be out of bed yet, so we tooled around a little," Joey said.

"Joey and I drove up and down, and I showed him all the things that changed while he was away," said Frankie. "But Patsy's pizza is still there."

"Damn," I chimed in. "Patsy's has been there since the 1930s. If that goes, forget about East Harlem!"

Rao's, the family-owned and operated restaurant on Pleasant Avenue at the edge of Jefferson Park, had been there even longer than Patsy's. It was still hanging on with a solid neighborhood base of customers who loved the meatballs and the expertly poured cocktails, not to mention the Christmas lights that stayed up all year round. But, Delano's fruit stand was gone, and the two best delis in town had been sold.

Frankie and Joey had stopped for a sandwich at what used to be Mancini's but was now just some bodega. Joey didn't know who owned the joint. When Frankie brought Joey a sandwich from the former Mancini's, my brother threw it away. "Is this the shit they're eating in the neighborhood nowadays, Frankie?" he'd asked him. "Seems like nobody's got any pride in what they do anymore."

He used to tell me, "Vin, when I stare up at those buildings I thought I was looking at one big fuckin' ugly cinderblock! And the food! This neighborhood deserves better, you know? Even these new people, they live in projects, so what? Just 'cause they're not Italian, you're gonna make 'em eat shit?"

When I was upstate, I had a lot of time to think and remember.

It had been a relatively warm December day in 1957 when I went into Barney's Bar to pick up number slips from Aldo the bartender. Aldo was a numbers runner, one of the guys who took bets from people and turned them over to the member of a crew booking the action. Before I could say a word, Aldo stared at me for a brief moment and said, "Vinnie, there's no more action. I'm down over fifty percent on the full number, and there's no more single action, either."

Before I had a chance to respond, Mary, Barney's wife, yelled out to me to come over to a table in the back of the bar. As I started to sit down, she burst into tears.

"Mary, what's wrong? Is Barney all right?"

Through her uncontrollable sobbing she said, "Look around, Vinnie, our place is empty. All our people had to move out. All the buildings are coming down. We used to make four, sometimes five, hundred pizzas a day! Yesterday, we made twenty." In Italian she started cursing the city, the state, even the president. She cursed her son-in-law for moving to Yonkers with her daughter; she said he'd put a jinx on the neighborhood.

I almost started to laugh, but I could also feel her pain.

As I left the bar and starting walking uptown on 2nd Avenue, all of a sudden it hit me as if I'd been struck by lightning: The stores looked like a Tic-tac-toe board with all the "x"'s in white paint on the front of them. Buildings where my friends once lived were padlocked. As I walked from the north side of 106th Street to 107th Street, the south side of 108th Street, from the East River to 3rd Avenue, I pondered the fact that the place looked like the day after the end of the world, ready to be demolished and sucked up to make room for housing that would change our neighborhood forever.

Mary blamed the politicians. Joey put the blame on people in our world who he felt sold out. In my opinion, they both took it to the extreme. Change always comes, but it happened too fast in East Harlem. And to say the least, it was badly planned. All the other Little Italies in New York had evolved. The difference between their neighborhoods and ours was the choices people could make; they weren't forced out, and their community wasn't destroyed.

Though very few Italians live in the so called Little Italies of New York these days, their footprint remains: the shops, the markets, the restaurants are still there. Not so in East Harlem. Still, every summer, we have the father and son's annual stickball game on Pleasant Avenue. Boy, that really brings back great memories of our old neighborhood. I've often wondered how my life would have been if East Harlem had remained a vibrant Italian neighborhood.

Joey was always thinking about the future. "When you get back from upstate," he said, "I'm gonna put up some money so you can open a good old-fashioned Italian deli."

The more he and Frankie told me about what had been lost in East Harlem, the more excited I got about my prospects. I figured I could make a go of it even with all the changes in the neighborhood. At my hideout, I spent more time in the kitchen perfecting recipes and less time at the local hot spots; I had to think ahead to what the future held.

As fate would have it, I opened the Big V Deli a few years later, directly across from where Barney's, which closed in 1958, used to be. When I opened in 1961, the new people in the projects became my clientele, as well as the students and teachers from the Manhattan School of Music on 105th Street, just a few steps west of where Gino the Zip once lived. Thank God my business enabled me to bypass earning street money, keeping me out of harm's way. Then again, had the neighborhood stayed the same, I may have become the owner of Barney's Bar and Restaurant. I always loved the place.

Who knows? As my brother's main man Willy Shakespeare wrote, "What's done, is done. What's done cannot be undone."

After he got out of prison, Joey struggled to adjust to the new realities in East Harlem. First, he had to check in with Armondo. It was late afternoon by the time he and Frankie drove back to Armondo's, which had moved from 104st and First to a much bigger restaurant on Tremont Avenue in the Bronx, very close to Long Island Sound. After buying a former German restaurant and catering hall at a deflated price during the war years, Armondo had been fixing up the new place on the sly. It was in an area of mostly private homes—a great cover for what was now called Villa Armondo. Joey realized when he saw the plush interiors, with thick rugs and sparkling chandeliers, that Armondo had been plotting his departure from the neighborhood for much longer than my brother had suspected.

It was Al Hicks who told me all about Joey's homecoming, since he'd been there to greet my brother along with all the other players, old and new.

When Joey walked in, Armondo embraced him, as did Al. Joey got straight to the point and asked, "Is my brother's plea deal in the works?"

"It's gonna get done, I promise, and very soon," Armondo assured him. Joey had me covered, as he always did.

Joey nodded and proceeded to rave about the size and beauty of Armondo's new place. People came over from the bar to say hello and pay their respects. Al Hicks took my brother aside to introduce him to Paulie Sisto and Marco Salie, "two new friends of ours." The newly made men were in awe of Joey. Paulie and Marco were not from East Harlem. As Bronx bookmakers, or "pencil pushers," as Joey called them, they had no place in our world as far as my brother was concerned.

Armondo invited them all to sit down at the table for a meal of pasta and veal. Frankie joined them after he parked the car.

"So, Frankie, how'd you like driving my new Cadillac?" Armondo asked.

"Smooth as a baby's ass!" Frankie said with a smirk.

"Frankie, you're coming up in the world," said Armondo, grinning.

Al Hicks chimed in, "Now that Joey's out, you'll even be dressing better."

Frankie hugged Joey. "You don't know how much I missed you." He looked over at Al and said, "We all wish we could dress as sharp as Joey."

Outwardly, Joey was charming as usual, but inside he was fuming. After spending years in jail for the organization, here he was basically auditioning all over again, and for guys younger than him who'd barely been around for a year. Just because these assholes were big earners, he was expected to sit down and break bread with them, he complained to Al later.

After the meal, Marco and Paulie excused themselves and went back to the bar. Joey barely waited for them to be out of earshot before he exploded, "What the fuck is this life coming to? It's not what you are anymore, who your family is, or even what your quality is—now all you need to be is a good earner. Money, that's the whole thing. Look at those two: who would'a ever thought they could be part of our life? Look at the bar. Some'a them cocksuckers should be in a kennel! They're all mutts."

If Al was amused by the whole outburst, he couldn't show it, he confided to me weeks later. Armondo didn't exactly disagree and felt bad for Joey after all he'd been through.

Al let it pass and tried to pacify him,. "Joey, please… Don't talk like that, they're our friends now. You just got home, give it a little time."

"Time for what, Armondo? They were shit before they got made, and as far as I can see, nothing's changed. Don't worry, you know me—I'll recognize them. I'll show them respect.

But, before it gets too late, I got some catchin' up to do."

He said his goodbyes and left with Frankie.

Al offered to take Joey with him if Armondo felt my brother would be a problem.

Armondo stared at Joey as he was leaving. "Never—he'll always be with me."

"I know Joey; he's just blowing off steam," Al added. "Joey lives by tradition, so we have to forgive him."

Armondo nodded slowly. "Think of it, Al, how can we exist living by the true code of our fucking world? Traditions can only be kept by those who can afford to. When you're broke and hungry and have responsibilities, traditions go by the wayside. Survival becomes tradition—you have to feed your family, pay the rent, do whatever the fuck you have to do. Since time began, man's first and foremost goal has been to survive. So, you tell me, what in the fuckin' hell is tradition? I envy those who know."

Armondo looked up at Al, who saw sincerity in his face. "That's why I admire and envy Joey."

By then, my brother was well on his way back to the city. But, as it started to get dark, Joey remembered a call he had to make. He stopped at a payphone, set up a meeting for a few days away, and dropped in for a drink with Marty Lester at the car lot. Then, he went to see Carole, who'd just settled into a new place on Central Park West.

Over the years, it was Nadine who filled me in on what this East Harlem girl was up to: her career ups and downs, her relationship with my brother. On a pretty regular basis, Carole met her old friend at a convenient midtown coffee shop, since the old haunts in East Harlem were long gone. For all the glamour of her new life, Carole had a hard time trusting those who didn't grow up where she had.

Yes, her job was going well, she'd told Nadine. Though she hadn't yet been considered for promotion, her perfumes had sold well enough to earn her frequent bonuses. Carole had a knack not just for which essences would blend with others, but also how to market to a new kind of American woman, one who didn't necessarily see her place in the world defined strictly by marriage and motherhood. This woman might want a job like the kind Carole had herself—something that gave her a measure of independence.

Carole's boss could see what those who'd grown up with her already knew: Carole Reedy had been that type of woman since she was a young girl. She made her own rules and lived with a certain flair and style. Others who aspired to be this kind of woman would want a different kind of fragrance, too—and Carole would know exactly which kind.

After a successful year at Creative Fragrances, Carole had negotiated a hefty raise.

After cutting through Central Park, Frankie dropped Joey off at Carole's building, where he paid the doorman to get in without phoning up: Joey wanted to surprise her. She knew he was getting out sometime that day, but he'd played it like it would be too late—that he'd call her tomorrow. When she opened the door, she almost screamed before grabbing Joey and dragging him into the bedroom.

Between kisses, she asked, "Have you eaten yet?"

"Not too much, I just nibbled."

Carole smiled. "Good, I want you lean and mean right now, Rendino."

It seemed as if Joey made up for four years in a few minutes;

the next few hours flew by. Afterwards, he poured her a glass of wine as they stood together at the window looking out over the park. "So my girl got herself a place on Central Park West—pretty nice."

"It has its advantages, but it's not home, not really. Did you go back to the neighborhood yet?"

Joey immediately soured. "Yeah, we drove through it. I had to see some of my people. Barely recognized it; everybody's moving out."

"I had to, Joey. I need to be closer to work. But, Danny's still holding on to our old place, and–"

"Hey, hey, hold on, kid, I didn't mean you. You did the right thing. Don't look back, Carole, look ahead. East Harlem is behind you. It's over. Out there, that's your future."

"It's not like that. I love that place. If I hadn't grown up there, I would've never known you."

"Maybe you'd be better off if you never had."

She misunderstood his sentiment and frowned. Joey added, with a smile, "'Cause now that you do know me, you're gonna get to know me a lot better."

"That's more like it, Rendino."

Carole glanced at the bottle of wine sitting on the table, grabbed Joey by the hand, and dragged him into the bedroom. After four long years without the woman he loved and lusted for, Joey was raring to go again as soon as they hit the bed, Carole later told Nadine over coffee.

Nadine laughed. "You don't need to give me the gory details, honey. I've been there myself!" Over the years Nadine had dated more than one neighborhood guy who'd done time.

"Well," Carole said, smiling knowingly, "then you don't have to use much imagination to fill in the blanks on this visual!"

Nadine laughed so hard that she nearly spilled coffee all over Carole's new designer suit.

Carole Reedy may have been living on Central Park West, but in matters of the heart she was forever an East Harlem girl.

CHAPTER ELEVEN

I wound up doing my time in Allenwood, which some people call "the country club." I pretty much lived in the prison kitchen. I made a lot of friends because I made a lot of good meals. Everyone in the joint talked about my pasta with veal Milanese and mushroom and sausage risotto, even the mooks who'd never eaten risotto in their lives. But some had, given that "the country club" had its share of educated criminals.

Cooking made the time go faster. I don't know what I thought about more, Joey or the bullshit life I was going back to. At least my brother would be there when I got out. Joey wasn't able to get up to see me all that often, and he knew I wouldn't want him to, even it this was a minimum security place with mostly white collar guys. He remembered how he'd felt—embarrassed. I just wanted to put my head down and do my time.

In the joint, I thought a lot about the stories Joey'd told me when we were kids. It was in Orange County Correctional, the reform school they sent kids to when they did something bad, but not so bad that they'd be tried as an adult, that he met the black man he called Higg. Back in those days, Clarence Higgins wasn't really able to walk the streets of East Harlem freely, if you know what I mean. He probably wouldn't have had any real trouble, but every eyeball on the block was gonna be watching him. So, he understood that being seen with Joey would not be a wise thing; there was always the chance that somebody might start something, and that whatever happened would leave him in a bad place. So, he and Joey always met to talk business at the Bronx Zoo.

Joey'd show up at least half an hour early, and he'd always watch the lions. One time, when he took me there, he brought me to the cage. He said, "Look real hard at these lions. What do you see?"

The lion happened to be yawning, so I said, "The teeth."

Joey smiled. "Yeah, you gotta watch out for the teeth and the claws. But, you know what I see? This guy, he's supposed to be the king of the jungle, right? Uh-uh, wrong! Look at him. He's gone soft. What's the last thing he killed to eat? Nah, this guy wouldn't last five minutes in the jungle. And he knows it—you can see that. What I'm trying to figure out is, does he like it? He's getting fed every day. I can't tell if he remembers the hunt at all. I don't know if he wants to be here."

I didn't know what to say, so I tried to make a joke out of it,. "Yeah, but you still don't want to get in the cage with him."

He laughed and winked. "Of course not, kid. That lion's got nothin' I want."

If my brother were here now, I know what I'd say—those lions, they're still kings. They get kept in cages for a reason, and you still gotta watch out for the claws and the teeth, too. You want to believe that they're soft, but you have to remember that at the end of the day, even a lion that's gone soft is still a lion.

Of all the guys Joey knew that he actually considered working with, Higgins was the most reliable. Joey felt he could trust Danny, but Higgins was the main man, the one he could always depend on; Higgins was all business.

My brother wanted to have everything worked out before bringing Higgins in; Higg was the one who'd ask the most questions because he was as obsessed with detail as Joey was.

Some people would've been annoyed by questions, especially from a black criminal, but Joey appreciated them because they were always the right ones—questions he had asked himself while planning his moves. All Joey's planning, down to the last detail, I'd find out about years later from a most unexpected source.

For his part, Higgins had come to realize over the years that Joey would always have the right answers for him.

Higgins never would've noticed Danny Reedy at Orange County Correctional if not for Joey. Higgins kept to himself. The white boys hated him, of course, but the blacks ran as more or less a gang, and Higgins couldn't get along with any of them. They were always causing trouble with the guards, the white guys, and each other. Higgins didn't want any trouble; he just wanted to get out.

Joey and Higgins were in some of the same classes. Though they were different ages, the kids were divided up by aptitude rather than age, and both happened to be at the same level in history and math. Higgins didn't pay attention to the teacher but spent his time watching the other kids. This started out as self-preservation. Not everybody could get there early enough to sit in the back row with only empty desks behind them. Eventually, Higgins knew all the kids in the class. Since he'd beaten two of the boys fairly severely, he felt confident that nobody was going to start anything. But, still he stayed in back to watch.

He watched Robbie draw pornographic comics and laugh to himself. He watched Leroy take notes, the only one who did. (He stayed up half the night copying the notes for any boy who wanted them; in return no one let on that they knew Leroy was gay.) Higgins watched Joey sit in the back, too, and take in every word the teacher said. My brother never wrote anything down and never cared enough about showing off to ace the tests. But, Higgins could see that Joey absorbed everything.

One day, Higg found my brother reading *Othello* in the library and started laughing at him. I found out many years later that Joey often called Higgins "The Moor." Realizing that they were both from New York, they argued, naturally. About what? Which pizza was the best in New York.

"Fuck you, the best pizza slice in the city is in Brooklyn."

"Ah, what the fuck do you know about pizza? You're an egg-plant! I'm telling you, East Harlem has it. It's not even close."

"Bullshit! When we get out of here, we gotta go to Carmine's."

"Fuck you and fuck Carmine's, we're going to Patsy's, I'll show you the best. And, it's the best because you can't buy just a slice, you gotta buy the whole pizza, ya cheap fuck."

"Fuck you talkin' about? I'm telling you, Carmine's is the

best."

"You wanna get on the subway and ride the train all the way to Brooklyn just to get to Carmine's, that's fine. You can walk to Patsy's, ya dumb black prick."

"Bullshit, you smart-ass guinea bastard!"

Believe or not, arguing over something they had in common like pizza made them fast friends. After they left juvie, Joey promised to keep in touch; Higgins was a little surprised that he did. Over the years, Joey used Higgins when it made sense. Whenever Armondo sent Joey to collect from a delinquent black numbers runner, he'd take Higgins along. Joey couldn't bring him in on everything he did, only in certain neighborhoods; but he made sure to work with him whenever possible. In Joey's new scheme, Higg would be even more important.

Joey knew that the first target couldn't be anybody from his neighborhood. In fact, he told himself that he had to wait; the blade had to be honed. More than anything, he wanted to take Armondo and the rest of the ones who'd sold out East Harlem for as much as he could. My brother also knew that at the least, he had to make sure that his crew knew what they were doing before going after the big scores. And, Higgins knew a lot of people on his side of town. He knew which ones were full of shit and which ones really were big spenders. Joey was considering a pimp for the first target but was open to whomever Higgins might suggest.

As always, they met at the zoo. Higgins was surprised one day when Joey met him close to the entrance instead of the usual spot by the lion's cage. He figured my brother was taking this even more seriously than usual. They walked for fifteen minutes, asking about each others' families and sharing gossip on a few mutual acquaintances. Joey always had at least one good "drunk Danny" story. Today's was a story about Danny getting up in the middle of the night at his girlfriend's apartment and pissing on the TV.

Then, Joey got down to business and laid out the plan. As soon as he brought up the Millers, Higgins got wary. "Joey, you sure you want to get involved with these crazy redneck pricks?

Remember what happened in Atlanta."

"Higg, you know what happens when their usefulness runs out."

Higgins wasn't entirely convinced and tried to push the point, "I like the idea, Joey, but why don't we use locals?"

"I want to use people from outside that don't know anybody here and won't be recognized. Just have faith, and let me handle it. It'll be like a piss off Pier Six."

"How am I gonna stand lookin' at these two wacky redneck motherfuckers?" Higgins said this more to himself than to Joey. In Leavenworth, he had grown to hate the Millers, though he had been as amused as Joey by their stories.

"Listen, Joey, there's one more thing. Is Danny gonna be part of this move?"

"Not yet, but if we ever need him, I'll let you know."

"Danny's stand-up all the way. But his lips, they get a little loose, you know what I mean?"

"Hey, Higg, first things first! Forget about Danny for now."

When they got to the gorillas, Joey and Higg stopped to watch them, honing in on a big one sitting beneath a tree. Joey recognized the animal's facial expression from his time in prison: The gorilla knew where it was, even if it didn't know why. And it didn't like it. Worse, it hated being seen this way in captivity. The animal snarled as Joey stared; my brother couldn't look away.

Higgins followed Joey's eyes. "Does he look like anybody you know?"

Joey thought for a second. Then they said together, "Fat Sam."

"I never did figure out where he was from," Joey added.

"He was Samoan," Higgs filled him in. There were a few countries that seemed important enough to Joey to remember their names, but Samoa had never been one of them. "Remember him? He's guarding Fattie Black Walters now."

"Fattie Black Walters? Who's that?"

Higgins smiled. "He's our first score."

Fattie Black was beefing with a pimp named Raul, who'd

been trying to sell drugs on the side. Raul hadn't backed off no matter what Fattie Black sent his way, and he'd brought in bodyguards after Raul shot up his car. Higgins had heard people talking about the feud and figured it would be the perfect cover for what Joey had planned. When he explained it, my brother agreed and adjusted his plan a bit to take advantage of the situation.

Once a guy's pissed off, who better to send him after than somebody he already hates?

CHAPTER TWELVE

When Joey had been back for a week or two, he spent a weekend up in Westchester. As far as Armondo was concerned, Joey wanted to take Carole somewhere private for a romantic weekend. And he did. But, Joey took a few hours on the side to walk around the neighborhood. He found a nice secluded house that the owner was renting out for the season.

The owner wasn't connected, just a regular guy. Joey didn't want to risk involving anybody who knew his world at all. My brother didn't want his name on any paperwork—nothing that could be traced back to him. No matter what, the guy wouldn't go for it. Even when Joey said he'd pay the whole thing up-front in cash, it was no go. Normally, Joey would've walked away and found another place, but he wanted to finish the deal then and there so he could get back to Carole ASAP. In the end, he signed for it as "Daniel Reedy."

In Joey's mind, this was a safe move. Danny wasn't involved, so what did it matter what some piece of paper said? Nobody was ever going to see it. Joey wasn't stupid enough to think there wasn't a chance that his plans might go wrong. He was only human, and plans get fucked up all the time. The trick was to anticipate where things could go wrong and make back-up plans. But, who was gonna trace the Millers, and then find the guy who owned the place? Even if the brothers attracted the wrong kind of attention, there was no reason to think any of it would come down on Danny.

Higgins was waiting at the airport when the plane landed. All of the other passengers stood aside to let the Miller brothers get off and away from them as quickly as possible. They weren't even causing problems; they'd been peaceful for the entire flight, mainly because they'd filled up on beer at the airport bar and passed out before the plane even left the runway. It was the smell and the way they looked that scared everyone away in droves.

Outside, the brothers spotted the car quickly and threw their luggage into the trunk. Seeing a black man in the driver's seat, they got in the backseat. Higgins hadn't meant to play chauffeur; but, since smell was still a factor, he didn't really care.

Though Higgins disliked the Millers, he got along better with Rusty than his brother. They hadn't spent a whole lot of time together in prison, but Joey had made sure they knew each other. And, Rusty had enough respect for Joey not to fuck with one of his friends.

Ronnie was tougher. It seemed like he wanted to start shit with Higgins specifically because Joey told them not to. Higg wasn't worried about taking Ronnie down if he had to, but he wouldn't have liked explaining it to Joey.

As they pulled onto the highway, Higgins looked back in the rearview mirror and said, "This is your first time in New York, right?"

Ronnie was lost in his own thoughts (what the ride would be like if the South hadn't lost, if guys like Higg knew their place), but Rusty nodded.

"What do you think so far?"

Rusty smiled. "I think I'm gonna love this city. Saw the skyline as we were landing. Looks like all the money in the world ends up on this island."

"Yeah, but you gotta be careful. My grandma always used to say, 'you look at gold the wrong way, and it'll blind you.'"

"That's true, but maybe I'll only lose one eye."

This, in a nutshell, explained the Miller brothers' philosophy on life: take the risk, no matter how stupid, and try to minimize your own pain; it had been working surprisingly well for them for years.

Higgins scowled. "If we do things the smart way, the way Joey says, then we're all gonna be happy. Nobody's gotta lose a thing. Ain't that right, Ronnie?"

Ronnie looked up, having followed none of the conversation, and blurted out, "Hey, yeah, that's right, I'm glad the South lost."

Higgins rolled his eyes. Quickly, he jumped lanes, slamming Ronnie's face against the window. "Yeah, me too, Ronnie."

Rusty slapped his brother on the back of the head. "Watch it, fucker, I told you!"

"You watch it." They stared at each other.

Higgins wasn't sure what to make of it: would these two crazy violent fucks be just as crazy and violent to each other?

Ronnie turned back to Higgins. "So, where we goin,' anyway?"

"Joey's got a place lined up." At a red light, Higg turned around and saw the large knife Rusty had tucked into his belt. "Damn, that's a hell of a blade."

"Yeah, I use it mainly for cutting cans."

"Cutting cans?"

"Yeah, you know… Mexi-cans, Puerto Ri-cans, even Ameri-cans."

Higgins smiled. "As long as you ain't cutting Afri-cans…" He laughed, but Rusty didn't get it.

About twenty minutes later, they reached Westchester. Higgins had a little trouble with some of the directions for the side streets. By the time the three of them got to the rented house, Joey had already finished cooking and was getting the table ready. The three men got out, stretched their legs a little, and walked in. Joey hugged Higgins and shook hands with the Miller brothers. With a grin, gesturing at the food on the table, he said, "You know, no matter how big or small a house is, Italians always feel most at home in the kitchen. Sit down, sit down, and eat."

Higgins replied, "I gotta hit the can first, Joey, I been in that car three hours. But, don't worry—I'm hungry as a motherfucker."

"No problem—down that hall, on'a right."

Rusty leaned in close, making sure his voice wouldn't carry, "How long you two know each other, anyways?"

Ronnie chimed in, laughing, "Yeah, I bet you didn't grow up

in the same part'a town."

Joey knew where this was leading; he had expected it. Careful to make his voice just a little louder than it needed to be, he calmly explained, "Matter of fact, we did grow up in the same part of town. Remember, when a man's a man, it doesn't matter what color he is."

Ronnie frowned. "Of course, Joey, fuck all'a that. What I mean is, do you trust him? This is some serious shit."

Joey stared at him. "I been doin' business with him a lot longer than I been doin' business with you two, Ronnie. You can be in or you can be out, but Higgins is part of it."

Ronnie didn't like this answer, but a quick look from Rusty killed any response.

Rusty said, "Joey, don't worry, we're in, and even my stupid brother knows that Higgins is a stand-up guy. He can't help what he was born."

When Higgins returned from the bathroom, they all sat down to the lasagna and salad Joey had prepared. Ronnie blew his nose in one of the napkins and then poured himself a big glass of wine before looking around, saying, "Uh, does anybody else want some?"

They spent the meal reminiscing about people they'd known in prison. "You remember that guard, Ralph Linson?" Rusty asked my brother.

"He's the guy that used to hate Italians 'cause his father died in World War II?"

"Exactly! Well, Ralph was working Harry down at the laundry, making him do double quota every day. He always pushed everybody, especially Harry. Finally, Harry couldn't take it anymore. Ralph says something about starch, and Harry turns around. Before anybody could do anything, he strips naked and gets down on all fours. So Ralph says, 'What the fuck you think you're doing?' And Harry says, 'Shit, Linson, if you're gonna work me like a dog, I'm gonna act like a dog!'

Higgins and Joey laughed, but Rusty shushed them. "Nah, listen, listen, so Harry's running around with his two-inch pecker hanging out, and everybody's laughing, right? Nobody's paying attention when Harry bites Ralph on the leg, and winds up getting two months in solitary. Ralph Linson, he left the job, couldn't handle it anymore. You get bit by a naked guy, and you tend to re-think a few things."

"But, that's not even the crazy part. So Ralph moves to New York because he can get a job there as a cop. He's working the late shift at the bus depot. Port Authority, Grand Central, whatever—walking around from midnight to eight a.m., mostly while it's closed, to make sure nobody's there. One night, Ralph goes in there with a friend, strips down naked, and just walks around wearing just his shoes and his cop hat, twirling his nightstick. His friend takes pictures. The next day the fuckin' moron drops them off at the photo shop like any other roll."

As he described it to me later, Higgins was on the edge of his seat. "So what happened?"

"What the fuck you think happened? Ralph got fired. So, what do you think the dumb prick does? He gets pinched selling drugs to an undercover agent."

While everyone else was laughing, Joey listened in disbelief. Rusty wasn't finished. "They were transferring Ralph into the can three days after me and Ronnie got released. Almost made me wanna stay an extra week."

After everybody had a good laugh, they settled into the meal, which was more than passable. For dessert, Joey had brought up a cheesecake from one of the few decent bakeries left in East Harlem. It was gobbled down in no time flat. When they'd finished eating, Joey filled in Higgins and the Miller brothers on how the whole thing would work.

"You're gonna go out in a van. Higgins drives it because he knows the streets. You two do the grab. I figure one of you does the approach, the other one keeps an eye out. Get him in the van as quickly as you can, but don't make any noise. No gunshots. If he resists, use the knife, but don't fire a gun in the middle of the night. New York cops still respond to shit like that."

"Afterwards, you take him back to the stash house. The

phone at the house isn't hooked up yet, so I scouted out a payphone on the way that you can use. He's gotta call somebody to arrange where the money is gonna be dropped off. One of you two rides out to meet his wife or girlfriend or uncle or whoever. Hey, Ronnie, you do it. We'll leave Rusty here with Higgins to watch this prick. By this point, he should be tied to a chair in an empty room. I don't think he'll be much trouble. Keep your masks on whenever you're around him, even after he's got the blindfold on, okay? This is important because you don't want anybody to see your faces."

Ronnie rolled his eyes. "Shit, Joey, we know what we're doing. We're not amateurs."

Higgins and Rusty both expected Joey to get angry, but he didn't. He stared at Ronnie for a minute and said, "I know, Ronnie. I know who I'm dealing with. None of us here are amateurs. We all live the Life one way or another. But, where did we meet? Prison. Every time, somebody was careless, the rest of us got fucked. I don't know about you, but I don't really want to go back there. I'm spelling this out now so there's no confusion."

Rusty nodded, though he hadn't been paying much attention. "So where are we gonna be stayin', Joey? You got us a room at the Ritz or something?"

"You two're gonna live up here for now. Higg can drive you into New York to pick up a few things. He'll fill you in on anything you don't already know." Joey punctuated this by dropping a set of house keys onto the table.

The brothers nodded in agreement. Higgins was silent. Then, Rusty had a question: "Where we gonna bring the targets?"

"I've got it all laid out. We'll be using four, maybe five spots. You'll get to know them all. I want you and Higgins to ride around a bit, just to get a feel for the area. You can make a few dry runs before we make the actual moves, so it'll all go smooth like we planned."

As Joey was leaving, he stopped and turned around. "One more thing, guys. You gotta find a barbershop, okay? You're gonna need to look a little more like New York City cops."

CHAPTER THIRTEEN

As far as everybody else was concerned, the plan was just to keep kidnapping drug dealers in the black neighborhoods, get a bunch of money, and then part ways. But, in Joey's mind, the kidnapping of Fattie Black was just a test-run. If the plan worked, Joey was already thinking about taking it to East Harlem, to any Italian who was paying homage to Armondo—maybe even that Irish fuck Jerry Shay. That was important to him.

I sometimes wonder what would've happened if it hadn't worked. If Fattie Black's bodyguards had done a better job, if one of them had just taken out Rusty Miller, maybe Joey would've abandoned the whole thing. Maybe there was still time for him to find another path. But, to Joey, it was either this or selling junk—and he didn't want any part of that. Maybe, if this hadn't 'a worked, he might have come up with something else. Just as Joey had planned, it went off without a hitch.

Joey knew it was a risk being there, watching the action. Everybody at the Pioneer thought he was with Carole, and Carole thought he was visiting me at Allenwood.

That week, Joey'd done a lot of the legwork himself, staying out late to watch Fattie Black's movements. Fattie always left his people around 2 a.m. and spent anywhere from one hour to four hours visiting his white girlfriend, who lived up in Washington Heights on a quiet, tree-lined street with bushes on both sides of the building.

Joey didn't need to be there; Higg and the Miller brothers could run the kidnapping without him. But, there was something about the thrill of seeing the whole thing come together that he couldn't resist. He tried to tell himself it was just this one, just to make sure the test-run worked out; but, as he watched it going down in front of him, he knew he'd never want to miss one. As long as they were pulling it, he'd stay close. The danger—the way it was stupid and unnecessary—was part of the appeal.

As soon as Fattie Black was buzzed in, Rusty got out of the van and walked down the street wearing sunglasses. Joey had told him they made him stick out too much and resemble a junkie. But, at least Rusty had gotten the haircut Joey insisted on. Rusty stopped at Fattie's car, pulled out his knife, and stabbed a gash in the front tire. Then, he disappeared into the shadows, staying behind some bushes near the car. Joey watched the whole thing and smiled: so far, so good.

Fattie came out a little before 4 a.m. He had a fairly light skin tone and wasn't very tall, but somehow he was huge from any angle you looked at him. If Louie Armstrong had been as fat as he looked with his cheeks inflated, he might have resembled Fattie Black.

Fattie was smiling and strutting large, but that all changed when he reached his car. Seeing the flat tire, he shouted, "Son of a bitch, this'a brand new car!"

Down the block, a white van slowly moved toward him. But, he was oblivious, continuing to stare down at the tire in disbelief, muttering to himself about how much he'd spent on the tires and the car, and how some dumb motherfucker was going to pay.

As the van got closer, Rusty started shaking the branches of the bush. Fattie turned suddenly as the motion stopped; he couldn't be sure anything had moved at all. It was starting to mess with his head, so he decided to go back upstairs. What the fuck, he was paying for the place; he could spend a night there.The bushes moved again; this time, Fattie saw the motion clearly. He took two steps closer just as the van reached the building and stopped short. At the sound of the brakes, Fattie turned to look. "Now who'da fuck is this?"

The side door of the van slid open, revealing only empty seats. No one appeared to be inside. Fattie couldn't see who'd opened the door and didn't want to get any closer. Behind him, Rusty silently emerged from the shadows with his gun. He waited until it was right up against Fattie's head to pull the hammer back so Fattie would hear the click.

"What the fuck is goin' on here?"

"Get in the fuckin' van or I'll blow your nigger head off!"

Fattie hadn't survived as long as he had by being slow. If somebody puts a gun to your head, you should probably do what he tells you. If he wanted to kill you, you'd be dead already. The best thing to do was just to see what was what. But, Fattie also kept an eye out for a slip up, a chance for him to draw his own pistol.

After Fattie got into the van, followed by Rusty, they drove off. Down the block, Joey started his car and followed. Wearing a ski mask, Higgins was driving because he knew the streets. The Millers stayed in the back with Fattie. They emptied his pockets and took his gun then tied his hands behind his back against the seat.

Rusty, in particular, seemed to enjoy slapping the black boss. The more it made Ronnie laugh, the more Rusty did it. He wound up punctuating every sentence with a slap across the face.

"Shut the fuck up and listen, you motherfucker. You like to push junk? You like fuckin' white broads? Young white broads like that girl upstairs? Well, it's time to pay—two-hundred grand or you're gonna die. Call whoever you gotta call, or we can just go back up to your cunt bitch and pick it up right now. It's up to you. But you're gonna pay."

"Tell you what, shit-head, let me out of the van right now, and I might be able to forget this whole thing long enough for you to get the fuck out of New York."

At this, Ronnie laughed even harder, while Rusty broke one of Fattie's fingers.

"Are you dumb bastards outta your minds?"

Ronnie smiled. "Yeah, Fattie, we are." He held up Fattie's gun and slammed it against the side of the drug dealer's head.

Higgins looked at them in the rearview mirror. "Hey, easy,

back there! Keep him conscious."

"Yeah, Fattie, that's right, don't pass out yet, okay? You've got to make some phone calls."

Joey continued to follow the van for several more blocks. Higgins took him around to the Warehouse District just west of Jerome Avenue in the Bronx, which he knew would be deserted this time of night. Finally, after circling the area for fifteen minutes, the van's blinker came on, and both vehicles pulled over.

Higgins got out and walked over to Joey, keeping his ski mask on until they were face to face. Joey rolled down his window as Higgins approached.

"He says if we'll take $60,000, he can get it tonight. Jus' gotta call his girl. He's got it in his house."

Higgins delivered the news coldly, anticipating Joey's negative response. On the one hand, he definitely wanted more money, but he didn't want to give the Millers any excuses to get rougher. The problem with a move like this was that once you hit a guy like Fattie Black hard, he might stay away and lick his wounds and not want to talk about it. You piss him off too much, he's gonna come after you looking for vengeance. Fattie Black was sharp, as smart a businessman as you'd find in any Wall Street office; but pride can interfere with even the strongest business sense, especially in the business of the street.

Joey thought about the offer and then dismissed it,. "No good. Tell him a hun'red or we chop off his head. You show him that blade that Rusty's got and he'll remember another stash of cash he can get his hands on, guaranteed."

"Sounds good!" Higgins pulled the mask down and walked back to the van as Joey lit a cigarette and waited. Sure enough, before he could finish the last drag and put it out in the ashtray, Higgins had leaned out the window and given him the thumbs up. Joey signaled with his headlights and started his car again.

Higgins drove Ronnie to the spot Joey had picked out in advance, next to a used car lot Marty Lester had a piece of, where they'd stashed a tan rental car. Joey had planned the locations so that Ronnie would have no chance of getting lost. Once he reached the parking lot, Ronnie would pull the bandana he'd tied around his neck up over his face.

Higgins pulled over at the phone booth Joey had picked out. They knew the phone was clean, and it was in the same abandoned area, where nobody would walk by and cause a scene. The last thing they needed was Fattie Black causing a ruckus and attracting attention while Rusty Miller held a gun on him. One thing Joey hadn't accounted for was Fattie's girth, which made for a tight squeeze in the phone booth. Rusty had to stand outside leaning in. Joey was already figuring that by the time he did this again, he'd have a scrambled phone installed at the house.

Fattie's girl Candy didn't answer the first set of rings. Rusty wasn't happy and raised the gun to threaten him. Fattie Black looked up at him: "Fuck man, what can I do? Bitch won't answer the phone."

He redialed, and, after six rings, she picked up and immediately started cursing at whoever was calling her in the middle of the night.

Fattie jumped in, "Listen, bitch, shut the fuck up."

Candy immediately apologized. "I didn't realize it was you, honey! You woke me–"

He interrupted her again to explain the situation. When she realized he actually had a gun to his head, Fattie could barely calm her down long enough to listen.

Then the operator chimed in that Fattie's dime was running out. He patted his pockets—nothing. The rednecks had picked him clean. He looked up at Rusty. "Hate to ask, brotha, but they say I need another dime, and I know you want me to keep talking, 'cause she ain't heard a word I said since I mentioned a gun."

Rusty stared at him, breathing out slowly through his mouth. He wasn't good at improvising, but thankfully this didn't require much independent thought. He shifted the gun to his other hand, pulled a dime out of his pocket, and slid it in the slot. After three attempts, Fattie was finally able to explain to Candy where the money was and where she needed to bring it.

Candy was still hysterical, "I love you baby! Everything will be okay! I'll do whatever you say."

"Bitch, just bring the money!" Fattie shouted, and slammed the phone down. Rusty slapped him, just for the hell of it, and dragged him back to the van.

About twenty minutes later, Joey saw Candy pull into the designated lot. He recognized the blue car from staking out her apartment. As instructed, she circled the lot once and then parked in the exact middle. She hadn't even taken the key out of the ignition when Ronnie climbed into the backseat. When she started to turn, he forced her head back. "What are you, stupid? You want to die, bitch? Don't look at me."

When she glanced in the rearview mirror and saw the gun in his hand, she quickly closed her eyes tight.

Ronnie picked up the suitcase at his feet and counted the money: it seemed to be all there. When he looked up into the rear view mirror, he could see that the V-neck sweater she was wearing showed off her huge tits. He started to get a hard on. If this had been just him and Rusty, he'd probably have taken the time to fuck her right there and then, but he knew Joey wanted this to go smooth, and probably would be pissed if he did something stupid. It was easy to look down on a guy just trying to get his nut off when you could go home with a girl like Carole any time you wanted.

"Hey, hey, Candy, listen, it's gonna be okay. You want to fuck a nigger, fine. I can't believe a pretty girl like you needs to, but shit, it takes all kinds. One thing I know is that if a woman wants to fuck a nigger, you better believe she's gonna. We got the money, so we'll let him go as long as you listen to me. You'll be able to fuck your nigger again real soon, okay? Stop crying, I'm being a nice guy tonight for a change. After I take off, you wait here fifteen minutes. Don't move! Don't even turn the car on to get the heater going. Somebody'll be watching. Then, when you get home, he'll call and tell you where you can pick up your nigger. One more thing, doll: you have to tell him that 'Raul says thanks for the money.' You got it? Say it back so I know you understand."

She nodded slowly. "Raul says thanks for the money."

Ronnie got out and walked over to his tan car, pulling off the bandana just as he got there. Joey wouldn't have liked that sloppiness, but he was keeping his eyes on Candy's car. He thought to himself, "Easy as a piss off a Pier Six," just like Joey always said.

CHAPTER FOURTEEN

Almost everything I'm telling you about now, I found out after the fact. I would've never believed in a million years that Joey was part of what happened. It was against everything our life was supposed to be. And, knowing how my brother loved the Life, I never thought he would be involved with something like this. When I heard about the nappings, as they were called in East Harlem, I had no idea they involved Joey. I thought that the people doing this must be the worst kind of lowlifes.

I found out that Joey did the same moves a few more times with guys that Higgins picked and then started switchin' it up. He started planning to go after junk pushers, the ones he knew were paying tribute to Armondo. His first target was going to be Butch "The Shadow" Ombra, Armondo's policy man, who did big narco deals with the Puerto Ricans. Joey knew he was going to have to be even more careful now that he was dealing with people who knew the same ones he did.

In the meantime, Joey had a lot of cash on hand from these jobs because they'd been even more successful than he'd expected. There was one thing I had to learn on my own—how to save money. I certainly didn't learn that from my brother. He was always a good strategist, but he could never plan too far ahead financially. Joey was like Houdini; he made money disappear. Yet, he always seemed to have some. It was just that he never saved it; he believed money was there to spend.

Now that he had a little bit extra, it was burning a hole in his pocket. He wanted to use it to impress the only person he ever cared about. So, one Friday night, he picked up Carole at her office on Third Avenue, not far from Bloomingdale's, and drove her out to Bronxville for a romantic surprise he'd planned, one that would con-

sume their whole weekend.

Joey was pushing Carole's patience. "Keep your eyes closed," he'd been telling her from the minute they'd gotten in the car. As soon as he'd seen the traffic around Central Park, he'd relented a little. But, my brother made her close her eyes again when they reached the Henry Hudson Bridge.

After about five minutes, she was frowning. "This better be worth it, Rendino."

If the asshole in the silver car in front of him had been driving any slower, she probably would've peeked. "Just lean your head back and relax."

After thirty minutes filled with more promises of satisfaction, Carole could hear the car pull onto a gravel driveway, slow down, and stop. When Joey opened the door of the car and led her up the walkway, he made sure her hands were still over her eyes when they entered the house.

"Okay, you can look now. We're here."

"Finally!" She opened her eyes to an empty room with beautiful wood floors, but not much else. "It's… nothing?" She looked around, not angry at Joey, but confused. "Where are we? Whose house is this?"

Joey moved his hands from behind his back and placed a piece of paper in Carole's hand—the deed. "It's yours. I wanted you to have it."

Her first instinct was to pull back: Carole told Nadine afterwards that she was taken aback at this lavish display and wondered what else Joey had up his sleeve. As a woman who liked to think she controlled her own destiny, she wasn't keen on surprises, but Carole couldn't help but feel touched that Joey had gone this all out to please her. Still, she enjoyed being a little coy with my brother.

"Always keep them wondering," Nadine Chiaro had advised Carole the last time they'd had a cup of coffee together. "Keep the mystery intact or you'll lose some of the allure." It was the same thing Carole tried to keep in mind when planning the launch of new fragrances. The independent new woman wanted to attract her man but on her own terms.

"It's perfect, Joey," Carole said with great excitement as she looked around the room. "Now, could I persuade you to throw in a ring, just a small one? Maybe an itsy-bitsy diamond?" she laughed, holding up her fingers.

Joey laughed, too, as he usually did when she tried to bust his balls. "You're a crazy kid! *Madonna*, what a crazy kid."

"Oh, Joey, it's beautiful, but…"

"What is it?"

"The house is beautiful, I love it! But I can't commute all the way into the city during the week." Given her rapid rise at Creative Fragrances, Carole couldn't give up a job she loved even to settle down with Joey, her true love—not that my brother would have wanted her to. Still, Carole wanted to make sure of his motives for giving her this extravagant gift.

"Nah, keep your place, Carole. You gotta great thing goin'. But, maybe you can get away and we can come out here on weekends. You know me, always loose as a goose."

Joey knew he shouldn't be flashy like this, buying a house, but even while he told himself that he was the wrong man for Carole, he clung to her desperately. Knowing how much she was making, he wanted to make a big, extravagant money-is-no-object gesture. But, he wasn't going to propose. He didn't want her tied to the neighborhood, nor did he want her to be a widow at thirty.

She showed her appreciation with a deep kiss but pulled back.

"What's wrong? You know, there's a furniture store about fifteen minutes away if you're worried–"

"No, it isn't that. It's just… I've been worrying about Danny lately," Carole said, deflecting her disappointment at Joey's reluctance to discuss giving her a ring..

"What's he into this time?"

Carole was holding back tears; she'd promised herself not to cry anymore over Danny, always telling herself that he couldn't help being who he was. "He's the same as he's always been only more so, you know? When he's flush, he shares with everybody. But when he's losing, he starts betting like crazy to try to make it back. Ever since Pop died he's been hanging around the pub. Danny says he's running the place, but really he's just drinking all the profits."

Though she couldn't admit it to herself, Carole knew she was pressing Joey for more of a commitment partially because of the instability in her family life. Her job and my brother were her anchors, along with a few friends from the old neighborhood, like Nadine.

"*Madonna mia*, your brother… okay, I'll talk to him, but he is what he is."

He looked up at her, smiling. "Thank God you are what you are…"Joey started kissing Carole's hand, going slowly up her arm. She enjoyed it briefly, and then leaned back again.

"Joey, what do you feel for me? Be honest."

A few days earlier, Carole had asked Nadine to meet her in midtown for lunch. She'd decided this was the time to confront her lover and wanted Nadine's opinion. It was a bit of a risk, Nadine had counseled, fully aware that Carole would do it anyway. Carole needed assurances from Joey at a time when her family wasn't providing much comfort. Nadine knew Carole would do what she felt she had to and reflect on it later.

As my brother continued talking to Carole, he punctuated his sentences with little kisses on her arm, getting closer and closer to her heart, "You know, Carole, feelings can be confusing simply because we feel so many different things. I had devotion for the way of life I chose, but it's gone. In a completely different way, I loved my mother very much. Although I was very young when she died, I can still feel the hurt. My father was a decent man who did the best he could considering the circumstances. I love Vinnie. I tried to advise him, but he's his own man, and I respect that. But you, how can I describe my feelings for you? If I see someone touch you, even your brother, I wanna tear them apart. If someone looks at you in a certain way, that disturbs me.

I want to tear their eyes out. Carole, I know I've loved you since the first time I saw you. But, my love for you is selfish because of who and what I am. You deserve much more."

"It's all I ever wanted, Joey, to be with you!" Carole told him, her voice wavering. "Yeah, I love my job—but I need you in my life to make it all real."

When he reached her shoulder, he stopped. "You know, I did make sure they set up a bed with the softest mattress in the store. Want to go take a look at the bedroom?"

Carole thought about it for a moment, and then shook her head as she regained her footing. "I've got a better idea. Let's take a look at the kitchen."

Joey said, "Why, all we do in the kitchen is cook."

"Uh, huh," said Carole suggestively, arching an eyebrow.

Though my brother had the foresight to buy a bottle of champagne, in a rare oversight, he'd forgotten to buy glasses for the new house. After he and Carole made love in ways Joey'd never imagined a kitchen could accommodate, the two of them drank straight from the bottle, still sweating and breathing hard.

After the weekend, Joey dropped Carole off at her apartment and then sped over to Lucky Chang's on Lexington Avenue just in time to see the Miller brothers dressed as detectives dragging Butch "The Shadow" Ombra into the back seat of a black car. Lucky Chang's, a famous Chinese restaurant, was a favorite of The Shadow and his Latina girlfriend.

Joey had finally decided to make a few moves in his own part of town. Butch was earning big bucks, not only in the Latino area of East Harlem, but also in Black Harlem, where the junk trade was flourishing. The Shadow had good relations with both the Puerto Ricans and blacks. He was so dark skinned that many people took him for a Puerto Rican, anyway. Butch was running five or six numbers spots in the *barrio*, and some heavyweight heroin dealers were scoring from him. As usual, Armondo looked the other way, as long as the tributes kept coming. Butch was nobody to fuck with, but he was everything about the Life that Joey detested.

Ombra owned a bar and grill on Third Avenue run by his father and two brothers. At first, Joey had planned to snatch Butch when he left the bar. Higgins clocked him for about two weeks and reported back to Joey that it was too risky because there were always people around. Two or three nights a week, Butch and his lady friend went to Lucky Chang's. Joey checked out the location and gave the go-ahead for the move.

Higgins and the Miller brothers tailed Butch to the restaurant on a Monday night. The street was quiet. When The Shadow and his girl left, Higgins pulled up in front of his car. Butch slowed his pace when he saw the Millers dressed as detectives.

Rusty walked up to him first, flashing a gold badge. "Hello, Butch, I'm Detective Koch. This here's my partner, Detective Adams. Why don't you send the pretty lady back inside while we talk a while?"

"Talk about what? I got nothing to talk to you about, go fuck yourselves." He looked to the girl and said, "Come on, let's go. Fuck these two jerk-offs."

Ronnie pulled out his gun and pointed it at the girl. "Get the fuck back in the restaurant, bitch, or I'll blow your fuckin' cunt head off. And don't make a fuss." When Butch saw the rage in Ronnie's eyes, he ordered her to go back to the restaurant. Scared shitless, she did as she was told.

Rusty had a hard time closing the cuffs on Butch's thick wrists. When Butch started to struggle, Ronnie punched him square in the nose, just hard enough to stun him.

Then, Ronnie said, "Get in the motherfuckin' car, or you're gonna become a fuckin' ghost." After blindfolding him, they pushed him into the backseat.

Higgins noticed Joey's car idling down the side street. Neither the Millers nor Butch had noticed Joey, which put Higgins at ease. Too many people knew Joey's car, but my brother couldn't resist the action. He would've loved to abuse the fat bastard for a few days, but that wouldn't have been good for business. And, by then, business was looking pretty damn good.

CHAPTER FIFTEEN

The Lester family had seven kids, but Mrs. Lester figured it was as easy to cook for a dozen as for seven. She was always taking in strays. While the courts were trying to figure out what to do with us after our dad died, Joey and I hung out at their brownstone on 106th between Park and Fifth Avenues, across from Fifth Avenue Flower Hospital. I remember the hospital well because I was stitched up there after Fredo Balducci smacked me on the head with a stickball bat.

Once, when Joey was talking about our mother and father, he mentioned that the Lesters became the closest thing we had to a family. It was a rare moment when my brother got sentimental. Of all the Lesters, Marty and Mel were the closest. They weren't twins. (Actually, they weren't even in-a-row; their sister, Minnie, was in-between.) But, they had the same kind of connection some twins do. Sometimes, it seemed as if they could read each other's mind. They always did business together. Years later, they died in the same month, even though they weren't even living in the same state. They had both retired, but Mel wanted a beach, and Marty liked the mountains. They spoke on the phone a few times a day. Once Mel died, Marty's wife said that Marty just deflated. She knew he wasn't gonna last.

I don't know what the secret is to surviving the death of a close family member. I got through it somehow, but I can't explain it. It wasn't a plan. It probably helps to be young when it happens. I've seen a lot of people live a long time, then somebody dies, and it's like the straw that broke the camel's back. All the people they've known who pass away pile up on them. Once they've lost too many, they give up on life. I've seen it happen a hundred times. The person left behind is gone within three months. I always wonder if God considers it suicide with something like that. It's not like they stick a gun in their mouth—they just give up. I hope God goes easy on 'em. People like that have suffered enough on earth already.

Marty Lester's car lot had a sign up that advertised, "The lowest prices in Yonkers." This wasn't true of every car on the lot. Much of his business was strictly above board. Mel handled a lot of that, and even if they'd only stuck with the new Oldsmobiles, they'd still have done very well. But, a few guys that Marty knew pretty well could bring cars by, and he'd pay cash, no questions asked. He could also produce paperwork that would stand up to scrutiny. Marty held onto his contacts because he never abused his privileges. He could sell these cars cheaper than anybody else and still manage to turn a profit.

Marty knew other ways to have a car lot generate extra money on the side; it was the perfect place to launder money. After a car went out overnight, if anything went wrong, he'd just report it stolen. Usually he charged quite a bit to keep names off paperwork; there was never any charge for Joey. Joey and the Lesters went way back. Joey was family.

Mr. Lester was a hands-on boss who wanted to know all his employees. He'd grown close to our father when the Lester's business was still in East Harlem. Since Joey and Marty were close in age, they spent time together. Mel was a little older. I just tagged along with Joey. The two families wound up hanging out, even off the clock. After our mother died, Mrs. Lester often insisted on inviting all of the Rendino men over for dinner. She and our dad would have passionate arguments over the respective virtues of Jewish and Italian cooking. Each one would insist that they were joking: that they loved the other's cooking, but their own was superior.

Over the years, I picked up quite a few cooking tips from Mrs. Lester, including how to make a brisket. Sometimes, I used tricks she taught me to entice my customers at Big V Deli once I opened the shop. They couldn't put their finger on what it was that I was doing that none of the other Italian cooks could duplicate.

When we spent time at the Lester's, especially after old man

Lester died and Mel and Marty took over the car business, Joey and Frankie would sometimes help out with collections if people got a little behind on their payments. Marty and Mel never went after anybody who'd had a bad break. If you lost your job, Mel would let you slide for a few months, but if you missed a payment and then went around splashing cash all over East Harlem, you better hope the Lesters didn't hear about it. My brother never actually needed to use violence to get the car payments; just the threat of Joey's reputation was all that was needed.

A few days after Joey got out of prison, he'd gone to see Mel and Marty Lester, who had a car waiting for him. Joey had left me his Olds when he went to the can. It helped my position with the ladies of East Harlem; in fact, that's how I met my girlfriend, Rosemarie Albano, who lived on Pleasant Avenue in East Harlem. Her father was a member of the Boys of Forever Club, a bunch of guys from the same union. The club was started a few years after the First World War, when Italian immigrants were being abused, working fifteen or sixteen hour days for very low pay. It took a mass of strength and courage to start a union back then; violent confrontations, even murders, were put into the effort to stop them. But, the Boys of Forever were unstoppable. They were resilient.

Rosemarie always cooked, and worked behind the counter at a pork store on 117th Street. One day, when I pulled up in front of the Boys of Forever on 119th and Pleasant, she was talking to her father, who knew both Joey and me. He was nicknamed Corky; to this day no one knows why.

Corky said hello to me, then goodbye to his daughter, and walked into the club. As I was getting out Rosemarie said, "That's a nice car! Is it yours?"

"Yeah," I lied casually, as if it were no big deal.

One thing led to another, and I asked her if she would like to take a ride. After we cruised around the neighborhood for a while, I took her for a hamburger at a White Castle on Bruckner Boulevard in the Bronx. In those days, that constituted an excursion.

I was twenty-three-years-old when we met; we've been together ever since.

At the time, Joey was already in motion with the Nappers. One morning, he stopped into Mel and Marty's lot in Yonkers, dodging the salesmen who were working for commissions. Carrying a brown paper bag, my brother walked into the managers' office, where Marty and Mel were playing a round of gin rummy.

"I got the best bagels, nova, and cream cheese in all New York. All we need's fresh hot coffee."

Marty looked at Joey with a disappointed expression. "Fuck the bagels. I was waiting for a nice sausage and pepper on some good seeded Italian bread. Bagels—he brings bagels! What does he think he is, a Jew?"

Mel rolled his eyes.

Joey looked at him. "You must be beatin' the balls off him, Mel. The prick's in a bad mood. You don't wanna eat, Marty? Good, more for us."

Mel stood up, shaking Joey's hand. "How are you, my friend? Please excuse my ill-mannered brother, who's losing very badly as usual. He should kiss you for walking in. You saved him from another *schneid.* I had him, seventy-seven to zip—schmuck."

Marty waved his brother off and gave Joey a hug. "He's got two four-leaf clovers up his ass, this guy. A blind man could win with the cards he gets. And he's not cheating—he gets 'em no matter who deals!"

Marty knew that Mel liked a salted bagel with a *schmear* of cream cheese on it. Mel knew just how much butter Marty liked and how much was too much. Joey enjoyed watching them prepare each other's bagel, a ceremony they had first performed at the insistence of their mother. Over the years, they had started to enjoy the ritual for its own sake, reinforcing their status as equals. They only did it for the first bagel, though; to do it each time would be a waste of time, and the Lesters were always efficient, especially when they were on the clock.

Mel was so excited this morning that he hadn't even taken

two bites before he started complaining. Any problem they had with an Italian, Joey heard about. They didn't expect him to do anything about it; they just liked to bust his balls. It was the same reason Joey called Marty "The Jew."

The Lesters told Joey that a friend of Armondo's named Little Larry Orsino had been by a few days ago. Little Larry was a player in the New York to New Jersey narcotics trade whose 5'3" stature and a noticeable twitch didn't stop him from being a lady-killer. As Armondo used to say, "That little prick must have a big one."

Mel told Joey, "He comes in here with cash in pocket, and he thinks I'm gonna give him a better deal? I says, don't do me any favors. I make more money if a deal is financed. I know they're your friends, Joey, so forgive me—but I don't need that bullshit! They want good deals, don't want to pay the taxes, they know this one, they know that one. I say, good—I'm glad you know lots of people and have plenty of friends. Maybe one of them can give you a ride. Goodbye."

Mel picked up his bagel and started chewing. As soon as there was an opening, Marty chimed in, "So what you think happens? He comes back the next day. We think he's ready to deal... he offers five hundred more then he did the day before! I tell him, that's not even the right number of zeroes. We're talking different ballparks. For the price he's paying, I tell him the only thing I can sell him that we'll guarantee will run is a Schwinn bicycle."

Joey laughed in recognition.

"Yeah, you laugh at this, but Larry didn't even smile. This guy I never even heard of is gonna come to my lot and tell me what the price is gonna be? Orsino, what's that, Italian for tight-ass?"

Mel picked up right where his brother had left off, "I don't get these show-offs. They make and spend tons of money, not to mention how much they gamble away. Cars are bought for wives, girlfriends, whoever. And, they nitpick for a few bucks. If this is the new breed, my friend, your world is in deep shit."

Joey usually ate only one or two bagels, leaving the rest for the Lesters, who'd often send the remnants out to the sales staff. By now, he'd finished and was just listening to the brothers. Finally, he chimed in, "I know what you mean, my friend. I know what you mean, and I know who you mean. It's all about the money. Ten, fifteen years ago, we would never be having this conversation. Now, it's all exposed—wide open."

"I hope you're far away from the crap when the shit hits the fan," Marty said.

Even as a kid, Marty Lester had worried about Joey. He'd always felt that Joey's problem stemmed from spending his teenage years without parents. He'd never learned enough about discipline; now it was probably too late. Marty didn't want to know much about what Joey was doing, but he knew enough to know it was dangerous. The money seemed good, but there was always money to be made if you took a lot of chances. The trick Marty had found was sticking to small gains on sure bets, instead of big gains on long shots that could blow up in your face.

As if reading Marty's thoughts, Joey replied, "How can I be? I'm part of the crap." My brother never denied obvious truths to friends.

Marty nodded, knowing what he meant. "Mel, shuffle the deck up, we're gonna play one more game. I'm just gonna walk Joey out to his car, and then I'm comin' back here to take you down."

As Marty approached the door, Mel said with perfect timing as he shuffled, "He's been saying 'one more game' all morning. If I let you win this one, can we start selling cars?"

Walking to Joey's car with him, Marty Lester pulled an envelope out of his pocket. "This big shot just bought a brand new car, cash. Orsino sent him."

Joey smiled and put his hand on Marty's shoulder. "All right, Marty. Thanks."

Later, when Joey stopped by Reedy's Pub to talk to Danny, he bumped into Jerry Shay. He bought him a drink and showed all the proper respect; but, inside, he was remembering the trouble Shay's gang had caused for the Reedys. Soon, Joey would have a chance to settle a personal score.

CHAPTER SIXTEEN

Joey never told anyone the truth about the zoo, not even me. When other people were around he'd walk by the jungle cats and the bears, even the lizards and reptiles sometimes. But, when he was there alone, Joey went to the birdhouse. He could stay in there for hours. Walking around there reminded him of the Orange County Correctional Facility back in Warwick, New York, the first place he'd ever heard birds from his window.

Before that, it was only cars; even though he'd missed the car sounds the entire time he was gone, he began to miss the birds the first night he was back in East Harlem. They'd fly off somewhere for most of the day, but they'd always be back in the morning right when the sun was coming up. One morning, when Joey woke up and didn't hear the birds, he thought they'd all died out in the cold. It wasn't until the next spring, when they returned, that he learned where they'd been.

Since then, birds had always given him a good feeling. He liked to think about them flying off, having adventures in places he'd never heard of. Sometimes, he'd bring a few pieces of bread. When he walked through Central Park to see Carole, he'd stop and throw them some crumbs. When a bicyclist rode through a crowd of birds that had gathered to eat the crumbs he'd thrown down, Joey walked over, tore the chain off the guy's bike and threatened to hit him with it. The guy was so scared shitless that he ran away as fast as he could.

Carole knew he liked birds, though she didn't know the real reason why. She always said it was because the birds never shit on him. Back when she was in college, twice in one year, Carole bought a dress for a month's salary and got pigeon shit on it the first time she wore it.

People said it was supposed to be good luck, but it didn't seem like it to her. On the other hand, Joey could walk under all the trees in Central Park and never get a drop of bird shit on his shoulder. It was like the birds knew who he was and wanted to keep him on their side.

The Nappers made their next move on Little Larry on one of those misty New York nights where it hasn't quite rained, but it always feels like it's about to. The streets were empty, and the mist made for perfect cover.

Larry wasn't one of Armondo's guys directly, though he made moves with some of Armondo's people. Because he knew many of the guys who did a lot of moves, Larry had his fingers in plenty of pies. Even though he was only 5'3", Larry acted like King Kong. He was both street-smart and wise to the ways of legit business. He owned a few diners, a luncheonette, and an apartment building in Riverdale where he housed one of his lady friends. The Nappers clocked him near the place for a month before they snatched him. At first, they thought they could take him when he left his luncheonette, but that proved too risky.

At about 1 a.m. on a Wednesday morning, Higgins and the Millers were parked down the street from the apartment. They'd seen Larry's latest lady love enter a few hours earlier; his car was parked outside. When they'd made their first pass at around 11:00 p.m., the always thorough Higgins consulted the log, comparing dates and times with the notes he'd made on previous runs.

When they noticed Larry leaving the building, they drove past slowly and double-parked beside his car.

As Larry approached, the Millers, disguised as detectives, got out to greet him, "Hey, little brother, how's it going?"

"Who the fuck are you?" Larry shot back. "Get the fuck out of my face and move your car."

Ronnie started to laugh as Rusty said, "Well, well, aren't we a smart-ass little guinea?" He smacked Larry hard on the side of his face.

When Higgins opened the door, Larry could see his black hands on the handle as they pushed him into the car. Higgins was the only one wearing a ski mask.

"Hey, nigger, why don't you show your face?" he sneered.

After he stopped laughing, Higgins said, "I'm not gonna show you my face, but I'm sure as shit you're going to show me a lot of your money."

"Whata ya talkin' about? I ain't got no money," Larry said, still defiant despite the fact that Rusty had smacked him again.

Rusty put the big knife to Larry's throat and told him, "If you ain't got no money, then you don't got no head."

After Higgins had pulled over onto a dark, quiet street, Ronnie blindfolded Larry and made him lie down on the back floorboard. Then, he and Rusty took turns kicking him—pure joy for the Miller brothers. By the time they got Larry to the stash house, he was ready to do anything they wanted—another piss off Pier Six.

After the kidnapping was over, Joey gave a piece to Marty, more than Marty expected—just 'cause Joey thought it was the right thing.

My brother had arranged to meet Higgins at 3 p.m. but lost track of time and wound up running over to the cats' area about ten minutes or so after 3 p.m. Higgins was just sitting on a bench, not watching the animals, but focusing on a small boy throwing popcorn at a panther. The kid had a good arm, and the kernels were hitting the cat square on the nose. The panther would growl, sending the kid into a fit of hysterics. Every time the boy threw more popcorn, he'd move a little closer to the cage. Higgins was watching, waiting to see how close the kid could get before the panther lunged for him.

Joey and Higgins shook hands. Then, Joey pointed toward a sign near one of the enclosures: "Look at that—it says they had a white tiger all the way from China. Same stripes as a real one, but this one's black and white."

"Yeah, black and white, just like you and me, right? What's he, like a Chinese albino?"

"I don't think so. His eyes ain't red."

"True, true. So when's the next move, Joey?"

"Look, Higg, so far, so good. The word hasn't hit the streets yet, so I got a good target lined up."

They stopped in front of a leopard as the employees tossed it some meat. Higgins glanced back at the panther cage, but the kid was gone, and the panther was pacing back and forth as though unsatisfied.

"Take a look at these guys, Higg. All they want's to eat, sleep, maybe get laid once in a while, and just be left alone. Why can't we be that way?"

"Hey, m'man, you forgettin' they're locked up. It's totally different when these motherfuckers are in the wild, then they gotta be strong t'survive. We're the same way when we're locked up. Think about it, three hots and a cot, whack off once in a while, and we're good to go."

"That's a good point, but I'm talking about free men. In there, everything's provided for. Out here you have to find your own way. You have to live paycheck to paycheck or you're gonna starve. It shouldn't be that way. The big fish eats the small fish. In my world, the small fish are like ants. We do all the work so that the big fish keep getting bigger. You know, Higg, Shakespeare says in *King Lear,* "Distribution should undo excess, and each man have enough."

"This motherfucker Shakespeare was a Communist!"

Joey laughed. "Forget about that, I got a whole new plan worked out. You wanna stay with this, or you had enough?"

"How much longer you gonna go with this, Joey? Me and you, fine, but we're gonna have a problem down the road with the two crazy bastards, you know that."

"Three, four more good moves. Then, the rednecks disappear. This time, you're gonna be waiting in a diner on the west side, near Local 468."

Joey paused for a moment before adding, "Until you hear from Danny."

Higgins' eyes narrowed immediately as he interjected, "Hol' on, when did Danny get into this?"

Joey was firm but avoided sounding defensive about the subject. "He knows where the target's house is, somewheres off the

Palisades. I stand by him. I trust him more than the Millers."

"That's probably true." Higgins didn't like it, but he could tell Joey's mind was made up. He trusted Joey to keep Danny in line. And, with the money Joey was pulling down for all of them, he'd earned a little leeway.

"So, you an' the Millers are waiting for Danny's call..."

Danny was waiting outside Jerry Shay's house in Jersey to see when he left. As soon as the driver drove away, Danny drove over to the nearest payphone, one he'd found at a nearby gas station. He called the Millers, who were waiting in a booth at a diner down the block from union hall where Jerry supervised the carpenter's union, Local 468.

Joey made sure that Danny didn't have too much to handle the first time in. He figured it was best to ease Danny into it, make sure Higgins could see he was reliable. He might need Danny on later jobs. And, Joey didn't want to hear Higgins say what he felt deep down himself: that the moves were dangerous enough without Danny getting involved.

Higgins stayed in the beige van with a plumbing insignia on the side while Rusty and Ronnie simply walked into the union hall, loitering by the doors. Jerry was dropped off about ten minutes after they got there, but nobody walked him up the steps, and his driver didn't even wait around. The Millers grabbed him before he'd even walked through the door.

Since it was quiet at that time of the morning, nobody saw it happen. Jerry wasn't missed for several hours because he often didn't come to the office until after noon. Joey had gotten lucky again: the Millers could have been stuck waiting at the union hall for hours. If there'd been a crowd around, they would've left. Joey would've planned another day, but fortune often favors the over-prepared, and Joey was still getting lucky on the early moves.

They had to keep Jerry stashed in the house with the Miller brothers for more than twenty-four hours before they finally had the money. It took a while for his people to get it together because Joey upped the price. This one was going to bring in three times what Fattie Black did.

The next afternoon, a beige van drove through Hell's Kitchen and stopped in front of the union hall, waiting at a red light. When the light turned green, the back doors of the van opened, and Jerry Shay was thrown out onto the asphalt as the van sped off. Nobody thought to get the license plate number because they were too distracted by the naked, blindfolded union leader standing in front of them with his hands tied behind his back.

He struggled with the rope for five minutes before somebody recognized him and rushed to help. Down the block, Joey smiled as he turned into traffic. Even though he knew he'd never do anything as stupid as keeping a record of any of these moves, he had to admit that this one time, he wished he'd brought a camera.

CHAPTER SEVENTEEN

Frankie and Swifty Chiaro were as close as brothers can be—closer than even me and Joey. The thing was that as simple as these two guys were, they understood each other better than anybody else did. They were always together. They even lived in the same apartment building.

Then, Swifty got that dog and named it Nunzzio. It was a cross-eyed mutt with half an ear missing. Frankie used to tell his brother, "The dog looks just like you."

From the very first time Nunz saw Frankie, the dog would bark and growl: he just didn't like him. Everybody thought it was funny, and even Frankie laughed it off at first. One day, Swifty took Nunzzio into the Pioneer. The poor dog was so nervous when it saw Frankie, it shit right in the middle of the floor in front of him. This time, when everyone laughed, Frankie got so mad that he kept kicking Nunzzio in the butt until Swifty and his dog were out of the club. He didn't even give Swifty a chance to clean up his dog's shit. That was the beginning of Swifty letting his dog shit in front of the club almost every day.

Neither one of them ever talks about it; but, if they did, they'd each say the other one had to apologize. I used to think Frankie was in the wrong but I had to consider that Swifty still brought that dog by the club every day to do his business. Sometimes, Frankie was there and chased him off. Usually, Swifty was able to get there when nobody was looking. Suddenly, there was dog shit outside the Pioneer, always in the same spot. Most people knew where Nunz shit, so they avoided stepping in it. We put up with it mainly because it got Frankie so pissed that we had a good laugh about it, but I was starting to see his point. Swifty's been through four dogs since then, and he's done the same thing with every one of 'em.

We laugh at those two brothers and the dog shit. We treat it as a comedy but think about how sad it is. The two brothers, they probably still love each other. We laugh because they're not the sharpest knives in the drawer. Do we know how Swifty feels when he's walking away with the dog?

I know something neither of them knows. Right now, each one thinks the other will be the first to break. Right now, it seems like they have all the time in the world. One day, they'll have no time at all. One day, one'a them's gonna die, and whoever's left is going to regret the bad blood until the day he dies. That's the thing about family: when your brother's being a stubborn asshole, if he's not gonna give in, you're gonna have to because he's family.

While the Nappers were making their moves, Joey still had to make good with Armondo. He was spending more time than usual on the street, trying to find out whatever he could. Joey spent less time at his own club and more time at Villa Armondo in the Bronx because there was more action there. Being around, you could find out a lot if you just knew how to watch and listen.

Joey was sitting there at the bar one day drinking a club soda when Philly Agoglia walked in. A really likeable East Harlem guy, Philly was a sharp dresser, but not flashy. When he saw Joey, he walked over to shake his hand.

"Hello, Philly. Have somethin' to drink."

He shook his head. "Thanks, Joey, but I'm workin' the game tonight. You know Al."

Joey pushed him a little to see if he'd break. "Come on, Al's not around, just have a fuck'n drink."

"Joey, no disrespect of course, but I can't do it. Al's got rules, and I ain't tryin' to piss anybody off."

Joey smiled. Philly had passed his test. "Of course! Al's lucky to have people like you and my kid brother. So, what did you wanna see me about?"

"My cousin, you know, Benny? He wants to borrow five thousand."

Joey raised his eyebrow, saying nothing. Everyone knew that Benny liked to gamble, and was a sucker for the ladies.

"Joey, I'll stand behind the loan."

Joey thought about this and then nodded. "Tell him to come by my club any mornin', 'bout ten-thirty. I'm always there."

My brother rarely ate breakfast. He thought it slowed him down. Joey had two styles of dress: his more casual daytime clothes and more formal evening attire, both of which made him stand out. If Nadine was around when he walked out of our building to the Pioneer in the morning, she would break his beads, "Where's your 8 by 10 glossy? You act and dress like a fuck'n Hollywood fag."

If I was around for the show, I'd break out laughing.

Joey was always quick with his comeback: "Hey Nadine, do me a favor—go clean up your brother's dog shit in front of the club and stay away from here unless you're cleaning the apartment or leaving me and Vinnie something good to eat. People see you in front of the club, and they think I turned my joint into a pet store."

Nadine would look my brother straight in the eye, take a few steps back, spread her legs, put her two hands in a "V" shape by her crouch and say, "I got your pet store right here, fag. Oh I forgot you don't eat breakfast, Joey! You should try it once in awhile; you might like it."

We all cracked up. Those were the good old days.

Ten in the morning, when my brother started his day, was early to the old guys sitting in the Pioneer drinking coffee and playing cards. As Joey walked by, he'd acknowledge each one with a shake of his head on the way to the back room. While Joey drank his coffee, Frankie would give him any messages from the night before and fill my brother in on everything that had gone on in the club while Joey hadn't been around.

The Pioneer was alive with action. Everyone in the club—some way, somehow—was selling swag: jewelry, rings, watches, whatever else had been shoplifted, or, as we used to say, "fallen off the truck."

Who was shylocking, who was playing card and crap games a couple a times a week? It wasn't just Joey and Frankie who earned in the Pioneer: Al Hicks ran the crap and blackjack games and also had a piece of the shy money. Of course, Amondo got a piece of everything. Those were the days when Joey was a believer in the Life to the core: it was all he lived for. East Harlem was the mecca of the universe to him. Joey told wise guys from other neighborhoods that whenever he left East Harlem, he felt like he was camping out in some foreign country. They laughed as though he was joking, but he wasn't: he truly loved his neighborhood, and believed in the Life.

Joey gave orders to all of us. Junkies or lowlifes weren't allowed in or anywhere near the Pioneer. We knew all of them in the neighborhood. Despite the fact that we even knew their families, junkies were not allowed in or around the club under any circumstances. It didn't matter who they were.

I remember one afternoon when this guy whose name I don't remember came by high on H. He got nasty when Frankie chased him away. Just as Frankie was about to throw him a beat'n, Joey heard the commotion and rushed out to stop Frankie right in his tracks. Joey put his arm around the guy's shoulder and walked him down the block. I followed my brother to make sure this prick didn't do anything stupid.

Though I couldn't hear what Joey was saying, I saw him put his hand in his pocket and give the junkie some money. He hugged Joey and kissed him on both cheeks. He still knew enough to show respect. Joey walked back towards me and Frankie shaking his head, with a sad expression on his face.

As he approached, he said to both us, "This poor fuck was slated to be part of our Life, but look what happens when you get on that shit. He lost not only his own life becoming a junkie; he wound up not being able to be in our Life, something we all strive for."

I said, "Joey, are you serious, I can't fuck'n believe it. That's really a fuck'n shame."

Joey wanted to show his softer side the day Philly's cousin,

Benny, showed up at the Pioneer in a tight spot. Benny'd always been a master carpenter but had trouble making ends meet until somebody asked him to make a secret compartment under a throw rug in the living room. Being an honest guy, Benny hadn't considered this type work before; but he did it quickly. The so-called client loved it, though Benny knew it hadn't been very good because it was in the most obvious spot in the room. Since he knew where people liked to put these things, Benny would try to suggest a less obvious spot first.

If someone asked for one behind a bookcase, Benny was happy to oblige in houses, clubs, wherever. He knew he'd always have business; once a guy had one trap, you could always sell him on a few more—one for the apartment, one for the stash house. Benny was almost as good at sales as he was at carpentry. Everybody on the street called him "Benny the Trap." If you had enough money that you needed to hide, someone in the neighborhood could put you in touch with Benny.

"The fuck is busy all the time. You know how these people are, Joey, they'll spend half their money gettin' Benny to build 'em a place to hide the other half. But, them fuckin' horses are killin' him," Philly had explained when he and Joey met in Armondo's.

"So what else is new?"

"I'm glad you're here, Joey. I was worried I was gonna have to kiss somebody's ass and sign over my firstborn kid, you know?"

When Benny showed up at the club two days later, Joey knew he must be desperate. Frankie was at the door as Swifty approached with the dog; he ignored Benny. At the door, Joey could see what was coming. He walked out and signaled to Benny to stay quiet.

"Hey, Swifty, if that fuckin' dog shits in front of this joint one more time, I'm gonna shove him up your ass!"

Grabbing his crotch, Swifty yelled, "Shove this up your ass, you fuckin' hard-on."

Joey always got a good laugh watching Swifty and his dog. "Every day, the same argument," he told Benny as he invited him in. "Swifty, tie up the dog and come in for coffee. Frankie'll get it for you. Right, Frankie?"

"Fuck him."

"No, fuck you!"

"Okay, fuck the both of you. Come inside, Frankie, I need some coffee."

Frankie stared at Swifty, waiting for him to walk down the block. Swifty stared at Frankie, waiting for him to go inside. Because he felt he had to listen to Joey, Frankie broke first and walked in, muttering, "Always breakin' my balls. Ever since we was kids, all he does is break my balls."

Joey laughed. "You got a brother, Benny?"

"Nah, just my sister, and a few cousins on my dad's side."

"Let me tell you, nobody can bust your balls like a brother. My kid brother's got the edge on me, knows exactly what to say to fuck with me. And, I love him for it."

In the back room, Joey told Benny, "Look, I'm giving you the money for only two points, but I don't wanna hear about you owin' money anywhere else."

"No way, Joey, I swear. I'm gonna use the loan to pay off the bookies, then I'm clean."

"Okay, pal. If anybody gives you a problem, tell them to see me. By the way, Benny, maybe you can pay off some of this in trade. I'll talk to you about it sometime."

Poor Benny. He muddled through life, never amassing enough to bother anybody. Any money he had, he promptly blew. Though he was seriously planning to stay away from the track after the most recent loss, in another bad decision, he'd chosen to ask Joey for help.

In addition to full payment, Joey decided to have Benny install a trap in the house in Bronxville. Always very busy with her work, Carole was never happy at the thought of having to decorate the new house. Unbeknownst to Joey, she'd hired an interior decorator who worked for some of the top names in the fragrance business. The decorator had suggested converting the den into a library. Carole loved the idea because she knew of Joey's love for reading and Shakespeare. Over dinner one evening, she told him about the decorator, who would keep the charm and character of the old house.

Joey was extremely happy that Carole had made such a wise decision.

"Does this decorator know a good carpenter to make sure the library's done right?" Joey asked her.

"Not yet," said Carole. "Do you have someone in mind?"

This was a perfect opportunity for Joey to kill two birds with one stone: to get the library done and create a trap within it. "I have the perfect person for the job," he told Carole with a smile.

Carole was thrilled with the idea that Joey had become involved with her efforts to make the Bronxville house their own. A few days later, when Joey arrived with Benny in tow, she could see this East Harlem character was in awe. He knew class when he saw it. Benny measured the den carefully and painted a vivid picture in his mind of the library, so he could come up with some ideas on the drive back to East Harlem. Incorporated into the book cases and intricate wood work would be the all-important trap.

"I'm gonna design pivot hinges, Joey, and pressure hinges for the wood panels. When you touch a certain area, the panels are gonna open to expose the trap."

Though Joey had no idea what Benny was talking about, he acted equally excited.

Given that Benny had to travel to the house with tools and materials, Joey arranged to get him a van from Marty Lester. It took Benny about two months to complete the work in the den; this time he outdid himself. Joey and Carole couldn't believe their eyes when they saw the finished library. Since it called for a celebration, they took Benny, the decorator, and her boyfriend to dinner at the Town Tavern, a very special Bronxville restaurant.

As usual, when Benny drank too much he became talkative. Since Carole's world was so different than his, she'd had never known Benny in East Harlem. But, as Benny worked on the house and made a fuss about pleasing her, Carole grew to like him. That evening, when they returned to the house after dinner, she expressed concern about Benny's drinking.

Out of earshot, she asked Joey, "Don't you think it's a better idea to have Benny stay here tonight and drive back in the morning?"

Joey agreed; this couldn't have suited him better.

After Carole said good night, Joey invited Benny to have a nightcap. Before long, the Trap was blabbing away. Joey told Benny how much he trusted him, and how he'd let him do whatever he felt was necessary in the work on the library— he knew Benny would never let him down.

It was Joey at his best, and Benny became emotional. As Benny kept talking, he wound up revealing that on two occasions he'd been picked up, blindfolded, and taken to a house to install a trap.

"All I asked ahead of time was whether or not this was a basement and where they wanted the trap: wall or ceiling."

"So you never knew where you were working?" Joey asked him.

"Bullshit, Joey, I knew."

"How?"

"They insulted me, Joey. They had no trust in me."

"Okay, Benny, forget it."

"I'll tell you how I knew. The first house was Babe's. JoJo Black picked me up early one morning. He blindfolded me and made me lay on the backseat. We rode about a half hour, so I knew we weren't in East Harlem. And, we hit a little traffic, too. JoJo took me to the back entrance. When he took off the blindfold, he asked me to pick the best spot for the trap. I installed the trap in the ceiling above the bar in the basement. There was no insulation in the ceiling. I heard JoJo talking to someone, and I recognized the other voice—Babe Marsano's."

"Are you sure, Benny? Wasn't the sound muffled?"

"No, I'm sure. You wanna know the other house? It was Louie Dee's."

"How did you find that out, Benny?"

"Same fuckin way—I heard somebody call the name Ginny,

Louie's wife."

Joey kept nudging Benny without making it obvious that he wanted the information. "Did you hear the same way—while you were working?"

"No. I built the trap in a low wall under the basement staircase. As Sally Fat was walking me back to the car, I heard what must have been one of the neighbors call Ginny. She must have seen Sally and me. It spooked her. Joey, I'm telling you this shit because I trust you."

"I know, Benny. What's said here will die here. Go to sleep."

Everybody liked Benny; he wasn't the sort of person who would ever think of using what he knew against Joey. Of course, if he'd told anybody what had happened, it might have pointed out to Benny that he was now a loose end Joey couldn't afford to leave dangling.

Benny would've insisted that Joey wouldn't think that way: that's the sort of guy Benny was.

CHAPTER EIGHTEEN

Joey pulled another napping sooner than he would've liked because he was feeling pressure from the Millers. They were gambling away the cash faster than he could give it to them. Joey must've known it was a bad idea to do too many so close to each other. It would get people talking and open up too many eyes. The longer between kidnappings, the more relaxed everybody got. Joey knew that key people would be on edge if the nappings became too frequent.

It was a numbers game. Butch the Shadow wasn't talking to anybody, and Little Larry hadn't gotten a good look at their faces. Sooner or later, the Nappers were gonna hit enough people that somebody was gonna be smart and remember something. Or, sooner or later, one of Joey's boys would slip up—if not Danny, then Rusty or Ronnie Miller.

But, one thing that money always breeds is the desire for more money. Even as my brother's means increased, he could barely keep pace with his lifestyle.

Higgins had begun to lose patience with the Millers. For the first few jobs, they'd followed Joey's instructions. But, they got bored easily and if nobody was paying attention, they'd knock out a few of the victim's teeth while they dragged him into the van. They'd give the guy at least some punches and maybe break his nose or at least a finger—just because they could.

And they were getting a lot less civil. When Joey wasn't around, they'd make jokes to each other about what a hardass he was. Higgins never said a word, but they saw the looks he gave them. Higg knew that Rusty and Ronnie had been spending a lot of weekends at the trotters in Yonkers. When they couldn't make it there, they'd look for action anywhere. Just to be a nice guy, Higgins had passed along a tip he'd heard on a horse that was running five to one. The Millers won a bundle and hadn't even given him a little cut, a finder's fee. On one of their moves, Higgins had let Ronnie pick the radio station, but after fifteen minutes of shit-kicker music, he'd shut it off. Now, every time they were in the van, Ronnie would try to get them to put on some cowboy singing about the woman who left him. Pass the whiskey, pass the beer.

The more time Higgins spent with them, the less he liked them. It was getting to the point where he felt like he was going to have to give Joey his notice because he knew better than to work with guys you couldn't trust. The alarms were already going off in his head, but he balanced the well-advised caution against the money. In the short term, the money kept winning. When it was this good, the boys found it easy to make "just one more job" the status quo.

Next, Higgins and the rednecks staked out Vito Romano's apartment building in the Bronx, a job that was already more complicated than they'd expected. An ex-boxer with the crooked nose and eyebrow scars to prove it, Vito was a big earner in the narco trade who paid major tribute to Armondo every month. His substantial black clientele extended not only to Philly and South Jersey, but also Washington D.C.

Joey thought they'd be able to grab Vito at a diner he frequented for breakfast around noon, but when Higgins pulled up, there'd been too many eyeballs outside. Higg had waited for ten minutes until he saw the same two men walk by the van a second time. Then he'd honked the horn three times, a signal Joey had concocted. After the Millers heard the horn, they'd figured that there were too many people around to pull off the move. They'd disappeared into the shadows, making their way to the rendezvous point a few blocks away.

A few nights later, Higgins was in a different van but still anxious to get it done. He'd found an inconspicuous parking spot for scouting out Vito's apartment, figuring that the dealer wouldn't have a crowd with him while bringing his girlfriend home after a night out on the town.

As Vito pulled up outside an apartment complex in the Hunt's Point section, a gorgeous blonde got out of the passenger side. After she ran up the steps, he drove around to a gated parking lot and pulled in to park the brand new Olds he'd purchased from Marty Lester just the month before. He wasn't even used to the automatic transmission yet. Back at the gate, he fumbled the key and dropped it on the ground. When he bent down to pick it up, he was flanked by the Miller brothers.

Rusty stared at him. "That's a nice car you're driving, Vito. The white powder business must be pretty good."

Vito wasn't used to people talking to him this way. "Who the fuck are you? Whaddaya, wandering the streets at night giving people shit?"

Ronnie pulled a gun. "Get in the van, you little New York guinea bastard." He gestured to the street, where Higgins had pulled up the van as silently as could be managed. It was earlier than usual, but they'd been lucky. There was no other foot traffic on the street, even though they were only a few blocks from the all-night wholesale markets.

When they got to the back of the van, Ronnie grabbed the handle but couldn't get the door open. He started banging on it: "Hey, nigger, it's locked!"

Rusty took the gun and aimed it at Vito, "Hey, shitbird, put your hands behind you and hold 'em there."

Inside, Higgins cursed and pulled on his ski mask as he turned off the car off and jumped out. Angrily, he whispered to Ronnie, "What the fuck is wrong with you? Making a racket at this time'a night?"

"It's nothing. Just open the fuckin' van."

Once Higgins opened the door and Rusty put the handcuffs on, Ronnie tied Vito's blindfold far tighter than it needed to be. As Vito climbed slowly into the back, Rusty and Ronnie looked at each other and smiled.

"What's funny?" Higgins asked.

Ronnie signaled as if to say "Watch this," as Rusty slammed the gun down on the back of Vito's neck, knocking him to the floor. Both of the Millers laughed, especially when Vito started rolling around.

Higgins just stared at them both. "Is that shit really necessary? Come on, motherfuckers, let's get going."

The Millers rolled their eyes. In the van, they started whispering back and forth, telling nigger jokes. Higgins knew what they were doing. Mentally, he began to calculate exactly how many more days he'd be able to stand the company of the Miller brothers before he wound up killing at least one of them on general principle.

Just as Higgins pulled away, Vito's blonde bombshell girlfriend came down to see what was taking him so long. When she found the parking lot gate unlocked, her first concern was for the car; but, once she saw that it was safe, she started to wonder what had happened to Vito. She'd almost gotten around to alerting the police before the call came in.

CHAPTER NINETEEN

I remember the day JFK got whacked. I was busy cooking in my deli when Joey walked into the kitchen and told me, "Hey, Vin, they clipped the Irishman."

We had no television, and the radio wasn't on. None of us knew, not even the customers. I said, "Joey, what Irishman? What are you talking about?"

After he turned on the radio, everything stopped. There was total silence. Joey called to Nadine, who was helping out behind the counter. He gave her two hundred-dollar bills and said, "Lunch is on me today. If you need more, let me know."

Then, he said, "It should never have been the son. It should have been that zig-zagging shanty Irish father of his. That son of a bitch fucked everyone he ever looked at."

Joey couldn't vote and wouldn't have voted even if he could. Joey said all politicians were either prostitutes or pimps. He told me one day, you ask a politician what his favorite color is, he'd tell you plaid. Joey admired Martin Luther King. He respected his integrity but also said, "He's a man with all good intentions, and he's gonna wind up dead, same as the Irishman."

At the time, I didn't want to agree with my brother. But, what can I say now? Joey knew the ways of the street, but also how those very ways translated to a different level of power. It was all the same: the ones that had it would do all they could to keep it. Armondo did what he had to do, and if it hurt people, so be it… it was all part of the Life, a life that wasn't exclusive to the East Harlem where we grew up.

Before Joey left Big V's, he raved about Carole and how well her career was going. But, little did he know how it would affect their relationship and their lives in the not too distant future.

The first thing Carole told her assistant Laura when she hired her was, "Tell me if I'm being a bitch." Carole was still trying to figure out how to be an effective woman executive at a time when role models were few and far between.

Everybody else in her division at Creative Fragrances, even some of the people Carole supervised, were men. Their natural inclination was to think that any female boss was a bitch. Because they felt this way, Carole often found that she had to *be* a bitch just to get them to do their job.

Carole discussed this all the time with Nadine, who tried to advise her as best she could, given her lack of personal knowledge about office life. But, as Nadine told Carole more than once, men are men, no matter what their circumstances. A woman like Carole was smart enough to beat them at their own game.

Carole Reedy decided that if she was going to have to act like a bitch all the time, she needed an assistant who was willing to call her on it. Otherwise, she was going to turn into a *real* bitch. Whatever her methods, there was no disputing that she got results: the company had quadrupled its sales in the three years since Carole had arrived and gone to work in the laboratory developing new scents that became huge successes.

As Stephen Aronson had suspected when he took a shot on this Irish girl from East Harlem, Carole Reedy knew intuitively that the art of making and selling perfume was a form of consumer magic. She got into the field just as it was dawning on the people in executive suites that the average woman wanted to become a weaver of spells, too, when she dabbed on a special scent. Carole foresaw all of this and made her way up the corporate ladder in the process.

Carole's executive assistant, Laura Silvers, was a petite brunette who'd grown up in Forest Hills, Queens. Ten years older than Carole, she'd worked in offices in the Garment District in a sportswear company and for an accountant. She was stylish in a more conservative way than Carole, who favored well-cut clothes with a European edge. Laura understood the sexual dynamics in offices and helped Carole navigate the politics. She got coffee for the men at meetings before they had time to ask Carole to do it. Laura was quickly becoming indispensable.

Given their unusually close relationship, Carole took Laura to a fancy restaurant for lunch at least twice a month, often weekly. Some of the male colleagues had given Carole a hard time at the beginning; but, as time went on and they saw what she could do, they gained respect for her. The clients had been so happy lately that Stephen Aronson had offered Carole a job in Paris at Lennox, the highly successful European division of Creative Fragrances. Aronson saw a market in Europe for the kind of clean, healthy American scent that was associated all over the world with an independent woman.

When Carole heard the news, she promptly went downstairs and told Laura to cancel her lunch plans and get them a table at the French place on the West Side they'd visited a few months back.

"Boy, Carole, isn't it great?"

"What's great? Oh, wait, you got lucky last night, right?"

"Oh, stop! I mean you and me. Ten years ago, it would've been lunch in Bickford's. You remember as well as I do. Thanks for letting me tag along. You're a great boss."

"Don't get all maple syrupy on me, and don't address me as your boss. You do your job, and you do it well. And, you sure can handle your martinis. I always thought Jews weren't big drinkers."

Laura just laughed her throaty smoker's chuckle. "As long as we're talking business—are you going to France? I heard a rumor at the water cooler. Are you going to accept the position? I still can't believe it was offered to a woman."

Carole frowned and took a drink to avoid answering. "God, how does everybody in the office hear these things? I only just heard about it an hour ago. Does everybody know about it before I have a chance to say yes or no?"

Laura shrugged. "That's how it is in an office, Carole. Everybody spends so much time together, they hear things."

Carole leaned closer. "I'll tell you, Laura, I want the promotion. I've never even been to Paris, but I love the idea of it. Still, I love my Joey… I still have some time. I'll know by the time we finish up the Lennox project."

Laura kept her mouth shut about her boss' devastatingly handsome, but rough-spoken, true love. She was street-smart enough to size up Joey the one time she'd met him when he came to pick up Carole at the office to take her out to dinner.

Laura never volunteered anything about her own love life, mainly because she considered it all in the past—something that was over and done with before she'd ever met Carole. In high school, Laura had been the queen of the prom, and it wasn't because she was the most popular or beautiful girl. She was dating the president of the class, Jake Vance, who was so charismatic that it rubbed off on her. After they'd been going out for two years, Laura expected that they'd be married.

They'd gone to college together, but when she mentioned the idea of getting an apartment, Jake wouldn't commit. When she pushed, he said that his WASPy grandmother wouldn't approve of her because she was Jewish. Laura had immediately backed off; you can't fight family.

Though she stuck with Jake for years, even moving with him to Albany when he won a seat in the State Assembly, Laura was miserable. Albany was a backwater as far as she was concerned. Bored, Laura had enrolled in community college, taking art history and accounting: an ideal mix of her interests, and her need to have a way to support herself if it came to that.

For a while, she still felt that she could still make Jake happy. But, when he told her he had to stop seeing her for a while when the governor's race started up, Laura began to wonder if her sacrifices would ever pay off. Most of Jake's staff knew of their affair, making Laura feel like a kept woman. The night he won the election, at the celebration party, he'd pulled her aside and confided, "I have to level with you, Laura—I don't have the luxury of making my own decisions now. You understand, don't you?"

She'd never seen him again. Laura felt like she'd wasted her twenties pursuing a relationship at the expense of her own life. She didn't want to look back from fifty with the same regrets. She wanted to enjoy herself. After moving back to New York, she bounced around a few offices until settling in at Aronson's, a comfortable place to be a secretary with no deeper ambition. The men in the office never went too far. Over the years, she'd had a few short-term affairs outside of the office, but only once had she gone home with someone after a Christmas party. And, that was after she knew he'd been fired.

Joey knew how much Carole cared for her assistant, who was a real friend as well as a colleague. But, his charm always reminded Laura of Jake, though she knew Joey had more honor in one bone than Jake had in his whole body. Still, Laura couldn't help but compare Joey to Jake and judge him by the only standard she had for men.

At lunch at a northern Italian place in midtown, she told Carole, "You know, I'm as New York as anyone. Joey is street, and he'll always be. For some women, that might be okay, but not for you—and Joey knows it, too. Your love for him is not enough. You need more, more than you'll ever find with him."

Carole wasn't used to Laura being this confrontational on a personal subject, but she'd never lost anything by being open with her. "I've loved him all my life."

With more than one glass of fine red wine under her belt, Laura pushed the point more than she ordinarily might have: "That's right! He's the same man you loved when you were growing up—exactly the same man. Are you the same woman? Please, I'm older than you, I know. Don't let this chance to go to Paris pass you by. It may never ever come again."

"You sure you're not saying all this just because you like Frenchmen?" Carole teased her as she looked over her shoulder: "Oh, waiter? Two more glasses of wine, please."

Laura took the cue and changed the subject to which of the chemists was going to blow up the lab first if Carole didn't make it back from lunch.

A few weeks earlier, Stephen Aronson had taken his rising

corporate star to dinner at a four star restaurant that wouldn't have been out of place in Paris itself—a not so subtle hint of what he had in mind. He and Carole had grown friendly in the years they'd worked together. A Bronx native himself, Stephen Aronson appreciated self-made people.

When Carole joked that the waiters were flirting with him, he retorted that she only fell for film noir characters. After laying the groundwork with Bombay martinis followed by bottles of French wine, Aronson started laying on the charm.

"Carole, my lovely, before we get to the serious talk, I have to ask you something."

"Ask away, my favorite boss."

"Carole, please, I've told you never to call me your boss. It insults me."

"You're full of it. Okay, ask away, Stephen my drinking companion."

"I've often wondered, why do you spell your name with the extra 'E?' Most people spell it C-A-R-O-L, like a Christmas carol. It may seem trivial to some, but not to me. It's like your personality, extended."

Carole laughed. "Oh, you are good. You're very good. Well, my mother was an avid fan of Carole Lombard, the actress. You may remember she spelled her name with the extra 'E,' so my mother extended the 'E' to me."

"That's perfect. Mrs. Gable would be very proud. And, of course, Miss Lombard loved Paris. You're a pacesetter, Carole, like she was. You'll make us proud in the City of Lights."

CHAPTER TWENTY

Between the plea deal set up by Jack Friedman and a little bit of time off for good behavior, I spent a little over a year in Allenwood, right down from Williamsport, Pennsylvania, where they have the Little League World Series. At least I knew both Joey and Rosemary would be waiting for me when I got out.

Once I was back in East Harlem, Joey never mentioned the Nappers at all. Anybody in a position to know anything about it wasn't gonna say much to anyone including me, right? But, some stories get around. People hear things, they get curious, and they talk. Most of it is made up. Lots of dirty laundry was tossed Joey's way after he was gone. Unfortunately, I wasn't able to clean up any of it.

There was definitely a point when Joey went too far; it was like he couldn't help himself. Maybe he started to feel invincible. Each time he had to take a bigger risk just to make it worth doing.

The money must've been great. I mean, if you had all the money you could spend, how much would you pay to get your son back from the Miller brothers?

Louie DeSalvo Jr. was at the junior high school playground where a crowd of people had gathered to watch the football game. He wasn't playing. Though he threw the ball around once in a while, he was too careful with his clothes to get them dirty tackling other kids in the muddy schoolyard. Usually, he just cheered his friends on from the sidelines. Today, his heart wasn't in it because Mary Reilly had come to watch. She went to the Catholic school across town, the one his cousin went to. Louie had met her a few times. He was pretty sure she even remembered his name.

When he turned around, there she was. She didn't seem to

be with anybody specific, though a few of the boys in the game were watching her more closely than they watched the ball.

First, Louie started to drift closer to her; then he panicked. What if she *didn't* remember his name? If he had to remind her, it might seem like a desperate move. He tried to remember what his cousin had told him about Catholic school. Just as he turned in Mary's direction, he saw her wince. Louie's best friend, Billy, had just been slammed between two other boys and knocked to the ground in a daze.

Louie watched Billy being carried off the field. By the time he turned around again, Mary Reilly was looking at him.

"Hi, Lou."

"Hey, Mary, how are you?"

"Fine. How come you're not playing?"

"By the time I got home to change, they'd be all done."

"That's a nice sweater."

"Oh, thanks. Uh, I, that's a pretty skirt."

"I hate it, but they make us wear these."

"Well, it doesn't matter, you look great in it."

She smiled at him!

After the game, walking home and reliving the moment over and over in his head, Louie was too distracted to notice two guys dressed like police detectives following him nonchalantly. Higgins had dropped off the Millers about twenty minutes earlier. But, Danny was the one driving the getaway van. When Rusty asked why Higgins couldn't do it, Higg had just rolled his eyes.

"Think about it, moron, a big black ex-con driving a van around a junior high picking up kids? Somebody's gonna notice."

When the Miller brothers got out of the van, fresh air blew in. Higgins let out a sigh he'd been holding in for the last fifteen minutes. "By the way," he called after them, "It'll be fine for now, but y'all gonna wear those suits on another job, you really oughta send 'em to the dry cleaner first."

He rolled down the windows and drove off.

Ronnie looked at his brother. "You believe that black motherfucker?"

Rusty took out the notepad Joey had given him, the kind he'd seen police detectives use. Joey knew that two guys standing around would look suspicious; people might stop and ask them questions. But, two guys that looked like cops, pointing at houses and looking at their notes—nobody was gonna say a thing to them. Nobody would even look them in the eye. Even honest people feel guilty when they see two guys in plainclothes who look like they might come knocking.

Rusty saw Louie first and grabbed Ronnie's shoulder. "That's him, right?"

"Yeah, I'm pretty sure. Shit. Where's Danny?"

Danny hadn't thought he'd need a map. He'd also thought a few drinks would calm him down and make the job go smoother. Neither of these thoughts proved to be correct. Even though Danny had the directions written down, all the streets looked the same. He wanted Forest, but the streets he was driving past had state's names: New York, Pennsylvania, Delaware, the whole damn East Coast.

He looked at his watch. He was already running a bit late; he didn't know how long he'd need because he didn't even know where he was. He looked down at the directions again as he passed a crossroads. Then, he saw the street sign just as it was too late to stop: F-O-R-E-S-T.

He slowed down to get ready to make the turn, but he was going 40 mph. Halfway down the block, a car pulling out of the driveway forced Danny to slam on the brakes. He let the guy pull out and took a swig from his flask to calm his nerves.

The other driver leaned out his window and yelled, "What the fuck is wrong with you? This is a one way street!"

Louie was about halfway between the school and his house when he realized he was being followed. He wasn't worried because he knew he hadn't done anything wrong. When the Miller brothers saw him looking over his shoulder, they knew they were running out of time. They crossed the street and followed directly behind him, removing any subtlety from the pursuit.

Louie turned again. When he saw how close they were, he

began to speed up a little. Ronnie called out, "Hey, DeSalvo, wait a second."

This only made Louie go faster.

"Louis? Hold on, we're police officers. Stop where you are."

The fact that they knew his name threw him off. He turned around.

As Rusty got close, he lifted his hand as if to smack Louie: "What are you running from, stupid kid?"

Ronnie grabbed his brother's hand. "Hey, there's no need for that. It's all gonna be okay." He leaned in to be face-to-face with the boy. "Believe me, kid—it's gonna be all right."

Louie just stared up at him. His father had always taught him not to talk to the police, and nothing about the Miller brothers suggested that they'd warrant an exception to the rule.

Just as Ronnie worried that he'd have to stare the kid down, the gray van Danny was driving finally appeared, racing down the block. "Ah, thank fuckin' Christ."

Ronnie turned to Louie and said in a soft voice, "Listen, kid, you're gonna get in the back of that van with us, and you're gonna do everything we say, or I'm gonna kill your mother."

Though Louie wanted to cooperate, by now he was too petrified to move. Ronnie and Rusty dragged him into the van and pulled the door closed behind them.

Immediately, Ronnie moved to the front seat as they sped off. "What the fuck happened? Where were you?" he asked Danny.

"I went down the wrong street. I'm sorry! Don't mention this to Joey, okay?" Danny whispered, remembering Joey's warning not to let the kid hear their voices.

Ronnie nodded and grabbed a flask from the seat. He took a big swig. Danny caught a whiff of something fowl and asked, "Did the kid shit his pants or something?"

In the backseat, Louie looked up at Rusty. "You didn't have to pull on my sweater, mister. You stretched it all out."

CHAPTER TWENTY-ONE

The only thing I can say in defense of my brother is that I know no matter what happened he never would've let them harm one hair on that kid's head. Higgins was a stand-up guy, too. Joey wouldn't have done anything without being sure the kid was safe. I know that because I know Joey. But, don't get me wrong—I'm not saying that makes it right.

Even so, when the story came out, it took me a long time to accept it. I thought it was bullshit. I thought they had made it up to justify what happened to Joey, the same way they spread stories about Gino the Zip. It was years later that I was able to confirm the story. I talked to one of Louie Dee's drivers, and it turned out that he was the guy who drove Louie Dee's kid to therapy every day for years. He had nightmares about that kidnapping even as an adult. I don't know if he ever got over it.

This time, the plan was a little more involved. Joey organized it so that the Millers had as little contact with the kid as possible. Higgins and Danny were going to stay with Louie Jr. at the stash house. The Miller brothers would keep on their detective outfits and pay a personal visit to Louie Dee, a former dock worker good with his hands who was now one of the biggest dealers around. Though his club was in the Bronx, he kept his East Harlem roots. Louie Dee was a little more flamboyant than Armondo would have liked.

The plan was to drive Louie Sr. to a payphone and dial the house, where Higgins would hold the phone up to Junior's head.

Joey took no chances with the Miller brothers and gave one final lecture before they left the house, "Make sure you make the call from the payphone on Boston Post Road. I checked it out. The phone in Louie Dee's house might be bugged. Don't take any chances, and don't get lazy. I'll be ridin' shotgun."

Ronnie and Rusty looked at each other, sharing a private joke about how much Joey over-planned these moves, "Hey, Ronnie, let me stay at the house with the wife."

When Joey reached a certain level of anger, he became incredibly calm. He looked both Miller brothers in the eye. "Are you fuckin' nuts? You don't even know this woman! And we never, ever touch women! You hear me, you redneck cocksuckers?"

Rusty started to laugh first, and Ronnie cracked almost immediately afterwards. "Lighten up, Joey—we're just playing with your head."

Back at the house, Danny and Higgins were babysitting the kid. "You wanna play some cards or something while we wait, Higg?"

"We gotta just wait for the call. Once that's taken care of, sure, I'll kick your ass at gin rummy, dollar-a-point."

By the time the Millers reached Louie Sr.'s house, he had already started to worry about his son. When he saw two detectives at the door, he expected the worst. When Rusty and Ronnie had told him to come with them, he'd gone numb. Louie Dee hadn't told his wife what was going on because he knew the appearance of the police must mean their son was dead.

He just leaned his head back into the house and said, "Ginny, I'll be back in a little while." He'd figure out how to tell her later, after he'd had a chance to compose himself.

After they got to the designated payphone, Louie got out of the car, confused. As they held the phone to Louie's ear, a voice at the other end said, "Pa, give 'em what they want! This guy says he'll put a nail inta my skull if you don't!"

Initially, Louie Dee was relieved that his son was still alive. But, as he realized what was happening, he got very, very angry. He managed to hold it back as he tried to soothe his son: "Stay calm, Louis, stay calm. I'll take care of it. You just do what they want, and everybody's going to be just fine. I'll straighten this all out, buddy, don't worry. Just leave it to me."

As they drove, Rusty explained their demands. Louie didn't seem to be paying much attention to what they were saying; all he could think about was his son. Rusty was so pissed that Louie wasn't listening, he screamed, "You angry 'cause we got your kid or 'cause we're gonna get your fuck'in money, you guinea prick?"

Louie just stared out the window. "You never should've brought him into it. He's just a kid."

"You hypocritical cocksucker! You ever think about all the kids whose lives you ruined with the junk you push? You want your kid, you get us the money."

Louie turned and stared at him, his eyes fixating on Rusty's fake mustache. "All right, take me home." Several blocks later, he spoke up again,. "You'd really hurt a kid, wouldn't you, you lowlife fucks?"

Ronnie waved the gun at him. "Faster than I'll blow your wife's head off if you keep runnin' your fuckin' guinea mouth. Relax, relax. Be nice or that fuckin' nail's gonna go deep."

Louie scowled. "How do I know you won't hurt him anyway?"

"One thing you know for sure is that we'll kill him if you don't give it up. Then, we'll also have to kill you and the missus. The house'll be a fuckin' mess. We could always torture you till you tell us where the money is, but, all things considered, this way seems easier, don't you think?"

Louie didn't say anything, but it was clear that he agreed.

Back at the house, Higg tried to calm the kid down after Louie Jr. got off the phone. He gave Louie a soda and told him he'd done a good job. Danny had gone to call Carole to let her know he wouldn't be around for the weekend.

Ten minutes after they got to Louie's, Joey saw the Miller brothers come out of the house with a shopping bag full of cash. He'd stayed behind to make sure no cars had followed them. Within the next half hour, three cars pulled up and parked on the street, but Joey had never expected to drop the kid at the house. Louie got a call at midnight that his son was on the steps of his school. Louie Jr. was so scared that even though he wasn't tied up, he hadn't taken off the blindfold.

Two days later, Louie did something Joey hadn't expected. Joey knew Louie would never go to the police, but he thought he would be too ashamed to involve anybody else—too afraid of looking weak if word get out. Instead, an enraged Louie called a meeting of several of his friends at the Continental, Louie's club on Westchester Avenue near Pelham Bay. In the 1950s and 60s it was a working class area, Irish, Italian, and German. Louie and his cousin and partner, Sally Fat, a massive man with the arms of a weight lifter, used the club not only for drug deals, but also for gambling.

Nobody wanted to speak first. Finally, Vito Romero asked, "You're sure this place ain't bugged?"

Sally nodded. "Positive. I had the joint swept yesterday. The place never closes, how the fuck are they gonna get in to bug us?"

Dominick Nappi was the first to speak on the subject, shouting, "What the fuck is wrong with your kid, Louie? Didn't you school him? How the fuck could he get in a van with strangers?"

Dom was a major dealer and gambler in East Harlem whose crew included Babe Marsano. He made sure all the dealings never involved Armondo, who reaped a good part of the profits.

"Dom, for Christ's sake, he thought they were cops. They showed gold badges. What's he know, he's a kid."

Sally Fat leaned back in his chair, smoking a cigar. He'd been hearing about the Nappers here and there, but he'd never heard of one involving a kid and his family. But, he was also sure there were more he hadn't heard about. He wondered whether it was the same guys or copycats pulling it off.

There seemed to be two logical options:. Either these guys were really stupid, so stupid that they thought kidnapping Louie Dee's kid would be an easy snatch; or they were really smart, so smart they knew their plan would work out perfectly, in which case they'd also be smart enough to cover their tracks. If it was the first one—or if it was just the two idiot rednecks that hit Louie up for cash—the crowd then sitting in the Continental would track them down soon enough. If it was the second, it meant this was the same crew that had taken Little Larry a few months back.

Sally figured that they should concentrate on the second problem because the other one would solve itself. He knew that time was on their side—that the Nappers would hit again. But, how did they always know the right people to take out? Why did their targets all come from the same neighborhood, all paying tribute to the same guy, Armondo?

Sally finally took the cigar out of his mouth, breathed out the smoke he'd built up, and said, "I figure this's gotta be comin' from somebody we do business with."

Louie Dee slammed his fist down on the table. "I only want one promise from whoever finds these motherfucker—I wanna do the work! Not because all rules were broken, but because of what they did to my son."

CHAPTER TWENTY-TWO

Right after Joey got out of prison, Carole and Danny's father, Mike, passed away. My brother helped Carole get through it, as he had when Katie passed. When people like Carole's assistant warned her boss about Joey, Carole felt like saying, "And which one of the banking stiffs who tried to pick me up at that bar last week could know my family? And which one would be comfortable coming with me to check out things at the pub?"

Now, Danny was in charge at Reedy's. Technically, Carole had a half-interest in the bar's ownership, but she was low-key about it. She made a good salary, and she knew that the income from the pub was all Danny had. So, she turned a blind eye to the fact that he was taking all the money.

Spike the bartender was basically running the place. Having Danny in charge with no Mike around to keep an eye out was like letting a rooster loose in the henhouse. Danny made a few decisions and showed up every day; mainly he was drinking his way through their stock. If Danny was suddenly feeling generous, most of the night's profits might disappear into free drinks for his "friends." He wanted people to like him—a little desperately. Once his father was gone, Danny just wanted the pub to feel like it had when Mike was still alive.

Mike Reedy and Joey made their peace right before Mike died. Joey told Mike that he'd make sure that Danny and Carole were okay, but he also gave Mike his word that he'd never marry Carole. Joey meant it; he'd never tie her down to all the neighborhood baggage like that, no matter how much he loved and needed her.

At that point, I was still hiding out upstate. Later on, I got the lowdown on Carole and Joey from Nadine: I would have been in the dark without her.

Danny had been serious about Bridget O'Malley for a few months now. Also the child of a saloon keeper, Bridget held her liquor as well as any man. She and Danny often saw each other across the bar at last call at 4 a.m. at Reedy's. From this convenience, a romance gradually developed. After Danny's father died, Danny had to think more seriously about his future, which included Bridget. Danny was rarely entirely sober, but the dinners he paid for were nice. And Danny had a wounded puppy thing that made her want to play nursemaid, a hangover from her own family life, in which her mother had always acted as caretaker for her seldom sober father. In the O'Malley clan, drinking was a way of life that spanned generations.

When Carole finally decided that it was time to get to know Bridget, she arranged a double date at Reedy's. Since she had to come from her office in midtown, by the time she made it over to Eleventh Avenue, Danny and Bridget had already gotten a booth with Joey.

As Carole walked in, she said hello to Timmy Green, who was sitting at the bar talking to a construction worker whose name Carole could never quite remember: Alan or Albert or Alec? It was something like that.

Danny spotted her first. "There she is. Spike, we're ready for food now."

The brisket and corned beef and cabbage at Reedy's had been known all over Hell's Kitchen until Mike died, and Danny turned his attention almost exclusively to the bar.

"So, this is where my brother takes his dates to impress them? I have to tell you, Danny, the food in this place isn't what it used to be," Carole said.

"You hear her, Joey? Every time she comes in, she raps the food. Always complains. My own, and she complains."

"My own? My own, my ass! The food stinks. If it weren't for the local drunks and local morons who don't know any better, you'd have to burn this dump." She stared at Danny for a beat, and they both started to laugh.

She turned to Bridget and said, “Hi, I’m Carole, you must be Bridget.”

Carole and Bridget got along immediately. Bridget loved the way Carole busted Danny’s balls, and Carole could tell that Bridget really cared for her brother. Joey seemed to like her, too. At some point in the conversation, Bridget mentioned doing some acting in college, and quoted a few passages from *Macbeth.* She and Joey wound up doing two full acts before they realized how bored their dates were. If it had been any other guy, Carole would’ve thought there was something flirtatious about all the play-acting. She knew Joey better than that.

Bridget had to call it an early night and took a cab home. Danny stayed behind, pouring himself a large glass of whiskey and sitting back down with Joey and Carole.

“I like her, Danny.” Looking at his drink, Joey added, “Why aren’t you taking her home now?”

“I would, but she’s a teacher. She’s gotta get up early. I wanted to stick around and talk things out with you guys.”

“Talk about what? We’re getting out of here soon, too. How late are you gonna stay?”

Danny didn’t say anything but took a big swig of his drink. Then, Carole started in on him, too. “I was serious before, Danny. Since Pop’s gone, this place has gone straight to hell. What the hell’s gone wrong with you? Lord’s sake, you’re drunk by noon every day.”

Danny started to stand, muttering, “I don’t have to listen to this shit from my kid sister.” One look from Joey put him back in his seat.

Staring right at him, Joey said, “She may be your kid sister, but you sure as shit better listen to her because she’s right.”

This only focused Carole’s attention on Joey. She’d had some wine with dinner, and her emotions were flowing freely. “Don’t think I don’t know you’ve been bailing him out…”

Joey frowned. “Now you’re out of line. That’s between me and your brother.”

Carole adapted a tough-guy accent, "Oh, now I'm out of line, big shot! Tough guy Joey Rendino, Mister East Harlem, Mister Cast Iron Balls—no, no, you can't get out of line with Rendino."

In spite of himself, Joey smiled, hearing this rough-edged stuff from Carole's beautiful mouth.

She barely noticed. "What a crock. You like animals so much, Joey, I finally figured out what your cologne is gonna smell like… lion shit." On the last word, she finally made eye contact with him.

For a moment, Joey tried to hold back but couldn't. He turned to Danny and said, "You know your sister is nuts, right?"

When Joey stood up to embrace Carole, she looked up at him and laughed so hard that she started to cry. "Oh, shut up. Why do I have to love two nitwits?"

When Joey took her back to Central Park West, Carole invited him upstairs. "There's something… important. We need to talk."

"What's goin' on? You can tell me."

"I'm gonna have a drink. Can I get you something—maybe your usual club soda and lemon, Mister Excitement?"

"Let's go crazy. Give me a piece of lime instead."

Carole made the drinks with her back to Joey. "I'm not… it's about work."

"Is somebody bothering you?"

"No, no. I want to know… Joey, what are we doing?"

"Us?"

"Everybody's telling me I have to think about the future. My boss wants me to go to Paris."

Joey was shocked. But, by the time she'd crossed the long living room to hand him his drink, he was smiling. "That's great. You should. You're young, you're beautiful, you're smart and self-sufficient. Do what you gotta do."

Instead of being thrilled about Joey's support, Carole stared at him before bursting into tears. "I love you, you love me… but what are we gonna do about it?"

"Carole, I've chosen the life I live. It's deceived me in many ways, but I still love it. I am what I am; nobody can change that. No matter how strong our love, we can never be enough for each other. How many nights in the can did I try not to think of you? It was one thing I could never control."

Carole buried her face into a pillow, sobbing deeper as he continued.

"Every time I closed my eyes, I saw your face, and I couldn't help myself—I wet my cot. Can't you see how selfish I am where you're concerned? I can't walk away from you. You have to be the one to leave. You made it, Carole—you got out. Keep going, okay? Don't hold back on account'a me… Please—walk away. If it were me, I would."

"You never would, I know you. You never would, Joey."

"I would, that is, if I had somewhere to go. I don't, Carole, and I never will."

CHAPTER TWENTY-THREE

Even though Joey didn't need the money he was earning from the new crap game set up by Al Hicks, he went along with it, just to keep up a good front. Most people in our world are not really good earners. They need the crap games, the monte games, even the hole in the wall poker joints, to generate some income. But, they had to get the word around as to where the crap games and the monte games were being moved. Otherwise, "the regulars" would be left out in the cold.

My brother's earnings in the crap games were dwarfed by his other source of cash. That was his biggest problem: Joey always needed more money. Somehow he could never get enough.

Knowing all the things my brother did, as I've learned over the years, I think Joey could've gotten away from the Nappers even after the Miller brothers fucked up, big time. If he'd taken them out, I think he could've stepped back, taken cover, and gotten through all right.

Maybe Joey thought the Nappers crew could just lay low for a little while. Then, after things blew over, he could run the same game again in a few months, maybe even six, for caution's sake. Maybe I'm wrong. Sooner or later, the Miller brothers were going to fuck up, and they weren't just going to fuck up once. In the short term, they'd be okay, but life is long. Over time, they were bound to slip. Any plan dependent on them was going to fall apart sooner or later. Joey was vain enough to think he could control them, and by the time he realized he was wrong, it was too late to change anything.

Joey and Al Hicks stopped by Dominick's club to let him know where the craps game would be that week. Joey didn't think about why Dominick was meeting with Babe Marsano, Sally Fat, and Louie Dee all at the same time in the middle of the afternoon. He should've been more suspicious; instead, he saw it as an opportunity. Knowing where the game was, he decided to work out a quick plan.

Usually, Joey would've gone over the plan thoroughly with everybody. By now, the Nappers crew felt like they knew what they were doing. For once, Joey didn't go into all that much detail about who they were going after. Later, looking back, he wasn't sure it would've mattered—if the Miller brothers would've been paying enough attention to catch it. But, he still felt sloppy about the mistake.

Still, he did tell the Millers that Babe Marsano was one tough and ballsy guy who was respected by everyone in East Harlem, where he cruised the streets in his favorite cashmere sweaters and suede jackets, no matter what the season. Joey respected Babe as one of the toughest people he knew.

Babe always stayed out late losing money with the rest of them. Higgins and Rusty staked out his car outside Nappi's club, expecting a long night, and were surprised when he got dropped off shortly after 1:30 a.m. Dominick and Sally were going to another game, but Babe had decided to surprise his wife and come home before sunrise. The truth was, Higgins and the rednecks would've waited all night, but they just got lucky.

Rusty wore his detective's outfit, which he'd finally washed. Ronnie didn't wear his, since it was still at the Laundromat. It was so wrinkled and dirty that it had required extra attention.

Rusty flashed his wallet at Babe. "Come on, Marsano, we gotta talk."

"Talk to your boss, dick, Chief McCleary's a friend'a mine."

Higgins came out of the shadows behind Babe with a gun pointed at his head. "Let's just get in the van, okay?"

Since Rusty and Higgins were wearing disguises, the problem didn't come up until the van got to the house in Yonkers. Ronnie hadn't bothered with a mask, and when Babe got out of the van, they stared at each other for almost a minute. Higgins led Babe into a room where he tied him to a chair while Rusty held the gun.

Once Babe was tied up, Ronnie pulled Rusty aside in the doorway. "Shit, shit, shit."

"What the hell is wrong?"

"We were canned up with this guy in Atlanta."

"Are you sure? I don't fuckin' remember him."

"I fuckin' do. The fuck stayed bunched up with all the guineas before they moved him to Lewisburg. Fuck, I'm pretty sure he recognized me."

"Shit, this isn't too good. I hope Joey calls soon."

Higgins came out, locking the door from the outside. "What's goin' on?"

"I think we got ourselves a major problem. We were in Atlanta with this guy. I'm takin' the wig off and walkin' in with Ronnie. Let's get his reaction."

Higgins wasn't sure that was a good idea, but Rusty pushed past him and opened the door. Babe stared up at Rusty, his eyes consumed with hatred. "You lowlife rebel motherfuckers, you can suck my guinea prick. And you, too, you black cocksucker."

Rusty leaned forward and put out his cigarette on Babe's arm. "The only thing gonna save you is money, tough guy. You give us money, we go, and you live."

The rest of the night, as Higgins watched the door, the rednecks got drunk, cursing their bad luck.

Joey already knew what was going on by the time he got there the next morning. Before he even had his car in park, he started yelling at Rusty. "You fucked up! You got careless. You never blindfolded him… Is he blindfolded now, at least?"

Though Rusty hated being treated like this, he had to admit that he and his brother had fucked up big time. "Yeah, and we had to gag him, too. This ain't lookin' good, Joey. He says he's not gonna give up nothin', 'cause even if he does, we'll kill him anyway. This is one crazy fuck."

"I told ya, didn't I? Don't worry, we'll get the money. We just gotta change the plan a bit. Improvise." Joey had worked out the details during the car ride over. It was rough, and he would've liked to talk to Higgins, but there was no time, so he laid it all out.

Joey had Rusty call Dominick's club from a payphone. "Listen, don't talk. We got Babe Marsano. I know you heard about Louie Dee, and now we got Babe. Louie did as he was told and nobody got hurt. It would be smart if you did the same, for Babe's sake."

Dominick gestured to JoJo Black to pick up the other extension. JoJo, a short, quiet but intense guy, spent nearly all his time at the club where he was Dom's partner. He grabbed a pen and paper to write down the details. "What should I do?"

"Call Babe's wife and tell her to bring two hundred big ones to the parking lot of the Wakefield Diner. She'll know where it is. And, listen very carefully: she comes alone. Okay? I mean that. One a.m. If you, or any of your crew, fuck around with this, I promise we'll kill her and Babe."

"How the fuck do I know if she's gonna come up with the money? You're talkin' two-hundred here."

"Don't fuck with me, Nappi, you and your friend lost more than that last week shootin' crap. You ain't playin' with amateurs here. We know she's got that money in the house, probably under the rug somewhere. Make sure she gets there alone."

Joey made Rusty repeat what he'd said word-for-word. Shaking his head, Joey realized that Rusty had slipped. He wasn't sure if Dominick would catch it, but Joey knew that Benny the Trap was the only person who could've known for sure where the money was hidden. Joey knew Benny was a loose end he'd have to tie up sooner or later. Now it was time.

Benny was predictable. He walked home from the subway at about the same time every night. Though it was nothing you could set your watch to, he moved in a window of about fifteen minutes or so, depending on how the trains were running that night. Joey parked about a block from the subway. When he saw Benny come out, he started the car and pulled up next to him. "Hey, Benny, I thought that was you. Come on, get in, you gotta be freezin' your balls off."

A few days later, two policemen found Benny's body in the backseat of a car under the West Side Highway.

That morning, Carole had called the Pioneer. "Hey, Rendino? I'm not going to Paris. In fact, I'm heading back to my apartment to take a nice, long, hot shower. You better be there holding my towel when I get out."

Joey smiled broadly and asked, "Who the hell is this?" By the time he and Carole got together, the fate of Benny the Trap and Babe Marsano were the last things on his mind.

The next day, my brother met up with Danny in the back of Reedy's: "Joey, what the fuck happened?"

"The moron rednecks fucked up. I did what I had to do. Look, before Carole gets here… I need you not to drink or gamble for a while. Most of all, keep your mouth shut. Don't think that my feelings for Carole will influence other decisions I have to make—you know what I mean?"

"Joey, you know I'll never say anything."

"Yeah, yeah, I know that. But, I still gotta say it. This is too serious, Danny. The rednecks went back home for a while. I'm closing things down until everyone's relaxed again."

Danny made a bad poker face. He'd been depending on Joey for some time now, and he'd already borrowed money on anticipation that Joey would use him on more jobs. Even though Joey had just paid him, Danny was already broke. "That's a good idea, Joey—can't be too careful."

After Carole arrived and had a drink with her brother, Joey took her out to Luchow's on 14th Street. She studied the wine list then looked over at him. "I don't feel like wine, Joey. How about we drink some good old German beer? You know, the dark, heavy, foamy beer belly kind? I had a good day, I'm happy, and I'm not worried about calories. What I've got planned for us later, oh boy, we'll burn it off."

Joey shook his head. "You know, you're a real crazy kid. The only time I feel as good as I do now is when I'm with you."

Carole leaned in to steal a kiss before reaching into her bag and taking out a box with a green ribbon tied around it and handed it to Joey.

He was a little stunned. It was his role to present carefully wrapped gifts: Carole had turned the tables on him. "What's this?"

"It's for you, my love."

He opened it carefully, untying the ribbon and putting it aside. Then, he unwrapped the paper rather than ripping it apart. Carole looked across the room to signal a trio of violin players, who rushed over and began to play "All My Life." Joey opened the box and pulled out a bottle of cologne. The green glass was inscribed with the legend, "Just Joey."

Joey was overcome with emotion. "I remember you said you would do this, but I always thought you were just foolin' around, Carole."

"No, I never fool around when it comes to you."

"You mean this scent is just for me?"

"Like I said, 'Just Joey.'"

"Okay, then I'll wear it only for you, when we're together."

"Then wear it all the time because that's when you're gonna be with me."

Joey never showed emotion in public. If he did, it was on rare occasions and only when he was with Carole; even then, his displays were controlled. But, overcome that someone cared enough to make something that was just for him, Joey sprayed just a little bit of Just Joey on his wrist. Suddenly, he leaped out of his chair and went over to the maitre'd, leaving Carole at the table with her mouth open. He grabbed the maitre'd by the wrist, leaned over, and whispered in his ear. When he returned to the table, Carole was still sitting with her mouth open, shocked at what she had just witnessed.

Soon everyone in the place was having a drink on my brother. If anyone asked, he or she was told it was their lucky night: a good customer was sharing his happiness.

Later that evening when they were lying in bed, Joey asked Carole how she'd developed it. "Making love to you had a lot to do with it, baby." She reached out and grabbed his crotch.

Startled, Joey asked, "Why, did I smell bad before?"

"No, silly, there are so many ingredients that go into creating a new scent. It's very complicated. I actually used your body scent to develop the cologne. I've always loved the way you smell when we make love. You're a cross between a lion and… an herb garden. Not to mention your olive oil skin. I love all the ingredients, just love it."

"That's great, Carole. But you left out the lion shit."

Carole had just hit Joey in the face with a pillow when the phone rang. "Hello…? When…? Stephen, please—it's so fuckin' late. Now you have to tell me this, so close to the holidays?"

After she'd hung up, Carole turned to Joey, who could read her face. "I don't think you're about to tell me something I wanna hear."

"I have no choice, Joey—I have to go to Paris to deal with our biggest client. Laura's going to meet me at the office first thing in morning."

Joey acted as if he was expecting this news: "Nothing is free in this life, Carole. Being successful is great. But, even if the price I have to pay is watching you leave, we both know it's the right thing. You made it. It doesn't matter how good you make me feel, or smell, I stink from within. You'll never know how bad, 'cause you're all good. Tomorrow, go do what you gotta do. For Stephen to call now, he must really need you."

"All right, Joey, I'll go in the morning. But, you're gonna stay tonight?"

"Of course. Where else am I gonna go and get what I got here?"

"You bastard!"

CHAPTER TWENTY-FOUR

The first thing Joey did when I got home from Allenwood was take me aside and give me an envelope. "You're gonna buy a deli here in the neighborhood, you're gonna give these people the good food that you and I grew up on. They deserve good food. If you need more money, just let know."

I wasn't sure what I wanted to do, but I thought Joey's idea was good. "You're gotta be able to earn on your own. You can't depend on anybody in this life for your living. I'm serious about this. I gotta repeat to you again: use the Life, don't let it use you. Armondo's already gonna hold it over your head because Jack Friedman's his man. And, don't think because you didn't pay Friedman's fee Armondo won't think you aren't gonna pay another way. I told you, Vin, that greedy fuck bleeds green."

"Even though he put you in this position, he's gonna act like he's in the right. Those are the realities of this fuckin' life. In his position, he can make himself right, even when he's a thousand percent wrong. That's what you gotta understand. Your obligation is Al Hicks. He's your skipper. Armondo will never call you other than through Al Hicks, so you don't have to worry about him."

I listened carefully to what my brother had to say when I got out of lockup. I was home well over a year when Armondo Manna decided to throw me and a few of our friends a party. They had just graduated college, a term we use for people getting out of jail. Armondo went all out. I must say, he was a great host. The bash was held at his new place in the Bronx, Villa Armondo. He brought some of the best cooks in East Harlem with him when he made the move to the new place. Even though Armondo threw the party, he didn't argue when Joey insisted on picking up the tab.

Joey thought it was a good idea waiting for these people to get out and get home to have my belated homecoming party. He wanted me to meet and get to know more people from our world that he knew could help me in the future. These were people who my brother respected; as usual, Joey was right.

It was a good time for a party like that. Though a whole lot of people had left East Harlem, it was recent enough that they still wanted an excuse to come together. Over the next few years, people stopped getting together with their old neighborhood friends and started hanging around their new neighborhoods. Yeah, it was a loss; but that's how life is. I guess we're an exception, the ones who still go to the Pioneer and want to keep some remnants of the old neighborhood alive: me, Frankie, Swifty, and, of course, Nadine.

At the party, Joey stood next to me, beaming. "Winds up doing about fifteen months, and he's out! I told him, you didn't even need to take your socks off!"

Everybody laughed.

Dominick took Joey aside to give him the update on the Nappers. "Babe must've made them, Joey. We did everything they asked. These pricks know what they're doing. Only certain people have the number where they called me—that's the clean phone. They even knew where he lived. Joey, they were waiting for his wife when she left the house to go make the drop. An' when they took her back inside, they knew right where the trap was."

"Seems like these rat-bastards are readin' our mail, Dom."

"Yeah, we figure Benny the Trap was involved–"

"–And then they took him out. Yeah, it all makes sense."

Dominick stared at him. "What're you talking about, Joey? Babe's wife can't even bury her husband whole. So far, they only found his head. You think that makes sense?"

"You have any idea how many cocksuckers are in on this? What they drive, what they look like? Any fuckin' thing at all?"

"We're getting all kinds of different stories. They seem to

come out of nowhere. They flash badges, then they put you in a van or sometimes a car, somethin' different every time. They blindfold you and you're gone. I still say they were cops. Babe must've made them, so they cooked him."

Joey was a good actor. Instead of pretending to be angry, he took the real anger he felt towards Armondo and simply channeled it into faking his anger at the Nappers. "Motherfuckers! Listen, Dom, you let me know if you hear anything else. Babe didn't deserve this. He should be here now with us, celebrating. You're right, Dom, who else but rat cops would do things like that?"

"All right, Joey—thanks."

Joey watched him walk away and then sank against the bar, deep in thought. He was looking off, staring out the window, and didn't even notice Philly Agolia approach until he'd said Joey's name twice.

"Philly, I'm sorry, my friend, my mind was a million miles away. How are you? I'm sorry to hear about your cousin Benny."

"I wanted to talk to you about him."

"I appreciate you comin'. But, I want you to just celebrate my brother's return, okay?" Joey was annoyed, thinking Philly should've known better. "When somebody dies, the loan dies too, Philly, you know that. Benny's gone—so's the debt. Have a fuckin' drink and enjoy the party."

Joey appreciated those who came and showed respect because it meant they also respected him. He was disappointed that Danny didn't come. Joey had made a point of stopping by the pub, but Danny wasn't around. Joey had left word with Spike for Danny to come out and have one drink.

As it turned out, Danny had things on his mind other than my party. Instead of raising a glass at Armondo's, he drove up to Yonkers to the racetrack to meet with the rednecks, who were back in town. Together, their bad luck was even worse; they'd been losing money as quickly as they could bet it, all day long.

"Five fuckin' losers. Not one in the money. Un-fuckin'-believeable. Son of a bitch!"

Ronnie laughed. "You'd have better luck if you let Ray Charles read your horse sheet. You suck, man."

As always, Rusty was impatient. "Are we gonna sit here pissin' and moaning, or are we gonna talk about makin' some money? And I don't give a fuck about Joey. We can make our own moves. Fuck him and his guinea mob."

This was the thing Danny wanted to hear least; he already felt like he was betraying Joey to an extent. But, he also felt that Joey had left him with no choice. Besides, Joey always told him he needed to take charge of his own life. Maybe it was time. He could control the Millers and run this move.

The first trick was to keep them in line. "If you two are taking that attitude, you can forget me. You wanna go play Cowboys and Indians, do it without me. I ain't ever fuckin' with Joey. And, let me add something, you cocksuckers—I'll kill anyone, including either or both of you, if you ever fuck with Joey."

As Danny and Rusty stared at each other, Ronnie stepped between them. "Rusty's just letting off some steam. He hates losing more than I do. Of course, we all feel the same way about the man. It's just that we don't need him to run the jobs."

Rusty agreed. "Look, Danny, the three of us, we're all in the same bag. We drink, we like women, we gamble. If we can get a little taste without him knowing it, who's it hurt? You set it up. We'll do it however you want. Ain't that right, Ronnie?"

"Whatever you say, brother, I'm cool with it."

Danny smiled. Being a leader wasn't so hard. "Okay, I got a good target lined up. I was gonna tell Joey, but he hasn't heard about it yet, so we'll do it your way. But it's only because I'm jammed up."

"We understand, bro, so tell us what you got."

"This guy, Johnny Redda, he's a big junk pusher. He meets his connection in my dad's—I mean my—bar, once a month. I'll walk you through the whole move."

"How the fuck we gonna know the day of the meet?"

"That's easy. They always meet on a Friday between four and six o'clock. It's been a few weeks since I've seen them, so it could be this Friday or next."

"Okay, we're on for this Friday. Let's have one more before we go."

Of course, with Danny and the Millers, one more turned into several, and Danny wound up sleeping it off at the house they were staying in, driving back to Manhattan the next morning. They all met in Reedy's the next day for more drinking. The Millers brothers sat in a booth.

"I have alligator boots that'd taste better than this steak. I'd rather be eating Mickey Mantle's glove," Rusty whined.

"I know, but it'd taste a whole lot worse if we hadda pay for it, so shut up and hope the dude shows up." At the bar, Danny tried to look like he was avoiding the Miller brothers; instead, he always seemed to be going by their booth, stopping for a moment as he did.

"How much did Danny give you to pay the tab?" Rusty asked his brother.

"Fifty."

"He thinks too much of this dump."

A man dressed in construction clothes walked into the pub with a gym bag and put it on the floor next to the stool where Timmy Green sat.

Spike came over and greeted the man as "Allan." At the time, Reedy's was busy. The Millers didn't see the early signals. Danny had to get very close to their booth before he got their attention. Once they acknowledged him, he continued walking as if he'd just been going to the restroom. Rusty pocketed the fifty that Danny had given him and left a ripped-up twenty tucked under the plate.

When the construction worker named Allan left the pub to meet Johnny Redda, the Millers were already waiting in the garage where Redda parked his car. They did their usual fake badge routine and made them open the trunk to Redda's car.

Johnny had a duffel bag full of heroin, his monthly exchange for the gym bag of cash. "Look, take the junk and the money. It'll do you more good than this pinch."

"Okay, we will. Now, give me your keys and get in the trunk—both of you."

There wasn't much of a plan; the brothers were winging it. They'd decided not to bring the van. Why bother parking since they were planning on stealing Johnny Redda's Cadillac anyway? Lock two guys in the trunk of a car and drive for fifty miles as fast as you can on the highways, and they're gonna be pretty subdued. Rusty and Ronnie didn't even bother to tie up the two napping victims until later.

The Millers had been bored, cooped up for months. They took it out on these two guys. Danny never knew anything about it. He'd told the Millers not to kill anybody if they could help it; they didn't care. They took Redda and Allan into the basement of the house Joey had rented and cut them up, betting each other which of the two men would last longer and which of the two brothers would finally kill him.

Unlike the moves Joey planned, this one became public fast.

CHAPTER TWENTY-FIVE

I was able to buy a stake in a place on Second Avenue between 105th and 106th really cheap because so many people were selling their houses and moving out of the neighborhood. I found a spot that already had a good oven and a lot of counter space, so I only had to keep it closed for a few weeks to renovate before I could re-open. I decided to call it "Big V Deli." Okay, it's a little egotistical, but I built it with my sweat. And, Big V has a certain ring to it.

Right away, the word spread that the food was actually good compared to what most people were selling. The meatball sandwiches were talked about all over. We always had a good line around lunchtime.

I worked my ass off to make Big V Deli a success.

"Vinnie Rendino, he's a wise guy. He's with Al Hicks."

Yes, I was part of a family in East Harlem. In some ways, it was an asset because nobody fucked with me or Big V Deli. In the end, I took Joey's advice and made the Life work to my advantage. My deliveries were on time. My credit was good. Everyone paid when they were supposed to. The young tough street kids made sure there was no trouble on our block.

I remember late one morning when I was in kitchen making sausages and peppers for lunch. It was plenty hot, and the exhaust fan had quit on me. Though I had the back door open to relieve the heat, it helped very little. Nadine was supposed to work that morning, but she was late. So, my wife Rosemarie was working the counter. We'd gotten married right after I got out of the joint.

Here I was sweating like a pig, wondering where the hell Nadine was.

At about 11:30, in walks Nadine, cursing her face off, "Hey,

Vinnie, fuck you and your cunt brother! I can't be in two places at one time. Your brother is worse than a fucking whore. I can't believe that fuck."

"Hey, calm down, for chrissake, and tell me what happened."

"Calm down, you tell me! You be around your fucking brother for three hours and then see how calm you are."

Rosemarie brought in some coffee. The two women got along great. Nadine would tell me all the time, "You better hope she never leaves you. You and your asshole brother, you both got women other men would give half their dicks for."

When Rosemarie went back out front laughing, I kept cooking as Nadine gave me the details on her morning with Joey.

"Yesterday Joey told my retard brother Frankie for me to meet Joey at his apartment at eight a.m. The retard gives me this news when he sees me this morning at 7:30."

"Go on, Nadine, I'm listening,"

"So I go up to Joey's place and knock on the door. No answer. I head down the stairs. Then, I hear the door open. Out steps the fuck in his Sulka Fifth Avenue silk robe. Very nicely, I tell him I gotta be at the deli by eight a.m. and that I'd come by later to clean.

'Oh, no, Nadine, don't worry about the deli, I'll talk to Vinnie later. The place is a mess! I can't stand it. Do the shower first. I want it nice and clean before I go in. Come on, Nadine, you'll be out of here in no time.'

"I gotta tell you, Vin, he's become a real cunt since you put in the new bathroom and kitchen," Nadine went on.

"I know! We had to take the other apartment on our floor just to do the renovations."

"You know how your brother is, Vin. There's no telling him 'no' when he wants something. So, I make the two beds. I dust. I clean the kitchen, all while the prick is still in the shower."Nadine was on a roll.

"I mean, how long does it take to take a shit, shower, and shave? I cleaned the shower first, just as he ordered. Now, he's fucking it up again. Out he walks in his fancy terrycloth robe. I'll tell you one thing—he's a good-looking bastard."

"Hey, Nadine, did you get a tingle?"

"Fuck you, Vin. Well, as you would guess, I had to redo the bathroom. Then, Joey decides he wants a new set of sheets on his bed. I said to him, 'Why the fuck didn't you tell me this before I made the bed?'"

"Then, he lays on the fancy charm: 'It's warm, you know, and I was sweating last night. You're the best, Nadine. We all love you. You know that!' Well, Vinnie, what can I say? He got me again."

"Okay, Nadine, you did good! Now, please get behind the counter and send Rosemarie back. I'm sweating my balls off here."

"Hey, blame your cunt brother!"

As the song says, "you don't know what you got 'til it's gone." And it goes so fast.

CHAPTER TWENTY-SIX

I followed Joey's advice about Armondo, but a few months after I opened up, Al Hicks showed up saying that Armondo thought the deli would make a good numbers spot. When Joey heard about it, he went straight to Armondo, saying we could blow a good legitimate business with a numbers pinch. Armondo agreed, and that ended that.

The local grapevine was buzzing with more than food reviews. Within three days of the Millers's move on Alan and Johnny Redda, the bodies had been found, and the headlines were out. Even though the newspapers didn't mention that it was just one in a string of kidnappings, the word on the street was that the Nappers were behind this, and there were a few leads this time. After Joey put in a call to Higgins, they arranged a meet for the next day.

Higgins saw Joey standing by the fountain near the cheetahs. "Joey, we come here any more and I swear they're gonna let me adopt a panther. I think the people here are starting to suspect you and me are having a secret romance or something. They know me at the ticket booth already."

"I love to be around these animals. It's a change of pace after all the shit I see on the street. You always know where you stand with an animal. If they love you, they show it outright, same as if they hate you. Most of the time, it's the female that holds it together 'cause she does most of the work. Look at the male lion, the lazy prick. Just like us humans... think about it, Higg."

"My man, I know you a long time, and I know you ain't called me up t'tell me some shit about lions."

"Danny and the rednecks did the Johnny Redda move last week. The rednecks said they had to go home for a few weeks.

Danny paid a bookmaker's tab that he owed for two months. He's been at the track; it all adds up. And, Redda's a made guy. He's got people down on Mott Street already asking questions."

"Motherfuckers! Okay, but why'd the rednecks go back home?"

"I know for a fact that Redda made big junk moves. There hadda be three, maybe four keys on him when they got him. No way could they move that much weight locally without sending up red flags. Who the fuck would make a move with them, anyway? They don't know anybody around here except us."

"You trusted Danny…"

Before Higgins could continue, Joey looked up at him. It wasn't anger in Joey's face—just acceptance. He knew he'd made a mistake and already regretted it.

So, Higgins let him off the hook. "Okay, now I know what we're gonna do. All you got to do is let me know how, where, and when. Greedy motherfuckers."

"Slow it down. We still need them. I got a few more good moves planned."

Higgins was surprised. When he started to argue, Joey put his finger over his lips, signaling Higgins to be quiet. "From now on, I'll be there when the money drops are made. We tell the rednecks we'll divvy up after all the moves are made—just to make sure they think they'll be loaded when they go back home for good. Remember, we know nothing about Danny or Johnny Redda."

"Where we're sending them, they ain't gonna need no fuckin' money." Higgins had more to say but proceeded carefully, unsure exactly how to say it. "Joey, why you doin' this? For me, it's the money, but I know it's not only the money for you. You got other motives."

"No, Higg, it *is* about the money—the power of it. I wish I could've cut the cancer of drugs out of my world. But, it spread too deep. You know, Higg, I got a girl who earns more in a month than most wise guys earn in a year. It is about the green, Higg. It's always about the green."

"Okay, Joey. I understand. But, you got enough now. Why

can't you take the girl and go? Because this thing looks like it's starting to fall apart."

"I'd be lying to you if I didn't say I'd thought about it, and she would go. But, I could never do that to her, Higg. I know it would destroy her if she gives up her career. Besides, as fucked up as it sounds, I love the Life. It's the only life I know and could ever live. If I wasn't who I am, there would be no Carole for me... And, by the way, it doesn't matter that Danny's her brother, as far as this thing goes."

Joey couldn't get away from his association with Carole's brother. He was at Armondo's one evening when the big man called him over to his booth. They exchanged small talk for a minute or two before Armondo brought up Danny Reedy.

"He goes drinkin' in all the midtown joints, throws your name around, don't pay his tabs... fine. That's small stuff. Maybe some people get annoyed, okay, but nothing that can't be talked over. But, this Johnny Redda thing comes up with these Mott Street guys, and we gotta show them respect. Do you feel he could be involved?"

"No fuckin' way. Look, Danny drinks, he gambles, he's a fuck-up, true—but that kind of move? Never! He's not capable." Joey was a good actor, and knew not to overplay the line.

Armondo stared at him, trying to spot any falseness behind what Joey said. "Okay, then, he's your responsibility."

"Good. Now I'll tell those would-be tough guys to stay out of Danny's pub. If they ever go in there and start accusing without proof, I'll fuck them up, all of 'em." He played it as angry as he actually would've been if somebody had threatened Danny.

Armondo watched Joey rage a bit before interrupting, "Calm down, Joey, calm down. I'll take care of it. I'll talk to 'em. I want you to take a ride with Al Hicks."

Joey stopped cold. "Take a ride?"

"Yeah, you gotta see this joint Sonny Gold is running. He's got a hell of a setup. Al's going over there, take a ride with him."

Joey knew that Sonny Gold has been a casino boss in Vegas who'd been brought back to New York to operate exclusive private gambling clubs. The clubs were his idea in the first place. Whatever Sonny touched seemed to live up to his last name. Though Joey admired his earning power, now he wasn't sure what was going on.

Armondo might know everything, or he might know nothing. "Take a ride" could mean nothing, or it could mean everything. But, Joey knew he had no choice but to go along. If it came to it, he knew he could take out Al Hicks.

When he and Al walked to the car, Joey was relieved to see that Frankie was driving. Frankie would never betray him. Joey relaxed a bit.

Al had already been to Sonny's place twice before. "I'm telling ya, Joey, wait till you see this operation. Class all the way. I met this guy through Jack Friedman. I can't believe the clientele—some of the top people in the city."

"Too bad he had to be hooked in with them downtown nuts."

"Look, word came from the top. We observe, give them a play, and then maybe we set up the same kind of operation, far enough away so there won't be any beefs." Armondo was always ready to move in and rip off a successful operation.

They got out at a brownstone on 63rd between Madison and Fifth. The doorman came down to meet them. "Is your driver coming in? We'll take the car…"

"No, he'll be back to pick us up. Thanks, fellas." When Al waved Frankie off, Joey tensed slightly. If it's going to come, he thought, this is gonna be it.

He hesitated a moment before he opened the door, with Al two steps behind him. They were greeted by two men in tuxedoes and led into the dining room on the left. When Joey scanned the room he saw a lot of players. Then, he noticed the stairs and realized there were other levels. "I see the action is good—lotta money around. How many guys have pieces of the game?"

Al frowned. "Too fuckin' many."

A tall man with a full head of gray hair, also wearing a tuxedo, called them over to be introduced. Al said, "Joey, say hello to

Sonny Gold. Sonny, this is Joey Rendino."

Sonny smiled and held out his hand to shake. "This is a real pleasure. Before I show you around, let's have a drink, maybe some food if you like."

Joey turned on the charm. "How many floors are there? This is beautiful, just beautiful."

"We operate three floors above. On the first floor, we got craps tables. The second floor's for blackjack and poker. Third floor, we have a bar and a baccarat room."

"Joey's gonna be surprised when he sees some of your clientele, especially a few of the regulars." Al stopped to look around. "By the way, is Jack here?"

"Not yet, but he's comin' by tonight. I expect him soon. When he gets here, tell him I'm giving Joey the tour." He led Joey away then stopped, suddenly catching a scent. "Joey, I have to ask, what is it you're wearing? That cologne, I mean, where's it from?"

"It's one of a kind, from a special friend. Glad you noticed."

"It's very nice, very unique." Usually, Joey was the charmer; but, in this case, he enjoyed being charmed.

The casino operation was much more elaborate than the ones Joey had seen before: fly-by-night operations that changed location every week, if not every night. On the way back, he shared his excitement with Al.

"How the fuck does a class guy like Sonny end up with them downtown jerk-offs? Hey, Al, take a ride down there some Saturday. You're gonna see some hard-ons in their Robert Hall suits, standing on the corner in the morning, wanting everybody to think that they're wise guys. But, the only thing they spend in Sonny's is the afternoon. You throw a firecracker in front of them, they'll shit their pants."

Al Hicks laughed. "Jack tells me Sonny makes lots of money with them. And let's not forget, most of that downtown crew are stand-up people."

"I know, Al, but they have their hard-ons, just like we got ours."

"You put on a good show tonight, Joey. All the books you read paid off. You left a hell of an impression."

Al was trying to compliment Joey to get him to forget about his complaints, but Joey went right on as if Al hadn't said anything.

"We got too many deadbeats in our operation," said Joey, referring to the game Al had helped him set up after my brother got out of prison.

"They think somebody owes 'em a living. Some of them are good guys, but our friends with the cash—we know who they are—they play it close to the vest. They ain't giving up zilch. *Niente.* Nothing. Pieces of shit."

Joey threw his cigarette out and rolled up the window to keep out the cold air. Al Hicks just stared at him. He'd known Joey had been bitter since his time in prison, but he and Armondo had always figured he'd get over it. But, it was getting harder to earn, and the tighter money got, the less likely that Joey was going to get over anything.

Al figured Joey was bitter over money. But, come to think of it, Joey always seemed to have money. He was going to ask Armondo how Joey was doing money-wise: if anybody would know, Armondo would.

By the time they got back, Armondo had gone to bed for the night, and Al didn't really think about it again until a few months later. By that time, it didn't matter.

CHAPTER TWENTY-SEVEN

My brother told me many times, "Vin, you gotta look good, to do good."

I remember Joey in so many ways. Case in point: I was in the kitchen one evening as Joey was dressing. I was about to start eating when I hear him, "Son of a bitchin' cheap bastard."

I walked into the bedroom. Joey had black socks on the bed and one sock on his foot. I said, "Joey, what's wrong?"

Joey answered me, "Vinnie, I drive to Yorkville to this cheap bastard's laundry, and he can't pair the socks up right. Look, that slanty-eyed prick, he put this pair together. They're not the same pattern."

I said, "Joey, they're both black, who the fuck's gonna know?"

"I'm gonna know Vinnie, and that's all that has to matter. You think I can walk around knowing I don't have socks on that match?" I didn't understand it then, but I did later.

Two nights after Joey'd gone to Sonny Gold's place with Al Hicks, he took me to the brownstone. My brother was very impressed with Sonny and his entire operation. As Sonny gave me the tour, Joey spotted Alphonse Basso and Anthony Dippoli of the laborer's union standing by the bar. They were both charter members of the Boys of Forever club in upper East Harlem. Joey highly respected these men.

The Pioneer was more or less a gambling joint. Even though some of Joey's people pushed money out of his club when he first started, he never allowed drug dealing. The Boys of Forever put neighborhood people to work out of their club. Though the official office of the union was elsewhere, most of the members went to the BOF club (as they called it) when they needed work. The club always had, and still has, a very warm atmosphere.

When Joey was a teen, first out of the orphanage, Alphonse Basso's father had put him to work. He advised Joey to join the laborer's union and always to show legitimate income no matter what he did later in life. Alphonse Basso felt a deep affection for Joey, and Joey felt the same about him. Joey got to be close with the Basso and the Dippoli families. Though Joey had adopted a different way of life, they remained devoted friends. Joey would later tell people about the BOF club, how it started, all that they had to contend with, including players in the Life. The men of the Boys of Forever were the real men of honor—men of integrity, men who helped, not like the ones who sold out East Harlem.

After we'd left Sonny's, I told my brother that I was happy with my own modest operation. The Big V was mine, all mine—and I didn't have to pay off anyone to keep it running smoothly. I was my own man, the way my brother had always encouraged me to be. "You know what?" I told Joey over espresso in the back room at the Pioneer, such a contrast to the opulence at Sonny's. But it was home turf.

"You were right," I admitted. "We gotta do for ourselves."

"Your place is earning," Joey nodded in approval. "Like I said, if you need more start-up money, let me know. Remember not to let the deli become a hangout for our friends. No credit, everybody pays—everybody, even me."

"I have to ask you something, off the record, as a brother—the money, where'd it come from, Joey?"

My brother got angry. "Since when are you asking questions like that? You know better. It's nothing for you to worry about, Vin!"

I kind of expected this: I knew he'd need to be firm. So, I got right up in Joey's face. "I hope you're not fucking around with junk or any of that shit. This place is open every day, but nothin's goin' on. Armondo asked Al if he sees you up at the crap game, 'cause he doesn't see you goin' around his joint anymore. Nobody sees you that much. Joey, you know this life better than anybody. Be careful."

"Fuck them all. Don't worry about me, I know what I'm doin'. As long as I give Armondo his envelope every month, I got no problems. As far as you know, I'm makin' real estate moves. Oh yeah, Marty Lester and me, we're wholesalin' cars from Pennsylvania, too."

I was silent for a minute, weighing my options.

Joey used the pause to his advantage: "You're a big man, now, huh? Standing up to your big brother?" He had me in a bear hug, but in a brotherly, affectionate way.

Across town, I found out later, Carole was starting to get a bad feeling, one she couldn't put her finger on. She flashed to Danny—that something was wrong with her brother. When she called the pub, Spike said he hadn't seen him since the previous afternoon. She'd called Joey's, but Frankie and said he hadn't seen Danny, either. She couldn't concentrate in the lab, so she ducked out early, leaving an assistant to supervise the work. Given that it was pretty basic stuff, she knew she didn't need to be there. And, she wanted her staff to be a little more independent anyway, and not micromanage everything.

Laura rode the elevator down with her. "Are you all right, Carole?"

"I've been up half the night, worrying. You know, Laura, you were right. I got out of East Harlem, and I know I can never go back. But, I feel so guilty—like I've betrayed the memory of Mom and Dad. We never gave up the apartment in East Harlem, Danny and I—although nobody ever uses it."

"It's time, Carole. Get rid of the apartment and anything else that's attached to where you grew up."

"Boy, Laura, you're like a bulldog. You never give up, do you?"

"Only because I know I'm right."

After the doors opened and Carole got out, Laura called after her, "By the way, I called the service; the car will be here in a minute or two."

Carole smiled. A good assistant really can work magic.

She took the car over to the Pioneer, where she found me

and Frankie hanging out. I had a little time off from Big V, a rare occurrence. By this time, Joey was nowhere to be found. Looking around, Carole was amazed at the state of the neighborhood, how some of the buildings that had been so well-cared for now looked like they were ready for demolition, how the ice cream parlor she went to as a child was now a bodega selling mangoes out in front. The old Jewish haberdasher Maxie Levine was no longer at the corner near the club. She could no longer connect with the girl who'd felt at home on these streets.

When I saw the look on her face, I sat with her for a while.

"Things around here have changed, huh? It's not all bad, Carole," I told her. "I got my own place now on Second Avenue. You've gotta come by. The food is damn good if I do say so myself."

That got a smile out of her. "You could always cook, Vin. I promise I'll stop over when I'm uptown again."

"Yeah, when's that gonna be?" I teased her. "Between Central Park West and that place Joey told me about in Westchester, you got no reason to hang out with us losers in the old neighborhood."

As I said it, I realized how ashamed I was with someone like Carole that I'd done time. It was one thing to talk with the other wise guys about prison; it was another to sit like this with someone who'd done so well once she acquired a toehold south of 96th Street.

"You're like family, Vin," she said, smiling tightly as she admitted how worried she was about Danny and Joey. Even so, we moved on quickly to people we'd gone to to high school with: who was pregnant, who'd moved out of town. Not many to the last point.

Our little bubble of reminiscence was shattered each time the phone rang. Carole's gaze went immediately to Frankie as he answered. Finally, after several false alarms, she spoke to Joey. But, what he said was vague and only scared her further.

When she asked him where he was, he said, "Calm down. No sense in me coming back there now. Don't say no more on this phone. I'll see you later."

Before Carole could protest, Joey had hung up.

When she came back to our table, she looked dazed.

"Come on, Carol," I said, taking her by the elbow gently. "Let me walk you out."

After making sure Carole was safely back in the car, I returned to the Pioneer to keep an eye out. Later, Carole told me that was the night she'd decided to follow Laura's advice and give up the Reedy apartment on 106th Street. She had to cut her ties while there was still time.

CHAPTER TWENTY-EIGHT

Like I said, Joey always kept me out of the loop as far as the Nappers were concerned. The only time me and Joey ever discussed it was when word started to come down about certain people we knew that were being kidnapped. It came up, and Joey told me some things I hadn't heard. I started ranting about what was going on, how low people had sunk. I never realized when I was cursing the Nappers that I was cursing my own brother.

I'd heard a few things when I got back. I knew Babe Marsano had been taken. Me and Joey talked about it, but I never thought Joey was involved. Right up until the end, I figured he had to be pushing junk on the side, just not out of the Pioneer. It made a lot more sense. When Danny Reedy disappeared, I got even more suspicious. But, I kept my head down and concentrated on perfecting my recipe for eggplant parmigiana.

Danny was always like a dog. He was loyal, but he'd get up to mischief if he was left alone. When'd you come home and find that your puppy had torn up your shoes, he'd look at you with those eyes, and you'd know he didn't mean it. He couldn't help himself. It was the same way with Danny: no matter how he fucked up, you couldn't stay mad at him because if he was your friend, he was with you until the end. I guess not everybody felt that way because somebody out there sure was pissed off at Danny Reedy. In a dank basement somewhere on the outskirts of the city, a man chained to a pipe was being beaten by two other men.

"Tell us, you cocksucker. Who did it with you? You can save yourself. Tell us."

"How the fuck can I tell you what I don't know?"

Danny had been a year behind Joey in school; they hadn't known each other much at first. One day, Joey was on his way home when he saw two older boys bullying Danny. Danny had always been a scrawny kid, so it didn't look like a fair fight. Joey was about to step in when Danny launched himself off the ground and head-butted the bigger kid right in the nose.

At the time, my brother told me, "This kid's a little crazy, but he's got some balls."

When a teacher came over to break it up, she found Danny kicking the other kid, who was down on the ground. Danny never said a word about why he was fighting to the teacher, even after he was suspended for a week. Joey got a day's detention because he wouldn't say a word, either. Since the other two kids went to the hospital, the school didn't bother to punish them.

Danny did tell his father why he'd done it. Mike Reedy cautioned him to control his temper; but Danny was never very good at controlling himself, period. He'd make crazy bets and wind up running across the subway tracks when a train was coming or steal an apple from the fruit stand Pete Sessa owned (back then, everybody called him "Old Man Pete" because he'd gone gray very early). When he was betting on himself, Danny would always win. But, when he tried the same thing betting on cards or races, he didn't have much luck. He'd play the long shot, hoping for that fifteen-to-one payoff, and then watch while Joey and his friends collected on the sure thing. At only two-to-one, Danny wouldn't have even felt like he was winning. He had to go over-the-top every time to prove himself.

"Look, Danny, is this worth dying over?"

"Fuck you!"

"Cocksucker!"

Danny hadn't always been a drinker. In fact, even though his father owned a pub, he'd never had a drink until his high school graduation, when two of his uncles took him all around town and got him completely plastered. They treated him like a man for the first time, and even bought him a whore.

Danny took to booze like a fish to water. The closest he

ever felt to his father was when Mike took him in as a partner at Reedy's. They'd often stay for hours after the pub was closed, with Mike telling Danny stories about the neighborhood, sometimes bringing by his old drinking buddies. Danny just listened and wished he was more like his father: a good family man, good to his wife. He longed to prove himself to Mike Reedy; deep down, he knew he was a fuck-up.

Of course, to do anything in this world, to accomplish anything that could make his father truly proud, Danny would need a stake, and that was always the problem. Danny could never hold onto money. He would always drink or bet his way through it quickly. Joey was always willing to help him out, but Danny would never take charity. So, Joey would wind up taking him along on moves. None of the official ones; Joey never brought Danny along on a job that needed a shooter because Danny was Irish and thus an outsider. But, sometimes an extra hand could be useful, and Danny could be intimidating when he kept his mouth shut.

Joey tried to make sure he always had a few extra bucks, but it was never in Danny's nature to save. They were two of a kind. Joey lectured and criticized Danny, but it did no good. He came to realize that it was really himself he was judging. When Joey saw his own sins in other people, he criticized the loudest and the longest.

That was why he'd had the fight with Bridget. Bridget noticed that they always ate at fancier restaurants on double dates with Joey and Carole. Danny hadn't told her any details, but she did know that he and Joey had done some deals together, and she couldn't understand why Joey was always so flush.

She told Danny she thought Joey might be using him: "Fuck these dinners, you should be out earning more money on your own!"

Danny's loyalty kicked in. After they'd argued for an hour, he finally stormed off, slamming the door behind him.

As soon as he did, he knew he'd made a mistake. His sister had always told him to never let Bridget feel like his friends mean more to him than his girl, especially if they actually do.

Danny wanted to turn right around, but when he heard Bridget smashing dishes on the floor, he decided to let her calm down. His father had warned him that Irish girls were crazy, and he hadn't yet found a reason to disagree.

Bridget didn't call him for four days. On the fifth day, she'd come to Reedy's Pub; but she wouldn't look or speak to Danny, even after he told Spike not to charge her for anything.

He'd tried to follow her home, but she got in the taxi without saying a single word. Danny took the hint: it was too soon.

Though Bridget had to admit she enjoyed watching him suffer that night, she also had to acknowledge that she was already starting to miss him. Three days later, she called the pub. After Danny took the phone from Spike, they'd apologized to each other for the next five minutes. She'd known Danny well enough to call a bit early in the evening when he wouldn't be too drunk. He'd agreed to come over. Walking to the subway, he even stopped to buy flowers.

He never made it there. The guys from Mott Street followed him when he left the pub and picked him up right across the street from the flower stand.

"This guy may be a tipster—or maybe he's one of the Nappers. But sure as shit, he ain't no rat. He died tough."

CHAPTER TWENTY-NINE

When a brother dies, you get mad at the world. It doesn't seem fair. Danny wasn't Joey's brother by blood, but his emotion on the subject was the same as Carole's. It was probably worse for Joey because Joey knew he'd had a hand in it. He'd gotten Danny together with the Millers. He'd kept them on the hook for money, and then cut them off without warning when the heat intensified.

I know the sort of advice Joey gave. If Joey could've advised Joey, he'd have said to cut his losses and move on. Stop making moves, take out the Millers. He would've told that to anybody. By then, he couldn't have taken his own advice. His blood was already up against Armondo. Danny was dead, and Armondo still hadn't paid for any of it.

Some guys would've walked away, but Joey made a point of doing another job as quickly as he could.

Armondo and Al were dining at Villa Armondo when Joey stopped by to complain. "It's two fuckin' weeks. Danny's gone, we know it, and we let it happen."

Armondo was amused, and looked over at Al. "Can you believe him? Can you believe this guy? Joey, he did this to himself, this kid."

Al agreed. "We went as far as we could with this. I mean, after all, he wasn't one of us. What's right is right. We're gonna have to let it go."

Joey looked at each of the men and then down. "I just hope they buried him already—for Carole's sake."

Carole was still clinging to the hope that Danny might turn up somewhere. Maybe he'd just skipped town, and word would get back. After avoiding Joey for two weeks, she finally returned his call and agreed to meet him at the Bronxville house. Joey had just arrived wearing his cashmere coat when Carole pushed past him as he leaned in to kiss her on the cheek.

"Whaddaya say, kid?"

"Danny's dead, isn't he?"

Joey couldn't answer.

She kept on. "How long did you plan on keeping it a secret? A secret from me, that is."

"The nature of bad news infects the teller, Carole."

"Fuck you and Shakespeare."

Joey couldn't figure out how to play this. Deep inside, he knew she was right to be furious. Slowly, he stood up and walked over to the bookcase and opened up the trap hidden inside the second shelf, extracting a brown leather suitcase. One of the handles had been broken a long time ago, but it still worked as a suitcase as long as you didn't have to carry it.

"Look, Carole, what's done is done. Danny's gone. It's over. Some of what's in here belonged to Danny. Now, it's all yours… if something should happen."

"Doesn't anything or anybody mean anything to you? Are you so cold and callous to think that a suitcase full of money could console me? You hypocritical bastard! Is that all our life together means to you—a fucking suitcase? My love for you is ruining my life! Danny's gone, and it's because of you he's dead."

Carole began to cry. Joey didn't move; his face betrayed no emotion.

"Danny talked, Joey. You know that. He talked to me, but I never thought you'd let him go that far. But, the only thing that's important to Joey is Joey." Her eyes narrowed, and her voice got quiet. "Your soul is darker and dirtier than the people you say you despise. You need the same power, you have the same greed. How could you cause so much pain? How could you? Even though I've loved you all my life, I don't even know who you are."

"You don't know who I am? You don't know who I am? I'm a fuckin' animal. We're all fuckin' animals. We're animals with cashmere coats and brand new shiny cars. Yes, I'm deceitful—I have to be—but never with you. I was always upfront with you, Carole, so don't give me that hypocrite bullshit. I told you from the get-go that you were a winner. I wanted to be a winner. Instead, I've become everything I detested in life. You made it. Go before you get consumed. Go, Carole, keep going. Just keep fuckin' going."

He sat down, fully spent, then looked up at her. "You're the one thing in my life that ever meant something, and look what's happened."

They sat in silence. Finally, Joey stood up without another word and walked to the door.

"Okay, I'm a winner, Joey. I won. I'll keep going. But, where in the hell do you think you're going?"

"Me? I'm goin' back to the zoo. You should be going to Paris."

She tried to hold herself back, but when she heard his car pull out, she flung open the door, ran outside, and called out his name. It was too late. Joey Rendino, the love of her life, was already gone. Stephen Aronson accompanied Carole to Paris. She put up the pretense that it was a vacation, but she had agreed to meet with a major client while she was there. Stephen knew she'd be intrigued once she met Paul Pascal, a tall, good-looking American living in Paris, who met her at a restaurant for lunch.

"So, you paid for me to fly out here, you're paying for my hotel and this meal… You're laying it on pretty thick. You must be desperate." On the sly, Carole noticed that his eyes were a slightly lighter shade of green than hers.

"Miss Reedy, Lennox sent me to France twelve years ago, and I've never left. As a matter of fact, I have dual citizenship. You should be flattered that we're asking you to take on this project."

Carole was interested, but she looked around as if she couldn't have cared less.

Pascal didn't miss a beat. "Lennox is going into a joint venture with a world-famous Italian designer. We're going to develop a perfume line for women and one for men. You'll have total control of the lab, but we're on a tight schedule. Marketing, advertising, and so forth are already in motion."

"That tells me I wasn't your first choice, Paul. Lennox never puts the cart before the horse."

"We weren't sure you'd be, well, available."

"Well, since I am available, there is no schedule. It's ready when I say it's ready. They can't sell what they don't have."

Pascal stared at her. After years of dealing with French women, he'd forgotten how much he could be turned on by an American girl.

"Something wrong?"

"No, not at all. It's just—you're not what I was expecting."

When Carole cocked her eyebrow, Paul was quick to add, "In a good way, a good way. The way you cut to the chase. That doesn't usually happen at a business lunch."

"You're gonna have to get used to me."

"Well, enough with the business. It's time we drink some good French wine. Tell me, is this your first time in Paris?"

She nodded. "I spent some time in Europe after college, but I was only in France for a week, and it was down in the south."

Aronson's natural nose for chemistry had paid off as usual; Carole found herself responding to Pascal, Joey's opposite in so many ways.

"There's a lot for you to see while you're here. Oh, just to get back to business for a second, Ms. Reedy, there will be a schedule, which I will set, and it will be ready when I say it's ready."

Carole was surprised, but said nothing as the waiter arrived with the wine list. Pascal began to speak to him in French.

Stephen hadn't accompanied them to the lunch but called Pascal immediately afterwards to hear about how it went. He wanted to show that he had complete confidence in Carole, and Pascal agreed. "You were correct. I could see the fire in her eyes when she thought she was our second choice. But, we may have shot ourselves in the foot where the money is concerned."

"Don't worry about the money, I'll handle it. She wants the challenge, the competition. That's what turns her on. I'm more concerned about exposing her talent. She's very loyal, but I don't want to tempt fate."

Even as Carole's career was going to the next level, back in America, Joey was already planning three more moves.

CHAPTER THIRTY

Joey had made Carole a promise when she gave him the cologne—and he stayed true to it. The whole time Carole was in Paris, he never wore Just Joey. He kept the bottle on his dresser next to a picture of Carole, like a little shrine. He never had much of Carole's stuff there because he wanted her to stay away from the neighborhood, he always wound up going to her new place on the Park.

I know that Carole was happy in Paris then. I saw her a few times over the years. Whenever business brought her back to New York, she would make a point of stopping in to see me—and she always talked about how she fell in love with the City of Lights the first time she saw it. She had a lot of work to do that first trip, but she made a list of all the places that she had to see as soon as she had time to enjoy herself.

She told me that Joey would've loved the Louvre. You could sit and stare at the paintings for hours and nobody would bother you. She said that whenever she went anywhere in Europe she wondered what Joey would've thought—and there were a lot of places he wouldn't have cared for. She never said this to me, but from talking to her, I know that she really wanted to have it both ways. She wanted to bring Joey with her to Paris. She didn't realize that Joey could never really stay away from New York, from East Harlem. If he could, he wouldn't have been Joey.

Joey decided that Old Man Pete Sessa would be the easiest to approach first. My brother had known the Sessa family all his life. They were fruit and produce people who had an entire corner in the East Harlem markets. At that time, East Harlem had the biggest markets in New York, ones that stretched for many blocks and even covered many avenues. Joey and I both remembered the fires the workers started in garbage cans on cold nights to keep warm. We talked about the smell of wood and coal burning and the wonderful fragrance of chestnuts roasting, and most importantly, the good old days. Men even caught eels in the East River and cooked them on those fires. The market was the heart and soul of East Harlem, providing fresh fruits and vegetables all year round, including watermelons in the spring and summer.

Then came autumn, which was grape season for all the homemade winemakers. The vendors would call out in a singsong way the names of the produce they were selling as they competed with each other. It was a way of life in a vibrant community—and now it had been replaced by housing projects. In our minds, a neighborhood isn't bricks and mortar; it's all about its people, and what they do for each other.

Joey took this even harder than I did. After all, Big V was thriving, its offerings all based on old school recipes. But, my brother hadn't found a way to make the changes in the neighborhood work to his advantage. Looking at the contrast between the new East Harlem and the one where we grew up, he must have been consumed by bitterness and poison even to think about abducting Old Man Sessa. My brother loved the Sessa family.

The Nappers crew met in a house Higgins had rented in a multi-racial part of Mount Vernon." Joey turned to the Millers. "You two wanna stay here or where you're at now?"

"We're okay where we are. I rented the double motel room like you said. We can both stay there, okay?"

"Next week, we make the next move. Listen to me—because of what happened with Johnny Redda, the street's gotten hot. All the neighborhoods are steamin', and everybody's on edge. They're trying to make the Redda hit look like one of our kidnappings, but everybody knew he was a junk pusher. His people made an example out of him. Fuck them all. I advised Danny to stay away for a while. The agents knew Redda, and the other guy went to Reedy's all the time."

Joey had told Higgins about Danny, but he had to throw the

rednecks off. "I'm holding all the money until we make the last move. It's not like I don't trust you people; it's just that I feel it's the best way, considering what's going on. If you all don't agree on this, we pack it in now and say our goodbyes. What's your pleasure?"

Nobody said anything. They all looked around. Joey got stern, "Well, come on, what's it gonna be?"

Higgins was the first to respond. They'd discussed this beforehand—that Joey would give Higgins his share whenever he wanted it. "I'm good with it."

Ronnie looked to Rusty. "If it's good for my brother, it's good for me."

Rusty looked around and then nodded. "If we need anything, we'll let you know."

When the Miller brothers were alone, they agreed that they'd wait until Joey hit the big guy ("Mongo" was what Rusty called him, though Ronnie was pretty sure it was "Mundo"), and then kill them both. They'd take their time on the nigger and head back down South with a big stake.

They grabbed Old Man Pete, got the money, and let him go. After the last few jobs, it was a nice change of pace when nothing went wrong. Pete Sessa was JoJo Black's uncle, and had started JoJo in the junk business—as he had Dominick Nappi and a lot of other guys. Joey figured, why go after JoJo? The old man would be easier. He'd be so rattled, he wouldn't be able to talk about it when he was let go. JoJo was still the one who'd pay, but Joey knew Pete would be a piss off Pier Six. He was right. So often I've wondered how things might have turned out better for my brother if he'd been wrong more often early in the Nappers' binge of grab, collect, wreak havoc as you go. But, he picked his targets carefully.

As my brother and his motley crew went about their business, Carole called at least once a week. On New Years, she tried to phone Joey repeatedly. Because Joey knew it was her, he wouldn't answer it. He was tempted. Once, when the phone wouldn't stop ringing, he couldn't take it any more and ripped the cord out of the wall.

She started calling the club and left a few messages with Frankie. Joey stopped by in the afternoon, right as Swifty was passing by with the dog. Frankie was shouting at him, "You're a real piece of shit, you know that?"

Joey walked over with a smile. "Youse must all be nuts. It's fuckin' freezin' out and yous're standing watchin' this crazy prick and his dog. Unbelievable."

Swifty got pissed. "Who's a crazy prick?" He grabbed his crotch, gesturing to Joey. "Here, take this. Take this, tough guy. Here's my crazy prick."

A few of the club's regulars stood around, laughing. Joey didn't laugh, though. Frankie got upset. "What did I say? Just before you got here—he's a fuckin' disrespectful prick. Every fuckin' day I find dog shit in front'a the door. That's why I'm out here. I'm gonna chop his fuckin' dog's head off right in front of him."

"That's why you're all out here? You're waitin' for a dog to take a shit? Swifty, do me a fuckin' favor. Take your dog for a walk. I got no head for your dog shit today."

Swifty walked on as Joey went inside. Frankie watched him go, then turned to Joey and called after him, "Joey! Carole's been callin' all morning."

"Frankie, do me a favor, if she calls again, don't let on that I'm here, understand?"

Over the next hour, I stopped by, and so did Al Hicks. After hearing the whole saga of Frankie and Swifty and his dog from the regulars, we wound up sitting at a table with Joey.

Al had some bad news. "You were right, Joey. Tommy Marra's made a beef about you getting' too close to Sonny Gold. The prick went straight to Armondo."

Marra was the boss of one of New York's five crime families, a heavyset man who dressed very conservatively. Everyone knew that he controlled Sonny Gold, and the action at Sonny's club.

"Tommy Marra—a fuckin' zillionaire. He made most of his bucks puttin' up money for junk deals. Never did five seconds worth of time. I think the only thing he ever killed in his life was time."

Joey turned to look at me, even though he was still talking to Al. "How much ya wanna bet our boss gets a piece of Sonny's next operation?"

Everybody at the table looked at Joey. "Yeah, yeah, the old freeze-out move, and the bosses eat and eat and eat."

In the Bronx, another meeting was taking place in the back room at the Continental Social Club. Sally Fat, Vito Romano, Louie Dee, Dominick Nappi, and JoJo Black were sharing a meal and swapping the latest information.

Dominick chimed in, "We don't think the Nappers are cops."

JoJo didn't think it mattered. "Whoever they are, they know what the fuck they're doin', and their information is good, too."

Dominick thought for a second. "So, all of you agree that whoever their tipster might be, it's somebody close, somebody we all know?"

They all agreed. Dominick turned to Louie Dee. "Talk to your kid again. Maybe he can give a better description. You too, Vito, think about it."

Sally usually kept quiet; but, after swallowing a mouthful of pasta, he said, What about your uncle Pete?"

JoJo sadly shook his head. "He's still fucked up. It happened too fast. He's confused and embarrassed."

Louie Dee hadn't touched his food; just talking about the Nappers made him furious. "I'll know the motherfuckers if I see them again. Disguise or no disguise, I'll never forget."

A few nights later, Joey took me to Sonny Gold's again. He thought I was putting in too many hours at the Big V and needed some extracurricular activity. As fate would have it, Tommy Marra walked in with his entourage just as we were sitting down. Sonny jumped up to seat Tommy.

One of Tommy's men approached our table and asked Joey to come over to meet him.

"Tom, this is Joey Rendino, *amici norstra*, a friend of ours. Joe, this is Tom Marra."

"*Buona salute,* Tom. Good health."

"It's a pleasure. I've heard a lot of good things about you, Joey. Sonny talks about you all the time. You guys see a lot of each other, I hear."

Joey caught the implication. He smiled and nodded his head. He'd wanted to meet Tommy face to face at least once before they kidnapped him. He was that angry at him. Tommy had nothing to lose by Joey and Sonny being friends. They'd become friends honestly, just because they got along. But, Tommy didn't want anybody getting too close to Sonny while he depended on him.

Whenever Joey felt powerless, he grew even more bitter. As this bitterness had fueled his plotting against Armondo, it also fueled his targeting of Tommy. "Maybe with your blessings, I'll keep on seeing him."

Afterwards, Joey and I went back to our place. Even though I wasn't living there, we still considered it our place. For a long time, even when we had the money to do it over, we kept the linoleum on the floor; the milk box where we used to store vegetables on the fire escape; the metal table in the kitchen, the kind they have now in so-called "vintage" stores; the dented silver pot for espresso, permanently set on one of the four burners on the little stove. All this made us feel at home no matter what was going on in the streets outside, or in places like Sonny Gold's. Eventually, we renovated the apartment.

"Damn, that place is fuckin' unbelievable!" I said to my brother. "A casino on one of the most expensive streets in Manhattan; there have to be some high profile people on that street. Don't they complain?"

"Complain!" Joey lit a cigarette. "Why should they complain? It's like they can walk to their own private club and eat, drink, gamble, and rub elbows with some top mob guys. Hey, what's not to like?"

"Not to mention the entire chorus line of the Copa," I added, laughing.

Suddenly, I wasn't laughing anymore. "You know, Joey, once you start dealing with people like Sonny Gold and Tommy Marra and that downtown crowd, you're dealing with a different kind of money—which means trouble."

Though I had no idea then what Joey was planning, I could see that my brother was being seduced by all the trappings in Sonny's brownstone.

And, I knew that nothing good would come of it.

"Now my little brother's giving me advice on the Life, huh?" said Joey, grinning. "How well I've taught you..."

On his way to the bathroom to take a shower, he said to me, "Don't sweat it, Vin, just concentrate on those grosses at Big V. You got a good thing going there—don't blow it."

CHAPTER THIRTY-ONE

Years later, when I read the "The Federalist Papers," I saw a line in there that made me think of Joey and our life: "Nothing works without stability and order." That's always been true. No government can work, no financial institution, no business... nothing works without stability and order. It's even more so in our way of life. When Joey lost that, I lost my brother.

As Carole and her new colleague Pascal had grown closer over the past few weeks, their Paris luncheons had segued into dinner dates. Though she enjoyed Paul's company, Carole was torn between what Pascal represented and the fact that she still loved Joey.

Still, Carole had to acknowledge that she was developing an attraction for Paul the better she got to know him. Over and over again, she tried to dismiss it as revengeful emotion, reacting to the manner in which she and Joey had parted. But, as Carole and Paul began spending time together, she noticed more and more so many similarities to her Joey: how he conducted himself socially, how Paul acted at business meetings, how discreetly he handed money to the maitre'd. They were very subtle, little things, but Carole noticed.

His impeccable dress and especially his inner strength reminded her of Joey. It was like seeing his double. But, like Joey, Paul Pascal was very hard to read. Carole started probing to find out exactly what it was about him that attracted her.

"So, Paul, it seems you know so much about me; yet I know very little about you. Where are you from? Were you ever married?" She laughed at her own assertiveness.

Quickly Carole added, "I'm sorry, Paul. I have no right…"

"No, no, Carole—it's okay. Let me start from the beginning. I was born in Chicago in a well-known Italian enclave known as the Patch. My parents came from a small town outside of Palermo, Sicily, and settled in Chicago. In the old country, my father was in the extract business. So, when he got to the good old U.S.A., he was a natural to take advantage of the opportunities Prohibition presented—that is, he became a bootlegger."

"Paul, I love it!" Carol laughed out loud. "Tell me more. I'm sorry for interrupting."

Paul stared at Carole across the table, in the same intent way Joey always had. "Don't misunderstand, Carole, my father was well-educated. But, he was also very street-wise. I tried very hard to emulate him. Both my parents were huge advocates of education. When I was in my early teens, we moved to Oak Park, an upper middle class neighborhood. But, to be truthful, I missed the Patch. I missed all the action, I missed hanging out, I missed being on the edge of two different worlds."

"Yeah Paul, I know exactly what you mean," Carole interjected, nodding.

"As they say, Carole, the rest is history. I went to a parochial high school. Then, I was accepted to the University of Chicago. I did well in chemistry, so here I am today."

They both laughed.

"And Carole, I forgot to mention that when my parents got to Ellis Island, they were named Paualo and Adalina Pascule. When they left, they were still Paualo and Adalina Pascal—old school, proud of their heritage."

He paused and then looked over at her again, smiling: "Now you know about me, my upbringing, my education. And, to answer your question directly, no, I never married. How about I stop boring you and start showing you a good time?"

"Paul, I've been having a great time just listening to you. I feel so much more at ease knowing now how much we really have in common. But, let me be clear, our personal relationship will not in any way influence our business relationship. Fun is fun, work is work."

He leaned across the table and almost whispered, "Great! I feel the same way. Now, what do you say we have another drink?"

Just then, Carole gazed across the dining room and saw a man going down on one knee while a violinist played "I Love Paris" for the couple.

"I think he just proposed to her!"

"I hope she says 'yes,'" Carole laughed as she turned back. "I'm serious! Imagine, after all the trouble that guy goes to, she doesn't even love the poor sap."

"I think you're cynical. I happen to believe in true love."

"Sitting across from you, I can definitely believe in it."

"I'm just not sure people always recognize it. Some people don't realize what they have until a good thing slips away."

"Don't—don't push it, okay?"

"Stephen told me that you still had attachments in New York, Carole. I'm just asking you how strong they are…"

"Don't talk about New York—or Stephen. Talk about me."

"All right… should I start on your lovely eyes or your fantastic hair?"

"Boring!"

He looked over her shoulder and signaled. The violin player approached, and he slipped him a bill. "Carole, have you thought of staying in Paris for a longer time?"

A chanteuse began to sing a song of love and regret to the accompaniment of the violinist. Carole didn't react to the music immediately, but when it hit her, she stopped suddenly, staring at the bow, and the violinist's fingers. It was the song that she had loved since she first heard it. It was her and Joey's song: "All My Life".

Suddenly, she stared at Paul and then stood up: "Paul, I—I have to go."

"What's wrong? I didn't mean–"

"No, it's not—it's got nothing to do with that." She rushed away from the table.

He stood up, calling after her, "Carole, wait… At least think it over for a day or two." But, she was already gone, and he sat back down and finished his glass of wine.

It was just a few days later back at the Pioneer that Carole stormed back into Joey's life. Her limo pulled up at 11 a.m. She'd landed just before 9:00, but traffic had been terrible. She stepped out of the limo and shivered a little. Though it was still February, she was wearing her flimsiest, sexiest clothes without a coat to hide them. She carried a pink bag with French writing on it as she strode into the club.

Joey was sitting at the bar reading a newspaper and sipping his coffee when the door flew open, and in walked Carole. People having breakfast, planning out their days, or just engaging in idle conversation all stopped to look up when she entered. Gorgeous, green-eyed redheads hauling shopping bags from Paris weren't a daily sight at the Pioneer. Even the men who didn't know who she was were intrigued by what might happen next. The people who did know her were stunned by the anger in her beautiful face, especially to see it directed at Joey.

Before Joey could say a word, she pulled a red towel out of the bag, flung it across his face, and stormed back out. As he pulled the towel off, tires squealed in the street. Carole's driver sped off so quickly that he almost hit Swifty's dog.

On a note pinned to the towel, Joey read: "I'm on my way to Bronxville. Be there in one hour." He smiled.

Frankie looked concerned. "My father always told me Irish girls are beautiful, but don't get them mad. *Madonna*, Joey, she looks mad."

"That's good advice, Frankie. I better get goin', 'cause I don't want her madder than she already is."

He drove up to the house as quickly as he could, opened the door silently, and slipped his shoes off. He could hear the shower going. He crept up the stairs, getting closer and closer to the bathroom door when suddenly the shower stopped.

Before he could move, the door opened. Carole stared over at him. He held out the towel and opened his mouth to say something, but, before a word could escape, she was kissing him passionately. She scratched at him and pulled off the clothes she'd just soaked. Joey responded in kind, pushing her against the wall.

She bit his lip and dug her nails into his arm. When he grunted like an animal, she smiled. They slid to the ground as she slipped his pants off.

In the aftermath, Carole rubbed a scratch on her hip. "I can't believe you forgot to take the pin out of the towel."

"Do I still smell good after we make love?"

"You smell like a prick because you are a prick. Six weeks, six fuckin' weeks you don't answer my phone calls. I had that bad feeling about Danny, now it's about you. I can't shake it, Joey. I'm worried sick."

"Look, kid, relax. I can't blame you for feeling what you feel, but it's because of Danny. Me, you don't have to worry about. I said everything I had to say before you went to France. You know my street life is off-limits to you. The less you know, the safer you are. Never forget that."

"You're right about me getting out. I did. I can't relate to my young years anymore, even though sometimes I feel guilty about pushing it out of my mind. Sometimes, I even despise the memories from my youth. And yet, when it comes to you, Joey, I can't let go. Why? Please. Tell me why..." He kissed her softly. "Someday, you won't have to let go. It'll just happen."

CHAPTER THIRTY-TWO

By this time, the street was definitely talking. I don't remember when people started calling them the Nappers, but they'd become kind of an urban legend. Anybody who had any idea what was going on kept quiet, so there was a lot of misinformation going around. The weird thing is, for months and years after Joey died, every once in a while, somebody would still get kidnapped. The moves seemed the same, but they obviously couldn't have been orchestrated by my brother. That just made the urban legend stronger.

One thing I've always wondered about is if I'd known sooner, what would I have done? I never would've wanted to take part even if Joey wanted me to. But,,what if Al Hicks had come to me and asked me about it: if he'd said, "Hey, Vinnie, Joey is betraying our life." Even though I loved Joey, how long would I have been able to evade the inevitable? I'm not sure. Why did my brother put me in this position?

The Nappers met up at a diner to plan the move on Tommy Marra. "How are you all doin' with the money?"

Higgins hardly looked at him. "I'm okay, Joey, you hang on to it."

Rusty shrugged. "You been payin' all our expenses. We ain't gamblin' or drinkin' any, so we're good."

Joey saw through this but nodded as if he believed it. "I'm making a change of plans. Our next target is gonna be tough to snatch. He's a boss, and there's always someone around him. I'll need a little time with this one. But, it'll be well worth the wait, believe me."

"If it's gonna be a while, maybe we can go back South. No

sense stayin' around here if we're not gonna move. We weren't home for the holidays, you know?"

Joey had figured they would volunteer this and smiled across the table at Higgins, who chimed in, "I didn't know you Southern boys celebrated the holidays."

After the Miller brothers left, Joey and Higgins went out to the car, where Joey grabbed a bag from the trunk and handed it to Higgins. "It's yours. I don't want to hang on to it." Rusty and Ronnie were spending some time at Hallandale Beach in Florida, at the Gulfstream Racetrack, blowing money in the company of two girls they'd picked up in a strip club. Bobby Collins and a few of his friends were down there for the season doing some bookmaking. Though Bobby had come up in Hell's Kitchen in Jerry Shay's organization, he was close to the Bronx crew that dealt junk out of the Continental Club. Dressed in a sporty blazer and white pants with matching vinyl belt, he looked like the embodiment of the Sunshine State good life.

He asked his companion, Mike Tuna, if he recognized the two rednecks dropping some serious coin at the betting windows. But, Mike said he'd never met them.

Bobby couldn't place them. Since he didn't want to approach them blind, he and Mike slid over to the bench where the Miller brothers were comparing notes.

"Go bet the five horse, baby, to win. Maybe you can change our luck. Take a shot, easy as a piss off a Pier Six, like Joey would say. Right, Rusty?"

As Rusty laughed at this, Ronnie turned back to the girl. "Your girlfriend there ain't doin' too well for Big Brother."

Rusty's girl disagreed and snapped back, "Then talk to Big Brother. He's the one picking all the horses."

Since Ronnie was about to hit her, she headed off to the betting window with her friend. While they were gone, Rusty asked, "How much we got left at home?"

"Well, thank the lord we gave some to Mrs. Miller. We must have about sixty left."

"We better call Ma when we get back to the room. The call

we're expectin' should be comin' soon. You know Ma, she's gettin' forgetful lately."

Bobby approached Rusty with a broad grin. "You're the Miller boys. We were in Atlanta together, remember? It's Bobby, Bobby Collins. Boy, I been sitting over there trying to figure out who you were."

"Oh, sure, Bobby, how are ya? Fuck, I thought you was a friend'a that big bald cocksucker for a minute."

"Hey, you guys knew Joey Rendino when you were in the joint, right?"

"Oh, yeah, he'd vouch for us. So what're you doin' in town?"

Rusty was feeling friendly, but Ronnie was thinking that they might be able to hit Bobby up for a loan they'd never pay back. If not, they could always take him hostage; maybe Armondo or one of those other *guidos* would pay for him. If not, Bobby could feed the alligators.

While Carole was back in town, she stopped by the New York office, where Laura was still working. Carole had made sure that even if she stayed in Paris, Stephen would keep Laura on.

When Laura saw her, she looked upset.

"What's wrong, Laura?"

"You're here about the article, right?" she said to her old boss.

"I was in the country, and just wanted to say hi. What are you talking about?"

"The newspaper article Charlie Knickerbocker wrote?"

"Laura, I've been up to my neck in formulas, and you want me to read a newspaper?"

Frustrated, Laura flipped through the pages and held up the paper so that Carole could see a headline screaming: "KILLER SCENT!"

Just below it, in bold print: "Who is the New York mob figure who had a cologne made just for him?"

"Will it be JUST for him? Word's out that a world famous cosmetic company is very interested. BANG! BANG! BANG!"

Carole looked up. "Stephen! That bastard…"

"He knew all along. He played on your passion, and he was

right. You created something wonderful, but CFF owns it. It was their lab, their ingredients, and you were on their time."

Carole stormed into Stephen's office waving the newspaper. "What the fuck is this all about? This is mine, Stephen, this is personal. This is Just Joey. It was never meant to be commercialized."

As mad as Carole was, Stephen was completely calm. "Carole, you're young, you're exceptionally talented. But you don't own it. Anything created in this building belongs to CFF. For you, it was about love. For CFF, it's all about business. And a major cosmetic and perfume company already bought it."

Carole turned to storm out.

"Carole, don't worry… you'll get your bonus."

"You don't want to know where you can put your bonus, Stephen."

Carole wasn't the only person who read the article. In the Bronx, Louie Dee had seen the column, and it sparked his memory. He stopped up Dominick's club and talked to Nappi and JoJo.

"Look, I don't know if this means anything, but my kid said something about a phone conversation he heard through the walls."

"What did he hear?"

"This motherfucker was talkin' to a broad named Karen, Carrie, something like that. He was sayin' things about makin' cologne, and her surprising somebody. The kid was in another room, but this rat bastard spoke pretty loud."

JoJo leaned in. "I talked to Pete Sessa this morning. He said he heard one of them call the other 'Big Brother,' and he knows it wasn't the shine talking."

"So we got three guys at least, maybe four. One's black, two are brothers, and Danny Reedy fits in there somewhere."

CHAPTER THIRTY-THREE

It's a funny thing about closure. I've learned so much over the years about what my brother did. Too much of it horrifies me, even now. I wish I knew for sure where Joey's body was, so that I had a place to visit to go see him. I'll never know where. Because that's the way it is. It was nothing anybody was ever going to talk about around me, and obviously I couldn't ask.

I just know that to go after a guy like Joey, they had to be sure. There had to be real, hard evidence that he was definitely involved. Armondo and Al Hicks cared about Joey too much. They wouldn't have done it on just rumors and innuendos.

Joey was at the Bronxville house with Carole, but things were moving quickly. While Carole was asleep, he made a call to Higg. He tried to keep quiet and not wake her up. After he hung up, he walked into the bedroom just as she woke up in a cold sweat.

"What's wrong, Carole? You're drenched."

"I had a bad dream. It was about you and Danny. All in black, he was pulling you into a house. But, inside the house, there was nothing—only a deep, dark hole. Oh, Joey, I got such a bad feeling. Please, let's go away, anywhere."

"You had a nightmare, we all have them. Tomorrow, you'll forget all about it. Go back to sleep."

"Why won't you listen to me? Why won't you accept what I'm feeling? You're making light of it because you're feeling it, too. Goddammit, Joey, there's something wrong."

"Trust me, nothing's gonna happen. There's not a thing wrong. Believe me, you'll get over this."

"Bullshit. I'll get over nothing. My feelings don't lie."

Though Carole had never been to any of the social clubs Joey frequented, when she was younger, she'd snuck a peek once or twice into clubs on the block. Her dream that night took her inside a club much like the Continental Club; her subconscious did a pretty good job imagining it. She saw several faces she didn't recognize in the crowd, and somebody she couldn't see was holding her back. She couldn't get to Joey.

She stretched out her arm, getting closer and closer to him, but always being held back. He floated in the air for a moment and said, "Goodbye, Carole," and then was dragged backwards, disappearing into the crowd. With all her strength, she leapt towards him, unable to touch him. At that point, she woke up.

By then, Joey had fallen asleep, and she didn't want to wake him. Carole stayed in bed the rest of the night, trying in vain to fall back asleep; trying even harder and even more in vain to forget the dreams that had been plaguing her for the past week. They were never quite the same, but they always involved either Joey or her brother or both. And they always ended with her feeling the same way—empty and lonely.

Carole's dream wasn't totally off base. Devious forces were at work. Bobby Collins and Sally Fat owned two of the faces she didn't recognize in her dream. In reality, they were meeting up at the Continental, taking a walk to discuss some news.

As they strolled Sally said, "I know you still owe some time. My fuckin' joint's been hot these past weeks, so you can't go talkin' in there."

"I understand. I wanted you to know this. I met these two fuckin' whacko brothers while I was down in Florida. I was in the can with them in Atlanta. When they moved to Leavenworth, they hooked up with Joey Rendino..."

Years later, I put all this together, piecing what was told to Frankie and what Al told me as he lay dying.

Things started to move fast after that. Joey and Higgins met up, because Higgins had been watching Tommy Marra and discovered a few weaknesses. And, Sally took the information Bobby had given him over to Armondo's. When they got there, they saw cars parked down the block that were obviously FBI. Sally made sure his face couldn't be seen in any pictures as he rushed down the sidewalk.

Al Hicks led Sally into the kitchen where Armondo was waiting. Armondo didn't say anything, letting Al take the angry lead. "Don't you check to see if you're being tailed? I could'a spotted them fuckin' agents from the Triborough Bridge, for Christ's sake."

"We lost the agents that were trailing us. The car you spotted was here when we got here."

Armondo waved Al off. "Hey, fuck the agents. We been living with them for years, they're here to stay. If what you people're here to tell me today is true, it's gonna tarnish us all. That's why we have to be sure, and we gotta know everything. Now, listen to me very carefully. Whatever we discuss today is not to be repeated outside this room. And most important, if you run into him, you must act as you've always acted towards him. Now, Sally, let's start with you..."

Higgins and Joey met at the zoo the next day. "The brothers are back. When did they call, Higg?"

"Right before I called you. They said to tell you they got the message yesterday. Are we ready to go on this?"

"No, we're not ready. That wacky mother of theirs must've given them the wrong message."

"Fuckin' rednecks. You think maybe their father could be their grandpa, too?"

Joey laughed. "Higg, sometimes you can be a cruel bastard."

"Joey, seriously, why not just kill these two assholes and fuck the next move? I got enough money. You can keep my end; let's just end it."

"Higg, you know it's not about the money, m'man. On this move, we're gonna take the greedy cocksucker's money, then we're gonna send him and the rednecks on their last journey."

"Okay, but this is it. We pack it in after this move."

Joey just nodded, and Higgins assumed he was agreeing.

CHAPTER THIRTY-FOUR

Al Hicks came by the deli. We talked for a little while; it was like he was feeling me out on something. I thought he was going to try to get a piece of the register; it never came up. Still, I knew what was on Al's mind. We talked about people we knew; we talked about the Life; we talked about Joey. He even mentioned Joey's cologne and asked if it was made specifically for him. He passed along a message for Joey and asked if I would drive my brother to the new spot for the crap game. Then, he said something that always stuck with me. In the language of the street, you never say anything direct.

Al said, "I heard it's getting harder to find fresh tomatoes."

I answered, "I haven't had any trouble yet."

"Well, you've been lucky, then. You start havin' any problems, let me know. I can help you out."

Bobby Collins got close to Ronnie and Rusty, hanging out with them in a cheesy strip joint on Queens Boulevard. The boys were cheap dates.

He set up a move to hit someone he said would be an easy target. He showed them the house that they'd have to hit, and then drove them back to their motel room by the Whitestone Bridge. "I know he scored some shit last week. I figure we move in a few days. Give him some time to make his moves and collect his money."

After dropping them off, Bobby headed to the Bronx to see Sally. Given all the surveillance, Armondo and his driver took Al Hicks and Dominick for a drive to a secluded street where they could talk without being recorded. "You do the work on the brothers, Dom. Use whoever you want. Joey is mine. Me and

Al brought him into this life, and we'll take him out. You gonna have to make a decision on Philly, Al."

"Yeah, and what about Frankie? And Vinnie?"

Al shook his head. "Vinnie was on the lam when all this mess started, and then he went to the can. This kid's heart's gonna bust open, but he's true to our world. And Frankie? Forget it; he never leaves the club or the block. Joey would never involve him."

"So, just Joey?"

They all nodded somberly. Armondo welled up with genuine emotion. "I love Joey more than a brother. You too, Al—you, too."

Back in East Harlem in the apartment above the Pioneer, Joey was ranting about the job Nadine Chiaro had done cleaning our place: "Now you know why I never pay anybody in advance, Vin! Does this place look like it was cleaned yesterday? C'mere, go look at how she made the bed! I tell ya, I love Frankie, but the whole family's fucked up. I don't know who's crazier, the sister, the brother with that damn dog, or Frankie."

"His brother Swifty is some piece of work. It was a show this morning, Joey. Swifty's got a new dog, so he's training him."

"Training him to what, shit in front of the club?" They both laughed. "I hear you're expanding. Business must be good."

"Better than I ever expected. I'm gonna start catering soon. Rosemarie and her mother wanna do the cooking, so I figure, why not?"

"Well, take it from me, don't advertise it. Things are not too good with some of the deadbeats in our mob."

I hadn't told Joey that Big V Deli had already been hit up by a few deadbeats looking for a free meal. "Hey, fuck them. Let them go break their asses like I been breakin' mine this past year."

"Ah, now you're gettin' it. But, if your skipper tells you to help some of our friends, what are you gonna do? Hey, speaking of which, what did Al say when he stopped by?"

"He wants me to pick you up and bring you to the new spot for the crap game. He said to tell you the guy from the brownstone is gonna be there too. I'll pick you up about eleven."

"Oh, that's good news. Maybe we could start movin' with this guy. This time, I'll make sure you earn, Vinnie. As much as I despise some of our so-called friends, we got no choice. We have to deal with them."

"Hey, it's getting' late. I gotta get back. Where do you want me to pick you up?"

"I'll meet you in front of Carole's apartment."

Bobby met up with the Millers at their motel room. He'd gotten them set up in a different place, so neither Higgins nor Joey could find them. The Millers weren't suspicious; Bobby was another New York jerk-off they'd met in the joint, just like Joey. They didn't think much about it. The plan seemed sound. After Bobby drove them to the house where they were supposed to kidnap the dealer, they were buzzed in. Then Bobby led them through a foyer.

When they reached the end of the foyer, they were pounced upon from behind and quickly disarmed. They were hit with lead pipes on the knees and arms. These guys took their time. Nobody in the room had any respect for the Millers, outsiders who'd busted into the family business. Bobby was trying to prove himself, thinking he might be able to step up to the big time if this went well for him. He cut off both of Ronnie's ears with Rusty's knife. The crew continued the dismemberment for hours.

Rusty was the first to die. Ronnie was coughing up blood. Bobby held the others back. "You see what happens, you redneck cocksucker?"

Ronnie looked up at Bobby, stared for a beat, then spit blood right in his eye. That got him more beatings. He wound up in a body bag next to his brother, dumped in the garbage in back. That was the last anyone saw of the Miller brothers.

Across town, Joey was having dinner with Carole at Luchow's.

"We can't be with each other, Joey, but we can't walk away, either. All you had to do was marry me. Then, nothing else would have mattered."

"Carole, far and above the best thing I ever did my whole life was not to marry you. I told you you'd have to be the one to walk away. As much as you feel for me, and I know how much you do, your first passion is your work. So, go do what you gotta do."

"I'm so happy you decided not to use your car tonight, Joey."

"Why?"

"Did you ever get laid in the backseat of a cab?"

"You know, you really are a crazy kid."

Since it was a nice night, they held off on the cab and walked up 14th Street, where Joey made a stop at a flower shop just getting ready to close. "What flowers would you suggest I buy for a crazy girl?"

The old lady looked to Carole. "She would only enhance any flower she gets. But, I just cut some fresh gardenias. The scent is quite lovely…"

When the taxi stopped in front of Carole's building, she begged him to spend the night. "You made tonight so special, let's not end it. Don't go to your appointment later."

"It's important. It's Armondo. I have to go. I'm being picked up in a few minutes."

"Please call me later. I don't care if it's late. I just want to hear from you. Promise!"

"Don't worry. Everything is fine."

"Promise."

"I'll call. Good night, you beautiful, crazy kid."

Carole put all her love and charm into the goodnight kiss, trying with everything she could muster to get Joey to come upstairs. She couldn't save Danny, but she wanted to save Joey. In the end, she broke off the kiss, and walked away.

CHAPTER THIRTY-FIVE

I pulled up in front of Carole's apartment a little before 11:00 that night. Joey was still watching her as she entered the lobby. I sensed his uneasiness as we drove up First Avenue towards the Willis Avenue Bridge. "Vin," he told me, "a long time ago, I said you weren't born for this life. Well, now I know I was wrong."

I didn't answer. He knew I understood. I remember every detail of that night: How Joey looked after he saw Carole step into the elevator. How he looked at me. Life is full of what ifs. What if I didn't do this? What if I did do that? We could "what if" ourselves to death. You wake up in the morning, and you play the day as you would any game—as best you can. I recall my friend Jamesy's old man Aldo telling us when we were kids. He spoke to us in Italian, but I'll translate.

He said, "Hey, you two stupid bastards. Don't try to be heroes because heroes die. And, remember one thing. When you die, everybody dies. Think about it."

Talking to Carole had put Joey on edge about the coming meet. "When did Al tell you about this meet?"

"I told you, he stopped into the deli yesterday."

"Who was he with?"

"What's the matter, Joey, is something wrong?"

"Let's see how many cars are parked in front of the joint before you let me off." Joey was always cautious. He knew how things went, which is why he was so observant on his own. And, he schooled me the same way. If somebody had a beef, Joey would tell me, something they're willing to kill over, they can't just do it. At the very least, Armondo would have to approve. And, he knew that if Armondo did approve, Al Hicks would be involved.

There'd been a few times in his life when Joey thought something might be coming down. The first time, he ran a deal with Marty Lester on the side and didn't cut Armondo in, he'd walked on eggshells for weeks. When Armondo called him in for a private sit-down, Joey wasn't sure he was ever coming back. You never knew what kind of rumors could get started. Look at what had happened to Gino the Zip, all based on bullshit talk.

There were times when my brother saw Al Hicks looking at him a certain way before they went out together on a job, making Joey wonder if this was the night something might happen. He wouldn't have known why, but he'd been on the other side of the gun often enough to know that the poor soul doesn't always know why he's being taken out.

Joey knew he'd be with somebody he trusted when it happened; that was always the way. Al Hicks or Sonny Gold a few months back… and now here I was, driving him to the meeting. Joey didn't know what to think. It could be that something was coming, and I knew about it. It could be that Al Hicks was just using me. Or, it could be going down exactly like Al said.

When we rounded the corner, we saw four cars parked outside. I pulled up to the loft slowly. "That's Philly. Who's the other guy?" I asked Joey.

"That's Tommy Marra's driver." He turned to me to give me some final words of wisdom, just in case. "Never ever let your guard down, Vin. This fuckin' life of ours is treacherous. Sometimes what you're lookin' at isn't really what you're seeing. I love you, kid, and I respect you. Always remember that."

Seeing Joey's apprehension, I tried to console him, "Joey, fuck this, and fuck this meeting. Whatever it's about, don't go. I'll tell 'em I couldn't get in touch with you. Go away. I'll go with you. I'll meet you, wherever."

Even before I finished this sentence, I know how Joey would respond. "Vinnie, where the fuck would I go? You know I can't live any other life."

I saw Joey giving me a sidelong glance, maybe wondering if I was in on the plan. He couldn't ask me, of course, because that would be a sign of mistrust between us. And, in terms of blood family, we had each other, period.

Joey knew I would never betray him. I couldn't. He knew my conscience—and I did have one—would never rest if I did.

But, if I hadn't betrayed him, Joey's suspicions might tarnish his memory forever—even thinking about a double-cross on my part. Besides, Joey didn't really believe anything was coming. Deep down, he felt he was just being paranoid.

Joey took a last look at me, as if he was memorizing my face. Then, he got out of the car after insisting that I get on the road. I didn't feel I had a choice; still, I felt sick in the very pit of my stomach.

Philly led Joey inside. Al, Dom, and Sally Fat were all waiting, keeping up the pretense of the meet. Louie Dee was planning on bursting out of the bathroom with a six-inch spike and a lump hammer. Al actually admitted this to me after the fact—with a guilty conscience of his own, maybe. He'd known me and Joey all our lives.

Al approached Joey. "How do you like it, buddy? It's a nice space, huh?"

"Where's Sonny and Tommy?"

"They'll be here a little later. I wanted to talk to you alone first. Sit down here, have some coffee."

Joey scanned the room, looking from Dom to Sal, but talking to Al the whole time. "Alone? These two mutts don't even tell me hello. You got these two guardin' the door, and you tryin' to put me at ease? Al, a man only dies once. So, what the fuck are you waiting for?"

They all took turns trying to break Joey, except Philly, who watched the door but wanted no part in it. Louie came out of the bathroom waving the spike around; by then, Joey had already moved on. He'd let himself go. His body was still there breathing, but he was past the point of pain. They held him down and Louie held the spike against his skull, raised the lump hammer above his head, and POUNDED.

CHAPTER THIRTY-SIX

Carole called Joey's club every fifteen minutes, and she probably called my apartment too; but I was waiting around the Pioneer, so I wouldn't know. I wanted to get some word just as bad as she did, but I told Frankie not to give me the phone. I didn't have anything to tell her that she'd want to hear.

At that time, I was burning inside to know who was involved in killing my brother. But, in our way of life, we never ask. We have to let it go. There's no such thing as closure. Sometime after Joey was gone for a while, people would come up to me and shake my hand, knowing that Joey was gone but never mentioning it, because nobody was supposed to know. Even though we knew that they did know, they weren't supposed to say so. That's part of the bullshit of this life.

Al Hicks, who I know loved me like a kid brother, very rarely mentioned Joey. We had one private conversation prior to Al getting sick. I told Al that I understood why Joey had to go.

Al spoke to me because he wanted to assure me that none of this reflected on me. I knew it was bullshit because Joey was my brother: how could it not reflect on me?

A few months later, Carole got ready to say her final goodbyes to New York. Much of the furniture and other things around the Bronxville house had been donated to the Sisters of Charity, which saved Carole the trouble of sorting everything. She'd taken a few boxes of things that would be shipped out to Paris, along with the suitcase with the broken handle.

She stopped off at Reedy's Pub, bringing a few documents for Spike to sign. After he had signed them, officially becoming the owner of the Pub, she slid over the suitcase. "Here's the blood money Joey left behind for me, Spike. You know what I want you to do with it."

She took a limo over to our old place on 105th. On the phone, Carole'd said that she wanted to see me one last time before flying back to Paris.

"You know, Vin, in all my years with Joey, I've never come to this apartment. I guess the last time I was in East Harlem was when I threw that towel at Joey in the Pioneer."

She smiled but caught herself. "I'm so happy you still have this place. All things considered, you can understand why the Bronxville house couldn't go to you. It's in the process of being sold. That money will go to the Sisters, Vin. Are you okay with it?"

"Absolutely, Carole—Joey would've wanted it that way. Let me ask, what about the Pub?"

"All the legal paperwork's done. I left it all to Spike. I'm sure he'll find the means to renovate the mess that Danny left." She dug into her purse and pulled out an envelope. "Here's my Paris address and phone number."

She stared into my eyes and held her hand against my cheek. Just for a moment, she could see Joey in me, and she smiled. "You were always like a brother to me, Vin. And, I love you as much as I loved Danny."

I had to break off eye contact. I watched her walk around the place, taking it all in.

"I was wondering if you wouldn't mind…"

"Take all the time you need, Carole. I'll just wait outside."

I stepped out. Before she left for good, Carole told me how she'd relished the shelves full of paperback Shakespeare, flipping through the books and seeing the passages he'd underlined. She saw a line she'd always liked in *A Midsummer Night's Dream*, "Love looks not with the eyes but with the mind."

In the closet, she took in the way jackets were hung, arranged by color. She saw how clean he'd kept his bathroom. She saw the way he'd folded even his underpants perfectly. And there, at the dresser, she looked up and saw the bottle of "Just Joey," still about a third of the way full. Carole hadn't been sure how long it had been there or how long it would last; now she knew it had turned into a lifetime supply. She stood there and stared at the bottle.

Since I was right outside the door, I heard her say, "You're right, Joey—I'm doing exactly what you would've wanted."

Outside, I waved goodbye to her. "Have a safe trip. You know I'm gonna keep in touch."

After Carole had gotten into the limo and shut the door, almost immediately, I went over to knock on her window. She rolled it down.

"The show's about to start, Carole…"

When I stepped to one side, she could see Swifty walking down the street with his dog. Frankie was outside with a broom, already cursing before they'd even crossed the street. But, Swifty kept walking calmly, saying nothing. Frankie got confused, stopped talking, and lowered the broom.

Swifty leaned in close and spoke to his brother. We couldn't hear what was said, but Frankie burst into tears, and Swifty quickly joined him. They embraced as they hadn't for years. Though neither man ever revealed what Swifty had said, they would both admit that Joey's death had prompted the reconciliation. Swifty knew the pain Frankie was going through. On that day, he came to him as a brother.

As the hug broke off, Swifty looked down and saw his dog taking a shit. He tried to stop him, but it was too late. When he looked up, Frankie was sweeping the shit into the gutter. The two men petted the dog, then took him inside to give him some water.

Carole started to tear up. "You know, Vinnie, it's wonderful to see things change for the better, but it's also wonderful how some things always stay the same."

CHAPTER THIRTY-SEVEN

I learned many things as the years went by. But, Marty Lester, Joey's dear friend and confidante, shook my world up big time after Joey was gone. What he revealed was that my mother's name was Ida Bello. She was born out of wedlock to a Jewish girl from Forsythe Street on the Lower East Side named Shirley Doffinsky. Marty's mother arranged for my grandmother to take the baby. In East Harlem, only the Aurelios knew.

I never knew my mother, but Joey always said he remembered her well. His memories were vivid. He told me about a trip to the Lower East Side, when she took him to meet a woman who was a waitress in Ratner's Restaurant. She took some money out of her apron and put it in Joey's pocket. She was our grandmother. And, from what Marty tells me, she was Jewish.

Joey once told me about the day I was born. He remembered the midwife, how happy my father was, and how my mother looked after giving birth to me. Joey remembered getting into the bed next to me and my mother. It was the only time I ever saw him cry. We were in the orphanage at the time—he told me he could still smell my mother whenever he was close to me. How can I not still love him?

As a few months went by, things got quiet. Word got out that the Nappers no longer existed. There was still trouble in mob-land because of new indictments coming down and all the other bullshit on the street. A lot of people were trying to stay under the radar.

Armondo was trying, too. Ever since his heart attack, he hadn't been at his restaurant as much as he used to be. After the stuff with Joey, he stayed home a lot. But, he still liked to start the day right by cooking himself a big breakfast every morning. His driver never came to pick him up before 11 a.m.

As Armondo was about to sit down one morning, the doorbell rang. When he looked out the peephole, he saw a delivery man with a big cardboard box. He opened the door.

The man held out a clipboard for Armondo's signature. "Manna?"

"It's Mahn-na, not man-nuh."

"Sure thing! Sign here, okay?"

Armondo looked up from the clipboard and saw a tattoo on the man's arm: a heart with a dagger through it. "I see your tattoo—were you a sailor?"

"I was a Navy SEAL for four years, but I'm out. I'm trying to raise a family now."

"Good for you, son." Armondo signed his name. He hadn't been expecting a package, so he looked at the return address on the label. He figured it was tribute from somebody trying to impress him.

"From Joey Rendino." His eyes widened as he realized his fate.

The delivery man raised his gun and shot Armondo right between the eyes. He picked up the box and, at a fast pace, walked back to the van, drove away, then abandoned the vehicle a few miles away. He got into a car that had been left for him courtesy of Lester Motors. He still had the money he'd been given in his possession. He wasn't sure why Spike had given it to him in a suitcase with a broken handle, but it was good enough for him.

People from all over the city came for Armondo's funeral. There were even some out-of-towners in attendance. Four guys flew all the way from Italy to pay their respects. Even the Boys of Forever came out; they didn't like some of the business Armondo was involved in, but they respected the Life.

After the funeral, the hierarchy of the family went to Villa Armondo for a meet. There was much confusion because nobody knew what had happened, or why, or who was involved. Things had to be sorted out. They didn't know if this was another family's doing or an internal struggle. Even after he was gone, Joey stirred the shit.

As much as Carole was different from Joey, in many ways she was just like him. She took the suitcase Joey had given her and plotted and planned methodically, as he would have. She made sure Spike knew what to do with it and with whom. Carole made sure Joey's business was settled from the grave.

After all was said and done, she didn't ever really get away. She was a street girl after all.

CHAPTER THIRTY-EIGHT

When I think about my brother Joey, I remember all the private discussions we had, most of them about our world—how it was deteriorating and changing, like the neighborhood we'd lived in all our lives. Our patch of Upper Manhattan was like a chameleon changing its colors; morphing into something completely different—a foreign country.

During these conversations, Joey was always telling me what to do and how to act: my apprenticeship never ended, even when he was treating me like an equal in the Life.

He would say to me, "Always be respectful and never show weakness. If you ever have a problem with another wise guy, let him make the beef. It will only make you look stronger in the eyes of the powers that be. And, it will give you an edge if there is ever a sit-down."

Even if I didn't always understand completely what he was trying to convey, later on I realized that in his roundabout way, Joey was trying to tell me that he wouldn't always be around.

Word got to me that my name came up concerning Armondo's death. People thought I may have been involved with it in some way. When somebody of Armondo's stature is taken out without anybody knowing who or why, questions get asked. Naturally, I was being looked at. Al Hicks stood up for me big-time and calmed everybody's fears. That's why I'm still here today to tell this story. It's hard not to take the death of your brother personally, but I had to let it go. As much as I loved Joey, he deserved what he got. He tarnished our name beyond repair for what he believed in. I know—I've had to live with it all my life.

Frankie was still with me then. And, Swifty still came by

with his dog. Instead of bringing Italian pastries, he now brings Dunkin' Donuts.

I once belonged to a life that played like a beautiful symphony orchestra. Now, I belong to a life that plays like an orchestra with all sour notes. I gotta admit, even surviving is a triumph.

One of my strongest memories of my brother is of the day he walked into my deli one morning at about 9:00. There was a good-sized line on this bitter cold day. When I looked out from the back of the kitchen, I watched my brother rub his hands together and stomp his feet on the floor, trying to warm up. That morning, Nadine was behind the counter handling orders. I heard her tell Joey that I was in the kitchen somewhere.

"Damn, I could feel the floor vibrating when you stamped your feet!" I said as I hugged him the way brothers do—a little roughneck.

Since Joey always dressed to the nines, I had to break his balls first about his shoes.

"Hey, it's freezing out, what's with the thin socks with those fancy Italian shoes?"

"You dope, you wear heavy socks with shoes like this, you look like a *cafone*." As usual, my immaculately turned out brother had to lecture me about my clothes.

"Yeah, sure, Joey, I'm gonna wear a custom-made shirt here to dish out egg and bacon sandwiches on a roll…" I pointed to my greasy, splattered apron for emphasis.

Just as I was about to call a truce by pouring my brother a cup of coffee, John Lupo of Lupo's Bakery came in through the back door with the muffins and other morning pastries.

"Sorry I'm late, Vin!" he called out from behind a towering pile of bakery boxes. "One of my bakers didn't show up. I've been up all night filling in, and now I'm the delivery boy on top of it."

For whatever reason, Joey had a soft spot for John Lupo, a kind and pleasant man. After John left, my brother's demeanor went from joking and jovial to deadly serious.

I went out front to check the bread. John had left the receipt at the cash register; I made sure he got paid before he left.

Back in the kitchen, Joey was sitting, sipping his coffee. He looked at me with piercing eyes and said, "Vinnie, who are the men of honor and tradition?"

"What do you mean," I asked as I refilled his cup with fresh brew.

"John Lupo is a man of tradition and honor," Joey said. "Santo is a man of tradition and honor. Tino the butcher is a man of tradition and honor. The men who work all night in the markets are men of tradition and honor. How can we not respect men like Santo, with all that he does? He took a fifty-seat neighborhood restaurant and transformed it into a crown jewel of Italian restaurants."

Joey stopped to look around my kitchen, as if to say silently, "Vin, you've made it. You're outta the Life, with a legit place that's all yours. I'm so proud of you."

Even if Joey didn't say it, I knew that's what he felt. He honored men who worked their asses off so their families could live better than they did growing up. If their kids went astray, it wasn't their fault.

"Our father was a man of honor and traditions. Mel Lester always talked about how hard he worked. He wanted both of us to go to college and get a good education. The poor fuck killed himself working."

Then, my brother stood up and put his hand on my shoulder. "Vinnie, you can be a man of honor and tradition in a way I never will."

Joey walked out before I could respond; I didn't chase after him. I brushed it off, telling myself that Joey was just being Joey.

But, I was wrong. He was reaching out. Maybe he wanted me to dig deeper, to find the real Joey.

I'll never know.

CHAPTER THIRTY-NINE

Eventually I'd had it with "unorganized" crime in East Harlem. After Armondo's death, things really fell apart at the seams. By the time Big V had been robbed at gunpoint twice, I was ready to pull up stakes and move the business to Arthur Avenue in the Bronx, where it still draws crowds, thank God. My son Joseph kept the old-time feeling but also introduced enough new dishes to keep them coming in. It was my son's idea to get into the off-premises catering business. I still work behind the counter and help with the ordering a few days a week. The deli and catering business is a young man's game. I regret the fact that Joseph never got to meet his uncle and namesake. I kept the facts of Joey's death under wraps, of course. Even I didn't know how it had gone down until the day I had an unexpected encounter in a most surprising place.

"Conscience does make cowards of us all." For me, this partial quote from *Hamlet* is about the inner voice that keeps haunting day after day, night after night: the guilt that never ends, eating the soul the way a cancer destroys the body.

About a year and a half after Joey disappeared, I was putting up a good front, even if I was ripped apart inside. Yeah, I missed my brother; but I was also furious with him.

Why, Joey? Why, I kept asking? I knew it wasn't only about the money.

I found some solace at St. Lucy's on 104th Street, where I started going every Sunday, always towards the end of the ten o'clock mass. I'd wait for people to leave before I lit a candle to St. Anthony. My father Antonio was named in his honor. I'd say a prayer, leave money in the poor box, then go back to the Pioneer. It became a ritual.

One cool Sunday morning in November, close to Thanksgiving, I walked into the church as usual. It was almost empty except for the few elders who always stayed behind to pray. Strangely, on that day, I saw a large black man in the back with his head down as if he were praying. I admired the saddle-colored, three quarter length suede jacket he was wearing. I walked by him as I approached the statue to light a candle in the way I usually did.

As I headed for the exit, he was still there with his head down. I was about to pass him when I heard him call my name softly, "Hello, Vinnie." Though he didn't startle me, I felt a shiver go through my entire body as I looked at him.

My instincts kicked in: I looked around the entire church before I turned back to him and asked, "Do we know each other?"

"I know you, Vinnie. I've known about you for a long time; but no, you don't know me. At least I don't know that you do."

I looked him right in the eye and said, "What do you want from me?"

He answered in a very soft voice: "What say we go to the Bronx Zoo and talk? We'll say hello to the lions."

I was stunned, and he could see it.

He said, "Look, Vinnie, I didn't come here to do any harm. I just want to talk to you. I'm alone." He opened his jacket. "I'm not heavy," he continued, indicating that he wasn't carrying a piece.

"I wanna tell you about what went down with Joey—about all the things he told me about you." The big man paused but continued to speak in a soft voice that seemed out of context from his physical self.

"He loved ya, but it's up to you. If you want, I'll go. You'll never see me again. Your call…."

He knew he had me. "Where's your car?" I asked.

He smiled. "Right outside the church."

On the way to the zoo, we stopped at a diner. From a telephone booth outside, I called the club and then Rosemarie to tell her I was busy—that she could go ahead and eat without me. Sunday dinner was an all-day affair at our house. I made sure this guy heard everything. By now, I'd figured out that he must be the one Joey'd talked about, the black guy who'd provided my brother with "cover" in Leavenworth. It had to be the man Joey called Higg. He'd said Higg had a build like a Mack truck and a good heart.

When I went to the phone booth, I asked the man with skin the color of a midnight sky to come with me. He understood why I wanted him to hear what I was saying and to whom.

Once I'd finished my phone calls, he held out his hand. "I know you're everything Joey said you were."

I looked into his eyes as I shook his hand and saw the hurt and sorrow there. Before we entered the diner, he asked, "Are you good with this place?"

It was a typical Greek diner, the kind you found in every New York neighborhood. It was Sunday. Italians never eat in diners on Sunday: They're too busy getting ready for the type family dinners I had waiting for me. I was certain there was no one I knew in there.

When the counterman waved to him, I knew Higgins had been there before. "I'm okay," I assured the guy behind the counter.

My brother had never referred to Clarence Higgins as a shine, as we called most black people in those days; he always talked about him with a great deal of respect. He told me that Higgins was one of the nicest, toughest SOBs Joey'd ever met. He said he was a stand-up guy and wished he had more people around him like that. Joey spoke about him whenever he was reminiscing. Then again, he spoke about many people. Though I didn't pay much attention in those days, I remembered the big black guy.

We took a booth at the far end of the diner. Politely, Higgins motioned for the waitress to come over to remove some napkins and a few crumbs left on the table.

"Sorry for the mess!" she said. She cleaned up as we both sat quietly watching her. Higgins said nothing until she'd finished cleaning and took our order.

"So you know who I am? I figured you would. You probably knew back in the church."

I was taken by his gentle demeanor; it didn't seem to fit a stone cold killer. Then again, couldn't the same have been said of

Joey? Now, I understood why they'd gotten along so well.

After the waitress filled our mugs with coffee, I asked her to hold off on the food. She was a good-looking woman of about fifty with a slim figure.

I heard myself say out loud, "She can't be Italian."

Higgins laughed. "I was just thinking about how my girl is gonna look when she gets to be that age."

As I look back now, I must have just been trying to ease the tension—not his, but mine. He went on, "Vinnie, I got lots to say. I hope you got the time right now, 'cause we may never see each other again. If you don't mind I'm going to start from the beginning." He suggested we go to the Bronx Zoo, where he and Joey did their planning and talking.

"You don't want to eat first?" I asked him.

He said no, "There's too much I have to tell ya."

He knew I was chomping at the bit. I was trying not to show any emotion, but it was to no avail. "Tell me everything, Higgins." My voice must have been rising because he looked at me intently.

"Calm down, bro," he said. "I know what you're feeling."

My heart was racing in my chest: "How the fuck can you know what I'm feeling? He was your friend, but he was my brother—the only one I had." I broke down but quickly composed myself. As I started to apologize, I could see tears streaming down his face. We were both silent for a few minutes.

Then he said, "Vinnie, your brother told me if ever I needed something or someone to talk to, I should come find you. He said you would never double bang me. Let me start with when Joey came up to Mt. Vernon after he left you on his last day with us. I was holding a big chunk of money for him, but it wasn't only the money he came for. I think he came to tell me goodbye. Looking back, I guess my instincts were right."

He leaned across the table. "I'm going to tell you everything because I don't want you to doubt who your brother was. I still got my ear to the wall. Some people I know still do business with Louie Dee and Sally."

I said, "Look, Higgins, what Joey did was wrong. Don't try to justify it."

"I ain't trying to justify anything. All I wanna do is tell you what really went down. You need to know, and I need to tell it." Standing up to his full height, maybe six four, he slapped a fifty dollar bill down on the table. "Let's get the fuck outta here. The food tastes like shit, anyway."

On the way out of the diner, I stopped to take a leak. The coffee'd gone right through me.

Higgins was backing the car out of the parking space as I got to the lot. It was then that I saw the "Lester Motors" logo on the rear bumper of the 1965 Olds Cutlass. Nice, but very inconspicuous.

We were both silent as we drove to the zoo, which was less than ten minutes from the diner on Fordham Road. Needless to say, Higgins knew the neighborhood like the back of his hand. He knew all the side-street short cuts to the zoo's parking lot. The first thing he wanted to see was the lions, one in particular. She was a female he called "Joey's girl."

For a few minutes, we stood watching as she moved back and forth, always keeping her eyes on us. As we walked away, she growled.

I was amazed at how Higgins knew times, dates, and places. He could tell me how methodically Joey'd planned all the nappings. He cursed the Millers. He said they put the bee in Joey's bonnet. He cursed Danny, as he felt he'd double-banged Joey. He cursed himself, but he always praised Joey—which told me how much he and my brother loved each other. It may seem strange, but in a way I felt it was part of why Higgins had come looking for me. I was an extension of Joey.

It was getting late and a bit colder. "Hey, Higg, what ya say we go for a drink and some good food? I'm fuck'n starving."

In a tone full of grief, he answered, "Man, you sound just like your brother."

When we stopped into a small neighborhood restaurant near Bronx Park East, every eye was on us. Though the bar was full, there were only a few people in the dining room.

"Hey, Higg, they must think I'm your drug connection." He laughed.

The owner chef and his wife, the hostess, greeted us warmly

and led us to a quiet table. She said her brother was the waiter, and he'd take good care of us. We thanked her and sat down. Her brother was right behind her. I ordered a Stoli and Higgins asked for a J.D. and ginger ale.

When the waiter came back with the drinks fifteen minutes later, he said, "I forgot to tell ya's, my name is Mario."

He seemed more interested in the football game on the bar's TV than he was in serving us. We kept drinking, and Higgins kept talking. He told me the entire story in the order in which it had unfolded. The drinks made me mellow. I thought they'd have the same effect on him—but no.

Higgins continued his tale of kidnapping, murder, and mayhem in his soft and gentle voice. "Let me finish before we drink any more."

I just nodded—all ears.

"First off, Vinnie, Joey never held the spike to Louie Dee's boy's head. I did."

Higgins looked down into his lap. "Psychologically, I ruined that boy for life. Joey never intended to harm Babe Marsano, either. But, Babe recognized those low-life Miller brothers. We had no choice. It was those redneck bastards who cut him up.

I'm not making excuses: Joey's rage and thirst for vengeance got the best of him. I got caught up in it, too."

He paused and looked over at me. "I'm not free, Vinnie. I'm serving a life sentence. I lost my soul, and then I lost my only son." He began to tear up and looked away from me for a moment.

"How did you lose your boy, Higg?"

"He was killed last month in Nam—only nineteen. I never married his mother, but we always stayed close. This is taking a toll on her, too. I try to act as the strong one. I do the best I can."

Higgins composed himself enough to continue with his story: "Joey said something to me the last time we spoke… I keep on recording it over and over again in my head. He said, 'Higg, too bad we had to hurt the innocent to get to the guilty.' It haunts me. I hurt young Louis Jr. and God is hurting me. He took my son instead of me."

For the next hour, Higgins and I shared many intimate stories about my brother and, of course, Carole—whom Higgins never knew. Joey'd simply told him she was a neighborhood streetwise girl who grew up to become a successful, sophisticated woman. He told me how Joey was a completely different person when he talked about her. She was the love of his life and he of hers.

I knew me and Higgins would be seeing each other again. And, we did meet up several more times at that lion's cage. After all, the story of my brother's life couldn't end with him disappearing into the vapor—not Joey Rendino. Higgins' own story didn't have a happy ending, either. It took him twenty-five long years after we met in the diner and at the zoo for him to drink himself to death. He left this earth a lonely, pathetic soul.

It was Frankie who'd approached me first, about a month after Joey went missing. After he stopped crying, he said, "Vinnie, I gotta show ya something."

He seemed mysterious—so out of character.

"Vin, please come to my apartment with me."

When we got to his place, I said, "Okay, what's so fuck'n important here?"

He took me over to a trap that Benny had built; it was especially well-concealed. After Frankie opened it, he took out a large duffle bag and handed it to me.

"What the hell is this, Frankie? We're not playing hide-and-seek here."

"Joey gave me this the last time I saw him, just before I drove him to Carole's apartment. He said if anything should happen to him, I should give this to you, Vinnie. Then, Joey made me swear never ever tell anyone else about the bag. I never did."

"Loyalty and honesty, man can leave no greater legacy."

Altogether there was $150,000 in the bag.

I know there are still things I don't know about my brother. But, I know enough to know that deep down inside, he wanted to be a man of honor, in his own way.

And I will always love him.

EPILOGUE

I'm considered an old-timer now. Though I'm no longer active in my world, I am still respected. I used the Life to my advantage, and luckily it worked out. I never got too ambitious and always kept a low profile.

Once or twice a week, I drive into East Harlem and meet Frankie, Swifty, and a few other old-timers who still hang out in the Pioneer Club. Joey took good care of Frankie back in the day. Quietly, Frankie purchased two apartment houses in the neighborhood. And, it was Frankie, not me, who kept things going at the club. I bought the building that houses the club the year after Joey was gone. In the sixties, it was a steal. Not so now.

When I pull up at the club by 10 a.m. or so, Swifty is usually out front with his dog, who's as feisty as ever, making sure no other dogs go near the Pioneer. I can hear him yell, "Hey, Frank, Vinnie's here! Make the coffee."

I always bring cake from a good bakery on Long Island, where I live now. After we hug and kiss each other and have our cake and coffee, the stories start. All we do is reminisce about the past. We tell the same stories, over and over again. But, depending on who's telling which stories, it seems they always change.

We talk about how we could pick and choose which Italian bakery to go to; which pork store made the best sausage; and who had the best pizza. We remember all the good days. I can still smell the crumb cake and the jelly doughnuts from the German bakery on our corner on First Avenue.

We talk about the two day card games; who was fooling around with whose wife; how we could walk to get anything we wanted. We remember all the good people we loved and lost—and, of course, Joey.

Now, I live in a nice house on the north shore of Long Island and own a condo in Florida; I did good.

But, I would give it all away for just one day of how it used to be.

ABOUT THE AUTHOR

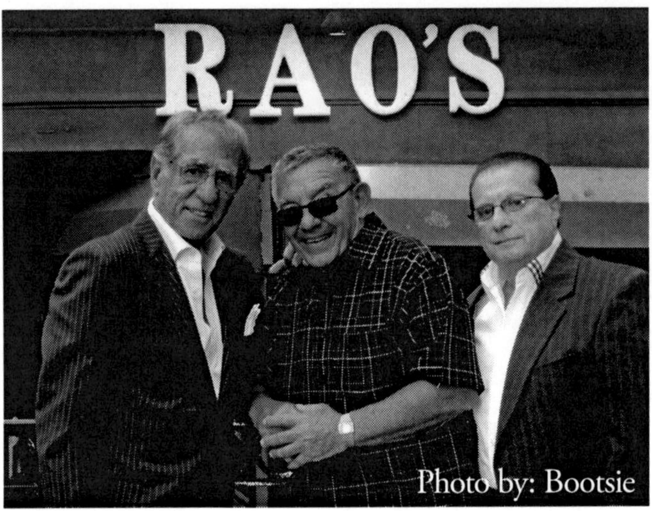

Left to right; Frank Pellegrino, Nick Rondi, Cary Alex, in front of the Internationally renowned Rao's Restaurant

The publishing of "The Nappers" would not have become a reality without the efforts of my dear friends, partners, and contributing writers Cary Alex and Frank Pellegrino. My love and gratitude cannot be fully expressed in words. Also, a special thanks to Lou Carvell, Howard Chesloff and Elizabeth Rosario for all their assistance..........Nick Rondi.

Nick Rondi was born and raised in East Harlem, New York, once the largest Italian enclave in the United States.

Nick was a union sheet metal worker in New York City and supplemented his income as a professional singer. Nick had the privilege of working on the original World Trade Center. Unfortunately, while working there, he was injured and lost the sight in one of his eyes.

Currently retired, he enjoys spending his time writing song lyrics and cooking traditional Italian dishes. He also takes pleasure in boating which provides an excellent atmosphere to reflect about the many ideas he writes about.

CPSIA information can be obtained at www.ICGtesting.com
Printed in the USA
BVOW07s0016280115

385178BV00002BA/6/P